CRITICAL ACCLAIM FOR JANETTE TURNER HOSPITAL'S NEWEST TRIUMPH— **THE TIGER IN THE TIGER PIT**

"Hospital delineates interior landscapes here with the same sense of rich detail she applied to her geographical setting, India, in *The Ivory Swing*, an award-winning first novel."

—*Library Journal*

"Her striking second novel is about a family's attempt to dig through years of repressed hostility in an effort to accept one another . . . It is a resonant, ultimately hopeful exploration of the melancholy way that familial love can constrict even as it sustains."

—*Booklist*

Janette Turner Hospital "is as adroit a prose stylist as Updike."

—*Detroit News*

"Exceptionally polished, brilliantly executed, and everywhere fraught with such intensity of spirit and sensibility and such richness of style that the results are consistently breathtaking."

—*Books in Canada*

"This book is even better than its predecessor, *The Ivory Swing* . . . The writer has one of the most elegant prose styles in the business.

—*The Times* (London)

The Tiger in the Tiger Pit

Janette Turner Hospital

Bantam Books
Toronto • New York • London • Sydney • Auckland

ACKNOWLEDGMENTS

Parts of this novel, in slightly different form, have appeared in the following magazines: *Saturday Night; Canadian Forum; Toronto Life.*

The section which appeared in *Saturday Night* (as the short story "Our Little Chamber Concerts") was awarded First Prize for magazine fiction (1982) by the Foundation for the Advancement of Canadian Letters in conjunction with the Periodical Distributors of Canada.

THE TIGER IN THE TIGER PIT

A Bantam Book / published by arrangement with E. P. Dutton Inc.

PRINTING HISTORY

First printed by McClelland and Stewart Ltd., Toronto, Canada, September 1983
E. P. Dutton edition published March 1984

Bantam Windstone Trade edition / April 1985

The epigram, "Lines for an Old Man," is reprinted by permission of Faber and Faber Ltd. From Collected Poems 1909-1962 *by T. S. Eliot.*

Windstone and accompanying logo of a Stylized W are trademarks of Bantam Books, Inc.

For information address: E. P. Dutton Inc., Subs. of JSD Corp (Dyson-Kissner-Moran Corp.), 2 Park Avenue, New York, N.Y. 10016.

ISBN 0-553-34164-2

Bantam Books are published by Bantam Books, Inc. Its trademark, consisting of the words "Bantam Books" and the portrayal of a rooster, is Registered in U.S. Patent and Trademark Office and in other countries. Marca Registrada. Bantam Books, Inc., 666 Fifth Avenue, New York, New York 10103.

PRINTED IN THE UNITED STATES OF AMERICA

O 10 9 8 7 6 5 4 3 2 1

ABOUT THE AUTHOR

Born in Melbourne, Australia, in 1942, Janette Turner Hospital began her writing career in 1975. She taught school in Australia until her husband's academic research took them to Los Angeles, Boston, London and South India.

She received an M.A. in Medieval English Literature from Queens University, Ontario. In 1974, she was awarded a Canada Council Doctoral Fellowship.

THE IVORY SWING, her first novel, was the winner of the $50,000 Seal Award in 1982 and was published to much acclaim in Canada, the United States and the United Kingdom. With her second novel, THE TIGER IN THE TIGER PIT (1983), "she fully establishes herself as a writer of remarkable talent who writes about family relationships with rare insight and compassion" (*Publishers Weekly*). She has also had numerous articles and stories published in such publications as *Saturday Night* (in which "Our Little Chamber Concerts" won the Magazine Fiction Award), *Mademoiselle, Canadian Forum,* and *Atlantic Monthly* (in which her story "Waiting" received an Atlantic First Citation).

Janette Turner Hospital lives in Kingston, Ontario, with her husband Clifford—Head of the Department of Religion at Queen's University—and their two children Geoffrey and Cressida.

The tiger in the tiger-pit
Is not more irritable than I.
The whipping tail is not more still
Than when I smell the enemy
Writhing in the essential blood
Or dangling from the friendly tree.
When I lay bare the tooth of wit
The hissing over the archèd tongue
Is more affectionate than hate,
More bitter than the love of youth,
And inaccessible by the young.
Reflected from my golden eye
The dullard knows that he is mad.
Tell me if I am not glad!

"Lines for an Old Man"
by T.S. Eliot

I Edward

Anger's my meat, I'll sup upon myself....

Lately lines from *Coriolanus* and *Timon of Athens* and *Macbeth*, the angry plays, had begun to surface in his mind like breath-starved divers rocketing up for air. And all his life he had been such a courteous and correct gentleman, right up until his seventieth birthday a little over three years ago when nothing remarkable had happened to make him so suddenly cantankerous – unless he counted a few discordant shrieks of mortality from his heart and the news about Adam who was, no doubt, a very ordinary boy. And perhaps he should count the occasional random reappearances in dreams of a woman who was not at all ordinary, whose face launched in him a thousand illicit memories and regrets.

O! full of scorpions is my mind....

These were his inspirational thoughts, soothing as whiskey. Ah yes, there had been a time when he used to indulge in classroom declamations of the more extravagant lines – Marc Antony's oration, Romeo's lament over Juliet in the crypt, Hamlet's anguish, that sort of thing – with the inevitable snickers from one or two in the class but with most of the children hooked, their eyes alight with theater magic. A long time ago, all that.

He wondered if Emily would bring Adam to see him on Sunday. How old would the child be now? Eight. He had an eight-year-old grandson whom he had never seen, of whose existence he had been unaware until three years ago. He could feel the rage of a lifetime rising in him like a thrombosis swelling and flowering and unfolding its clotted petals.

Hence, rotten thing, or I shall shake thy bones out of thy garments!

He recited that inwardly as his brooding eyes looked out on

yet another morning arrogant with early summer. And as though on cue, Bessie moaned a little with the abrasiveness of waking, rolled her old bones out of bed, and shuffled slowly downstairs to make coffee. He was elated, his blood unknotted itself, he felt gifted with arcane potency.

He kicked back the bedding, snarling at his legs so obscenely shrunken and gnarled. There were veins branching like deformed walnut trees. *Iago*! he hissed. He had begun to hold insulting conversations with his body since it had chosen to go its own defiant way. Just as his children had done. He was a well-mocked man.

With the help of his canes, he heaved himself across to his chair by the window. The pacemaker went berserk and he thumped the tin box in his chest with contempt. There was something pleasurable about the way it – Iago, his body – winced.

Bessie kept the row of little bottles on the windowsill and he shook from them, one by one, his daily dose. A red tablet, a yellow tablet, a capsule full of multicolored dots. For his heart, for his liver, for God knew what. Iago-fodder.

With his good eye he took a careful sighting and flicked them one by one through the rip in the screen. His flicking finger was as keen as it had been sixty years ago when he could win every marble in the ring. And then of course he used to give them all back, every last little colored glass ball, to the kids who looked crestfallen or pathetic. Or who looked as if they might *tell*. Oh he was a real Robin Hood, scared to death of not being good. His troubles had started early. By the tender age of ten he had already been hopelessly – and fearfully – committed to a life of moral rectitude.

If he missed the jagged tear in the screen and hit the mesh, the tablets would bounce back like concussed athletes off a trampoline. He punished himself by eating them. Though sometimes he cheated by enlarging the hole and trying again. He aimed for the forsythia or the lilacs that stretched in a shaggy undisciplined curve all the way to the old gazebo. He had to concede that the tablets were beneficial. His morale was certainly up at medication time, his energy level was up. He was hopeful of poisoning the bushes by the end of the growing season. The lilacs in particular enraged him, all that exhibitionistic flamboyance. They reminded him of his son, Jason, and of his younger daughter, Emily.

He watched a translucent cluster of pale mauve blossoms shudder from the impact of a crimson pellet. In a matter of days, he consoled himself, the lilacs would be nothing but foliage and unsightly brown cones. But he, Edward Carpenter, retired school principal of Ashville, Massachusetts, would still be there. Endurance was everything.

His wife came into the room with the breakfast tray. It seemed to him monstrous that Bessie, who had been sweet and stupid all her life, should be able to negotiate stairs alone.

Caged! he thought with a fury that was no good at all for his heart. Caged. With a senile smiling keeper. At times he had to restrain himself from punching out the screen with his bare fists and catapulting his body over the sill for the sheer pleasure of unimpeded movement. It was a seductive ending: to lie broken-backed in the smashed lilacs, mouth full of warm June mud, taking a host of living things with him, vengeful as Samson.

How delightfully embarrassing and humiliating it would be for Jason.

Dr. Jason Carpenter's father passed away floridly and florally in the little town of Ashville where he had been school principal for far too many years, having overreached himself like an aging Icarus and fallen to earth at last. He requested that there be no flowers....

"Have you taken your tablets, Edward?"

He saw her lips moving. He hated the way she had begun to mumble to herself.

"What? Speak up, Bessie! Damn it, woman, if you can climb stairs you can speak clearly."

"You're not wearing your hearing aid," she said mildly, pointing to it.

So. He had forgotten again. Not that he would need it if she didn't muffle up her words so willfully.

"If you would stop mumbling!" Shouting to give authority to a voice that reached his own ears on a fading note. He plugged himself in to the fractious world.

She smiled. And why the ironic tug at the corners of her mouth? Arrogant woman, nursing a fantasy of superiority all these years. To think he had wasted a lifetime being faithful to her. What had it profited him, this careful shepherding of his soul? What had he gained? A whole world, a life, irretrievably lost.

What I want, he thought passionately, is a last Faustian toss with the Devil. My exemplary life in exchange for the freedom to sin. Seventy-three years of keeping the rules bartered for one fresh temptation and the strength to yield to it.

Three children were rolling a rubber ball back and forth along his stretch of sidewalk while two mothers, their hands resting on occupied strollers, stood talking. The ball rolled on to his lawn and a little girl ran after it. Her laughter surrounded her like a cloud of bells. How beautiful children were, with their thistledown hair and their translucent skin. How he hated them. Perhaps he would even hate Adam whom he had vowed never to see. Surely Emily would bring the boy with her on Sunday. If Emily came at all. She must certainly realize that he had not meant... well, he had meant it at the time, the night he had raged in New York, but given half a chance he would not mean it. If she had any perception at all, she would realize that.

If Emily did not bring Adam he thought that the pacemaker would not help much. He would be too proud to reproach or beg. His systems would simply shut down.

Below him, the little girl had retrieved her ball but her attention had been caught by the gazebo, a domed octagon veiled in a tangle of honeysuckle. She climbed its rickety steps and stood on the bench that ran around the inside, her face peering out between swaying green tendrils.

Edward leaned forward, his forehead pushing against the screen so that it bellied out like a spinnaker before the wind. He did not know if he was more shocked by this intrusion into his past (he saw Marta's face, he saw Victoria's face, staring at him from the same gazebo, the same honeysuckle), or more afraid that the child would fall through the rotting bench-wood and injure herself.

He thought of shouting harshly: Little girl! If you set foot in my gazebo again, I'll cut off your legs!

The words eddied up from childhood nightmares. From old Mrs. Weston, neighborhood Medusa. Off my grass, she would scream, or I'll chop off your feet! You want to see my icebox full of legs?

She had had a leading role in bad dreams through which he heaved himself on bloody stumps, yelling for help. There was his drunken father, floozy on arm, trying to shush him, an unsteady finger to lips.

Hush, now, Edward. Don't want to bring mother rushing out. Don't want to upset her.

But mother, a fluster of hardships, would fill the air with beating wings, shielding her eyes from the blood and from father's woman. And always Mrs. Weston, old witch, was there – leaning casually on her gory cleaver with a manic smile on her lips.

He was terrified even to walk on her side of the block.

To his relief the little girl emerged from the gazebo. He let her run, unharmed, back to her playmates.

But his memory was full of Mrs. Weston. Such potency she had. The most powerful person in the world, the most dangerously alive. A lifetime later he could still remember her name. It was a kind of immortality.

The little girl was back in his garden, stepping on his lilies of the valley, foraging under forsythia boughs. He stared moodily at the mothers on the sidewalk. Listless figures, like color photographs that have faded.

Motherhood, he thought, is a hibernation from which most women never emerge. At least in his time that had been true. (In his time, indeed! Verbal litter. He did not easily forgive himself for succumbing to the clichés of the young, for this past tense view of himself.) Motherhood. He had lost Bessie in that steamy cave. Her bearings had been lost, she had never wakened again. It was supposed to be different now. So he heard. And so he read in the Sunday supplements. Women full of waking anger all over the place. Not that they were any easier to live with apparently. His daughters, for instance. One burned out and the other raging every which way like a forest fire.

But the two mothers on the sidewalk, he could see, were classic throwbacks to the old dormant order, slow and heavy-hipped, the movements of their heads and eyes languid, their voices bored.

And yet he had the power to energize them. He imagined how they would snap taut in outrage if he should hurl bolts of terror down upon the child.

"Little girl!" he roared.

The child looked up, momentarily startled. The slack bodies of the mothers tightened as though an inner spring were being wound. Squinting, the child located the face above and waved.

"Hi, mister!" A smile of delighted complicity.

Even children have changed, thought the old man with baffled anger. It is scarcely possible to frighten them anymore. It was not even possible to maintain the desire. Their amiable trust was so subversive.

"Can you find your ball?" he called gruffly.

The mothers relaxed and turned away. Indifferent to sacrilege, the little girl frolicked in the gazebo again. Edward wished he had been vicious. He would never star in anyone's dreams. He would never rampage, hugely alive with the threat of death, through the imaginations of the neighborhood children. He was not made of indelible stuff.

No one would mourn his passing extravagantly. Certainly not his own children. Not even Bessie for whom it would probably be conveniently restful. But he wanted to be mourned extravagantly. Things should have been otherwise. He should have been approaching death in grander style. There should have been a beautiful woman, desolate with impending loss, bending over him.

There should have been Marta. He whispered it like an incantation: *Marta, Marta.*

After turning seventy, one craved unremittingly for the roads not taken.

He had been restrained, at the moment of choice, by the laws of moral propriety, by what is expected of a school principal, by Bessie's need, by the claims of his eldest child, Victoria, by the approaching birth of his son, Jason. At thirty-three, he had done the right thing: he had chosen renunciation and responsibility. At seventy-three he wanted to retract. He did not forgive his family for keeping him righteous.

For several years now he had been devouring everything he could find on the final years of Sartre and Picasso. Napoleon on Elba obsessed him. Also Boethius. And the antic aging of Salvador Dali. He was an expert on geriatric fame.

In what objective sense, he asked himself, was this the dawning of his eighth decade different from their declining years? They had all dwindled and doddered into decrepitude, living in isolation, their past passions and achievements a wan glow in the debris of years. Or consider Dante, hallucinating in exile. Were they not alike, he and Dante, frantic dreamers of alternate autobiography?

Suppose he simply equated himself with the significant livers by an act of will? It seemed to him expedient now to edit and revise his life, to compose a variant past, to approach death from a different and more bearable direction.

He wanted to go back to that last night with Marta, to do things over. It was imperative that he find out, before he died, what had become of her. Forty years ago. That was before Jason and Emily. Let them go, let them go, unmake them. Yet Emily, wanton woman, had produced Adam whom he had not seen, his blood sullied but intact, his thin sad bid for dynasty.

It was not so easy to extinguish a son and a daughter, not even those two. They would not go quietly, they had always been importunate. It enraged him that they could sin with such impunity, without fear of the unspecified but awful retributions that had always haunted their father. He drew comfort from the fact that Jason at least seemed perpetually unhappy.

He could not forgive them. Victoria was a cross that he bore with fortitude, but he deserved better than Jason and Emily.

Had he not pledged himself to them, sight unseen, turning aside from temptation? He should have had a better return on his virtue.

Bessie came into the room, shuffle shuffle in her tireless slippers, blundering intruder in life and memories.

"So much to do," she sighed as mildly and maddeningly as she had done on that long-gone unforgotten evening, that other infringement. "Getting the rooms ready for everyone. And Jason might come a day early with Victoria."

Damned celebration. He wished he had put his foot down. He wished he had forbidden her to issue invitations. He was terrified of finding out who would not come.

"I don't want any of you badgering me. Get your hands off me, you interfering old woman."

"Do be calm, Edward." She tied a towel around his neck and put his shaving kit and a bowl of water on the table beside his chair. Insults, insults. The indignity of age! He gestured angrily with his arm and the bowl went spinning into the air, the hot water leaving it and rising intact, a crystal bird. Sounds: of shattering, of splashing, of a cry of pain.

"I didn't want to shave." Exonerating himself. "I don't intend to shave again."

"Does that include Sunday?" For a second, phosphorescence leaped from her eyes like marsh fire. Perhaps he imagined it. She was wrapping a towel around her hand, picking up pieces of the bowl, her eyes lowered. "You wish to be seen with stubble?"

It was not natural, her calm. It was perverse. It suggested a dimming of intelligence.

"Sunday," he mumbled, ambiguously.

"Fifty years," she said, enticing him. "It's a milestone nobody ignores. The whole family coming home. It's a ritual event. Like marriages and christenings and funerals."

Privately he thought: funerals indeed. I should be struck dead for choosing fifty years of this.

But he did at least deserve an award for staying power.

"At the very least, Edward, we should celebrate our endurance."

He looked at her in surprise. What cause had she to complain? Had he not stayed to honor and protect when he might have been blown away on a hurricane of passion? But of course she had never known that.

"Remember when the Pritchards had theirs? Three generations, all those grandchildren. . . ?" She faltered.

"Hah!" he said savagely. "Something peculiar about *our* golden years, isn't there? Not a marriage in sight. Not a single grandchild – unless you count Emily's bastard."

He did not know why he was doomed to say these things lately, he who had never let an improper word pass his lips in all his years of public office, he who would consent to walk peaceably into the valley of the shadow if only his grandson came. Lord, now lettest thou thy servant depart in peace, for mine eyes have seen....

Bessie said quietly: "Marriage is neither here nor there these days, Edward."

Surely the woman could tell he yearned to see Adam. She had lived with him fifty years, she ought to know what too many years of being a school principal required of him. They had all behaved abominably, hiding from him for all those years the birth of his only grandchild. When they finally told him, after Emily's concert in New York, he had been trapped into ultimatums. Bessie had flown to England for the boy's seventh birthday. He had not been invited. He would not ask. He would not give in.

"You should think of Jason's Ruth as a daughter-in-law," Bessie said. "They've been together a number of years."

"No hope of a grandchild there. That colorless woman is drying up faster than a pumpkin seed."

"Edward," she said, warning him.

They never could discuss Jason.

Or Victoria.

Or Emily.

Or anything.

Does the boy look like me? he longed to ask but could not. He could not ask whether Emily would bring him with her.

Bessie said nothing.

But he knew what would happen. They would keep Adam from him, knowing he was desperate to see the child. They were punishing him because life had required him to be unbending, a bastion of the moral code and the old verities. They would let him die with an unbearable ache in the gut, a petered out line, a dead name.

The old man pushed his splayed hands against the screen like a prisoner in agony.

The tiger in the tiger pit, he snarled to himself, is not more irritable than I.

II Elizabeth

What a mess! she thought. Though I suppose I've always had blood on my hands and been bloody-minded.

Perhaps the composition she was working on, final movement of a family symphony, was the bloodiest work of all.

She did not really believe this, though heaven knew all the evidence pointed to disaster. With a pair of tweezers, she picked needles of shaving bowl out of the gash in her hand, then held it under running water in the kitchen sink. The ending would be harmonious because she willed it so, she would write it that way, in the face of all the dissonance that had gone before. She sometimes thought she was infected with hope the way other seventy-year-old women suffered from perpetual chills.

Her hand was clear for a moment, white. Then the cut reappeared like a tracing on a map, diagonally across her palm, right in the crease of the life line. When she moved her thumb it opened like a mouth and drooled blood. Irritating. One of those surface slashes that take forever to stop bleeding.

In a copper pan hanging on the wall she caught sight of her face, out of focus, elongated by the dimples of beaten metal.

Ah grandma, she sighed theatrically. What hollow cheeks you have!

All the better to remind you, Elizabeth dear, that we're into the final movement, she made her reflection reply. And it had better be good. You had better make it work.

Easy to say, old copperface. But there's risk involved. We both know there's just as likely to be carnage.

It would start with Edward and Jason, words crossing like daggers. Then Tory would become so agitated that Edward would spit thunder. Which would cause Emily to flee in panic with Adam.

None of this would help. It would render no one's years golden. It would do nothing for the children; would be an appalling thing for Adam to witness. Exactly what Emily would be thinking, of course. (Without question the major difficulty: getting Emily and Adam to come. Her letter, a guerrilla tactic on whose content and timing she had expended weeks of thought, might still not be enough. She would need Jason's help.)

Her reflection stared at her with the somber authority of a copper funeral mask, its eye sockets black and shadowy: Are you sure you know what you're doing, Elizabeth? Do we really need this? Shouldn't we drift on in the more or less comfortable present, puttering in the garden in the morning, reading to him after lunch, playing the piano in the evenings? Coaxing him into serenity, tempting him with the little pleasures of each day, maundering toward death like two indolent after-dinner drowsers.

Not sure, never sure I know what I'm doing, copperface, but it has to be done. Not for me, but for them. She pointed an accusing finger at her shadow-self: You conceived this family gone so badly out of tune. Fix it.

Her finger made a red smear on the bottom of the pan. She had forgotten about her hand which was sloppy with blood again. Lifting it to her face, she drew rouge-apples on her cheeks. Like a clown. She grimaced. Leered. Stuck her tongue out at herself. Dipped her finger in the palette of her palm and painted a banana grin around her lips. Laughed.

Frowned with disapproval.

She said sternly: I find you guilty of appalling frivolity, clownface. Copper, copper, on the wall, who is the guiltiest bitch of all?

She struck the metal with her knuckles and it answered her like a gong: Ask not for whom the frying pan tolls. You are guilty, Elizabeth, guilty. You have committed levity and willful presentness.

She knew it; always subject to the moment. Anything could waylay her – the texture of blood; the shape of spilled water; patterns in shaving foam; an earthworm in the garden; a Mozart sonata she might play for hours, forgetting Edward's dinner. He lived, had always lived, somewhere other than the present. Once it had been in the future; now it was in the past. And for fifty years she had tried to beguile him with *today* – which inhabited her like an army of occupation. The inexhaustible variety of living, the sights, sounds, smells, chance encounters, the letters from England and New York and Australia, the bizarre cavalcade of human activity spilling out of newspapers: cornucopias of amazing event.

But it was more than this. She veered away from the past the way moths at the penultimate moment glance off the lamp that obsesses them. For fear of scorching. For fear that if she looked at it with the naked eye, she would be blinded. She feasted her eyes and stuffed her ears with the now in order to shut out the wolf howl of yesterday's griefs. As for the future, she had always been so impossibly sanguine about it, no thought in that direction seemed necessary.

Blood was dribbling down her wrist and absent-mindedly she wiped it with a kitchen towel and wrapped the towel loosely around her hand. She wandered into the living room and sat on the stool in front of the grand piano, dreaming out through the French windows: the gazebo, the greenery, the lilacs waited as always, composing themselves for her as though for a photographer's coffee-table book. It was difficult, with such a daily view, to believe that the drift of things would be other than benign. Without being conscious of her movements, she put the crumpled towel on top of the piano and began to play.

She played the family. An adagio for Victoria, a dark piece, haunted and mad. Broadening into long tranquil cadences, sweet with melancholy. (She loved to sit with her daughter in the gardens of her various institutions; they would thread flowers together while Tory ranted poetry or sang nursery rhymes.) This was one of her sins: the pleasure she took in Tory as Tory was, when no doubt anguish and guilt were more appropriate. Except that those goads – in which the others all wallowed – afflicted Tory like arrows. If Tory could come home and be at peace.... They would sit in the gazebo together, she would hold Tory's hand and read her stories.

If Tory could come home. Possible only if the furies in

Edward could be lulled. She played the taming of furies, the casting out of demons. She circled him with Adam, an intrusion of grace notes.

An allegro for Jason, the phrases restless, full of syncopation and discord. (Jason her well-beloved, who wore life like a hair shirt.) There were double pianissimo sections, fractured, but whispering of old intimacies. (Perhaps she had damaged him with closeness, with too much responsibility.) She wound the discordant strands into harmony, a soft coda. This was what she yearned for.

Emily: a scherzo life. (The one who escaped, but who, like the dove from the ark, fluttered across the breast of the waters finding nowhere to rest.) She played runs and arpeggios and the melody seemed scattered beyond the recognizing, a keyboard hide-and-seek. But sneaking up from the left hand came a persistent theme and it infiltrated the flighty right-hand phrases, subsuming them into its orbit. She played the homecoming of Emily and Adam, a stasis of chords.

In the final movement, a slow rich one, a resolution of all themes, they were all present and at peace, old and young in one another's arms. It will happen that way, she thought, her hands still resting on the keyboard. I'll write it that way.

She wondered idly why there were smudges of red ink on some of the keys and rubbed at them with a towel that had been left on the piano. Perhaps it was time to see if Edward wanted morning tea. She passed the hallway mirror where a garish clown's face startled her. She widened her eyes at it for a moment, shook her head at it.

Really, Elizabeth, she sighed. You're crowding the stage. You'll blow your cover. It's Bessie he's expecting. You want to precipitate another heart attack?

In the bathroom she washed her face and bandaged her hand. There was a watch on the side of the basin. Hers. Must have left it there earlier in the morning. According to the watch, it was a few minutes after one. In the afternoon presumably. Surely not? Had she forgotten his lunch?

He was drowsing in his chair, a hand on the windowsill, the head sagging on one shoulder. Like a skeleton daubed with clothes. Or perhaps a small tangle of barbed wire, braced against the marauder happiness in whatever stray guises it might stalk him in sleep.

She stood watching. If she could just bundle up his spikiness in her arms and croon away the jagged edges. It was this conspiracy that absorbed her, to sabotage him with contentment before the end. She remembered that it was essential to put a call through to Jason. Now. Before she forgot again, or dreamed that she had done it. She went downstairs and called him at his New York office.

"How is he?" Jason asked.

"Grumbling about it. But not actually refusing to let it take place. I haven't heard from Emily yet. I'm counting on you, Jason."

"I'll call her tonight. And you, mother, how *are* you?"

"I'm fine, of course, darling. I'm excited really."

"I hope you won't be disappointed."

"You think I'm bound to be. But you're wrong, I sense it somehow."

"It would be nice if you were right."

"Bye, darling."

"Bye, mother."

Yes, she thought, climbing the stairs again. It would indeed be nice. And she would be right.

He was still drowsing.

From the awkward set of his shoulder, she knew he would wake with pain. She crossed the room in slippered feet and eased a cushion behind his neck. He stirred, whimpered *Bessie* in his sleep, groped vaguely and made contact with her arm, the trusting gesture of a child. Half woke then, grumbled, threw the cushion on the floor, slithered back into his nap.

Elizabeth smiled. Wryly. Affectionately. A mother acknowledging bratty behavior and indulging it. For a moment she laid her cheek against his. Then she eased herself onto the windowsill, leaning lightly against the molding and crossing her arms. Still smiling, she observed him calmly: the air of a magician with an ace up her sleeve.

III Emily

Emily had intense relationships with a number of men – Vivaldi, Bach, Beethoven, Sibelius. She remained faithful to them to atone for earlier mistakes. When in the course of the past three years she had felt too sharp a need for lesser men, she had expended her passion on the more turbulent movements of violin concertos or soothed herself with Bach's austerity.

Or perhaps, if she were away on concert tour, she would spend a poignant but chaste evening with some member of the local orchestra or with one of the attendant music critics or academics who frequented the parties preceding or following engagements. These men were invariably married. They were gentle and sad and searching for some indefinable flicker of happiness which they seemed to believe Emily could provide.

She would be insouciant and compassionate but would excuse herself, when the drift of innuendo eddied toward the flesh, with the gentlest of regrets.

I have a little boy, she would say. His name is Adam and he's eight years old. I find it better to avoid involvements. You understand.

She thought of love as a kind of refugee act, akin to handling a live grenade, something to be engaged in while poised for flight. Always claustrophobia and imminent bloodiness waited in the wings like hobgoblins in a morality play while the euphoric pull of sensual comfort had its foolish little moment on stage. An old gazebo choked with honeysuckle would rear into her dreams, a shadowy portent, her lover's eyes in every leaf, his breath heavy in the creamy blossoms, his limbs in its throttling branches. She would have to break out, escape, flee the country.

England was her fourth country of residence.

And now already there were signs in the air, vibrations and patterns she recognized, temptations to warmth, indications that it might become necessary to move on. Or, more frightening, to move back. To Australia. To Dave. Her importunate physical yearnings kept up a whisper, raspily and obscenely, like ill-mannered concertgoers during a performance. She drowned them with music. Through insomniac nights she played Vivaldi and Bach. Eventually the prick of deprivation would mute itself and everything would return to normal.

She hoped.

Otherwise....

She knew that if she were ever to "settle down" somewhere, *belong* somewhere, for Adam's sake, she would have to cultivate impermanence; she would have to learn the knack of fragmentary affairs that went nowhere, that did not disrupt. But as old churches attract antiquarians, so men with a sempiternal itch burgeoned into her life. This was what she had against casual sex: that a lover could not be counted on to leave the next morning; that he might break the rules; that he might take root and expand into her days like a bewitched beanstalk, declaring his addiction to continuity and to her.

She thought wistfully that she would like to become the sort of person who would grow old in this little house in Harrow. She liked the sound of *London.* Of *Harrow-on-the-Hill* and *the Metropolitan line.* Of *near the little fifteenth-century stone church.* Tranquil and dignified identity labels. Perhaps if she made her performance schedule more demanding? It seemed to her that she would be able to tolerate a constant postal address if she were at it infrequently. Or if she never received any mail.

When her mother's letter arrived, London was pouting with summer rain and Emily was trying to open the French windows on to her garden. Not a simple task, everything wooden sulking from the damp. She applied her shoulder as a battering ram and went spinning suddenly on to the brick paving under the cherry tree.

For these she had bought the house—for the French windows and the cherry tree. House! Box, her father would call it.

Because of just such cramped tenements his forefathers had crossed the ocean to win for themselves the large Georgian houses and gazebo-enhanced grounds of western Massachusetts.

It was true that in the sliver of town house to which she held title she could barely turn around in the kitchen, that the bathroom was primitive by transatlantic standards, that the water heater had to be coddled as one might an eccentric wealthy relative, and that an insatiable gas meter gorged itself on coins all winter, blackmailing her with the absence of heat. Nevertheless she had fallen in love – with a bay window in the living room, a trellis of roses, the French windows, the cherry tree, and a garrulous upstairs neighbor who called her "luv" and was a marvelous nanny to Adam.

To see the cherry hung with snow, she murmured, reciting talismanic words (a prayer, perhaps, of appeasement), sitting under a drizzle of the last few wet petals and the finest powdering of rain, inhaling tranquility, holding unease at bay for a few more minutes. She thought of Massachusetts. The gazebo would be riotous with honeysuckle now, and what would mother be doing? She sighed, braced herself, opened the letter and read it.

I won't go, she thought immediately. I can't. Not even for mother.

She wrapped her arms around the cherry tree and tapped her forehead softly and rhythmically against its trunk as though exorcising a constant pain. Family, family. One could never escape. There were no pockets in the world distant enough. One was hooked at birth and no matter how far the line was played out one could always be hauled in again. Because of course one always consented.

> *I don't want to apply unfair pressure, Emily, and I'll understand if you feel you can't. But your father is frail and unhappy. I am having some trouble with stairs myself lately. We can't last forever.*
>
> *I know, I know. That's unfair pressure. I confess: I'll stoop to almost anything to see the whole family together for this occasion.*

Frail and unhappy. Your father is. Still is.

A guilty ache in the gut. A swooning sense of hurtling toward the death of a parent. Daddy! (Something she could rarely say to him; usually "father" in his presence.) An acute desire to put her arms around his wasted body, knowing that in his presence it would probably be impossible, that she would probably become incapable of making, and he of receiving, such a gesture.

Irritation, a merciful painkiller, coated her grief. Rage to the rescue. Why such short notice? Six days, for god's sake. It was impossible. Had mother waited, hoping against hope that Emily would think of it herself? Would just drop in for a spontaneous visit, crossing the Atlantic, parachuting from the bosom of Pan Am? Happy golden wedding anniversary, mom and dad!

Absurd. I wasn't around for the original occasion. Can I be expected to keep score for fifty years?

But perhaps it was a way of providing her with an excuse for not going? (She had always thought of her mother as a co-conspirator.) No. *I'll stoop to almost anything....* More likely a device to give her no time to think of subterfuge.

She wondered if Jason would go. I must phone him tonight, she thought, suddenly wanting to. Wanting quite intensely to see him again. Protector against bullies, binder of wounds. A year ago, when he came to London for that conference (The New Face of Freud? Psychoanalysis – Junger Than Ever? something like that; they had joked about it) how delightful it had been. A kind of intimate abandon as sometimes occurs after a few drinks between strangers who meet at a party, strangers who stumble into an agreeably vibrant comfort, happening upon esoteric but shared past experiences. And they were like strangers, new to each other after so many years. Foraging through childhood. Two archeologists unearthing long forgotten clues to time past. Do you remember...? No, no, that's not how it happened.... Don't correct me, Emily, I'm five years older than you. But not necessarily wiser, Jason.

Perhaps after all, Emily reflected, she should go.

It would mean seeing Victoria again. Of course she *should* see Victoria again. It was quite appalling...how much time had gone by? Eight, nine years since she had seen her sister. Montreal, that frightful scene at the airport. Oh god. The trouble with memory: pick up a pebble and an avalanche comes thundering about your head. Poor Tory, spinning her own sticky webs for the family, holding all of them in thrall, her poems fluttering around the mail routes of the globe like lost souls:

under dead honeysuckle leaves
there are eyes that glitter like quartz.
The bones are neatly arranged, all the bodies
folded and put away. Wherever you move
the eyes follow....

Wild and whirling words. Mentally, Emily crossed herself every day before she opened her mailbox. So far England was safe. Tory did not have her London address.

I can't, I can't, she told herself. I can't go back. I might never get out again.

She was smeared with Ashville and the family as with birdlime. She would never allow Adam to be tainted.

And please bring Adam. Yes, yes, I know what your father said. But your father's rages have to be taken with a grain of salt. They are a reflex action with him. He spent too many years with a switch in his hand. Besides, Emily, you cannot deny me Adam, surely you cannot. With your father so ill, I cannot travel to London again.

Bring Adam. You must give your father a chance.

A chance.

That was what Juilliard had been. New York and freedom. A chance to get away from a town where every boy had had your father as his high school principal, every boy had heard rumors of what old Carpenter did to anyone who messed with his daughters, every boy kept a wide and nervous distance. (Yet in later years, when she had met some of those boys in New York or Boston or wherever, they were always awash in nostalgia, sighing for Ashville High, sentimentalizing her father beyond recognition.)

In New York there had not been a soul to ask discreet prying questions about Victoria. At Juilliard, no one had heard of her father.

New York was chance itself – city of the random encounter, of the unexpected event, of the indiscretion without repercussions, of blissful anonymity. To be forever unknown and unmonitored seemed to Emily the most desirable of goods. To be free.

And now her mother was cajoling her back to the cage.

It had taken her until the age of nineteen to escape. She was now thirty-four. She had not been home in between.

Perhaps at last she could go back with head held high. The heroine's return. Even into the columns of the *Ashville Daily Chronicle* the news must have dropped like carbon datings: Juilliard; Montreal Philharmonic; Sydney Symphony; Harrow Chamber Orchestra; concert violinist.

She imagined wandering casually into Berring's corner store:

– Why Emily Carpenter! You haven't changed a bit.

– Back with your husband and child?

– Not married...? Ahh....

– Still traipsing around with your violin? Why yes, I believe now you mention it, I did read something....

– And how is your sister Tory, poor dear?

Even after fifteen years, not a chance.

No, she thought again, decisively. I can't do it. I'll plead concert engagements. I'll offer to meet them again in New York in a few weeks' time. I'll take them out to dinner. I'll bring them both over here for Adam's next birthday. I'll send masses of flowers.

No sense in calling Jason, no sense in stickying the web any further. It was hard enough to remain free as things were. She hugged the cherry tree and began murmuring to herself as though reciting an essential catechism: Stay detached. Do not capitulate. Do not be done in by sentimentality.

I know you think this is equivalent to throwing a party for the passing of the dinosaurs. I know you think it foolish of me to have stayed for fifty years. But for my generation, my dear, marriage is so much more complex and painful and satisfying than for yours.

Please come. And bring Adam with you.

Above all, stop thinking about mother before guilt itself decides the issue.

Run.

And through the French windows came Adam, for whom she would indeed run through fire.

"Oh Adam!" Hugging him, wanting to hold him longer, remembering father's stifling embraces and letting him go. "How would you like to see grandma again? And Uncle Jason? How would you like to fly to New York?"

Adam stared at her with wide uneasy eyes. He had reason to fear sudden departures.

Emily, glancing restively at the soggy dreariness of gray sky, warmed recklessly and involuntarily to the mad idea, to the thought of sun on Cape Cod beaches.

"We could leave tomorrow. An adventure!"

"We can't, mummy." Adam's voice was overly precise, as though he spoke a meticulously learned second language, the chiselled diction of a boys' school. (He had suffered greatly from arriving with an Australian accent.) "What about Verulamium?"

"Verulamium?"

"You remember." On a faltering note. "Our field trip."

"Field trip? Oh! Those Roman ruins near St. Albans."

"Mr. Price said to remind you that the parents have to be at the school at eight sharp on Wednesday morning."

"I have to go too?"

"Mummy, you promised. You signed it on the permission letter."

"Oh dear. I'd forgotten. Well then, that settles it. We can't go to New York this week."

Pass to freedom. A legitimate excuse.

Somewhere close to midnight the phone rang. Surfacing from sleep, Emily thought the sound came from the flat above.

"Mummy!" Adam stood in her doorway, ghostly in white pajamas. "Is it Dave?"

Because of the hour. One thought of overseas where time played games. Also, Dave called on Adam's birthday each year. And occasionally at other times.

"No, no, darling. It won't be Dave. Go back to bed."

She stumbled into the hallway, feeling for the receiver.

"Emily. Did I wake you? What time is it there?"

"Jason! Don't do this to me. It's somewhere around midnight, I think."

"Sorry. It's cheaper after six our time. This is to find out what day you're flying in and whether you want to be met in Boston or New York."

"Oh Jason. I don't know. Do we have to go?"

"Emily, really. Yes, I would say we have to."

"Here we go again," she said with mock despair. "Your Edwardian sense of propriety. The oddest notions. And so contradictory."

"On the contrary. Quite logical."

"Form is paramount, of course." A sardonic barb.

"It is. The psyche requires imposed order."

"Excuse me. Should I be taking notes?"

Order in Jason's life? Form, empty form. That sad marriage to Nina, and then this long strange thing with Ruth, whom Emily had never met. (Did Ruth really exist?) And who could keep count of the other women? But officially monogamous and filial always, that was the thing. Imposed order.

"You're very odd, Jason," she sighed, remembering his visit to the London conference, the long talks, the rediscoveries and amazements.

Love and passion, he had claimed, were absolutely matters of illusion. They had to be played against a backdrop of danger and betrayal or they did not exist. As for the rest, for daily living, one imposed a form. As necessary and as peripheral to the brief bloom of love as mulch was to the rose.

"Oh you're so wrong, Jason," Emily had protested. "So ludicrously wrong." Love was voracious, it could swallow one's life whole. "Look at mother."

"Yes. Look at mother."

"A stupid permanent vegetable love for father. Her life seeping into oblivion."

"What utter rubbish, Emily. Father has very little to do with her life, really. Just a frame for it."

"A cage, more like."

"No. She's indifferent to where she is. Unaware of it. That abstracted and absorbed way she plays the piano."

"Exactly. She might have been a concert pianist."

"That's not what's significant...."

"Hah! Is that so? You think I want to dispense with audiences and bouquets?"

"I'm saying they've never mattered to mother."

"Incredible! Incredible! Believe me, I know her better."

"Emily," he said quietly, suddenly turning to her and putting his hands on her shoulders. "Believe me, you don't. You don't know her as well as I do."

They walked in silence beside the Thames. Emily remembered a long-gone summer evening when she had been sitting in the gazebo listening to the music drifting out from the living room – her mother playing Beethoven. Quite abruptly the music had stopped, the pianist apparently arrested by some thought in mid-phrase. She had appeared at the closed French windows, her arms spread in entreaty or despair, a crucified figure against the living room lamps. A caged woman behind a barred window.

Watching her, Emily had held her breath in a kind of pain. I will never let myself be trapped like that, she had vowed.

Jason sighed heavily. "Do you know I was afraid to see you again? After your New York concert."

"New York! Please!" Indicating an event too awful to be dragged into discussion.

"I have this necessary image of you. A frame of reference. My little sister in her first white concert dress." He began picking up small stones, exploring them with his fingers, rejecting some. Classifying something in his mind. "It's to do with this sense of...of *murk* in the past – we both seem to have it – and the wish, the passion, for something pure, some unambiguous memory of childhood.... Thank God, you're always even more beautiful than I remember."

He began tossing his stones with a kind of violence into the river, not looking at her, and went on.

"It's because of Tory, I suppose. Because of everything...I require you – you'll have to forgive me – I absolutely require you to remain perfect and innocent and above reproach. And I was so afraid.... I nearly didn't call you. But somehow in spite of...no, because of Adam...you still are."

"Oh god, Jason, undeceive yourself, please. At Juilliard I was recklessly promiscuous."

"Yes, well. For us that sort of thing was inevitable on first getting out from under father's thumb. You seem...rather celibate at the moment."

"It shows? It's for complicated reasons, all of them impure. The world is strewn with my lovers. I'm as consumed with guilt and abandoned loves as St. Augustine."

"St. Augustine. Yes. Exactly."

"Jason," she now complained sleepily via transatlantic satellite. "I think I have conflicting concert arrangements. I only just got the letter today. There isn't time to make changes."

"You do not have conflicting concert arrangements. I called your booking agent."

"How horrid of you. But anyway, Adam has a school field trip that we both have to go on."

"When is it?"

"Is this an inquisition?"

"I'm trying to help. What day is the field trip?"

"Wednesday."

"Fine. You could get a Thursday flight. Or even Friday. We could still be in Ashville by Saturday."

"That's crazy. To go so far for three or four days. Anyway, it's probably not possible at such short notice. Summer season, remember. Booked out months ahead."

"On a cancellation or a standby it's always possible. Call me as soon as you have a flight number and time. And Emily: be there. You know, whatever else, certain milestones require tribute."

"I cannot imagine how you preserve these shibboleths. I mean, especially someone who scrabbles around in other people's libidos for a profession."

"That's exactly why. I *know* the importance of landmarks. And a golden wedding anniversary isn't something you can ignore. It's not just hugely significant for them. It's *our* lives too."

"Jason, I'm terrified of going back. I know that's irrational, but I am. Quite terrified."

"Listen," he said in a low and conspiratorial whisper of excitement. "The honeysuckle will be in bloom. Remember our midnight picnics in the gazebo? Remember sliding down that rope from my window? Don't you want to show Adam that?"

A wave of nostalgia crested over her.

"Not Adam," she said, resisting it. "Even if I come, I shouldn't bring Adam. Aren't you forgetting what father said in New York?"

"I would discount that entirely. You announced it badly. His only grandchild. And Adam can wrap anyone around his little finger in five minutes. We just have to get father to *see* him..."

"No. School's still in session here and it would be bad for Adam to miss any. Besides, he doesn't want to come."

"I don't believe it. You've presented it badly. As usual. You've carted him around the world like chattel and he's scared of moving. But he'll love the old house. He has a desperate need for roots."

"What rubbish. He's as footloose as I am. He just doesn't want to miss out on the final weeks of school right now."

"When I talked to him last year he asked incessant questions about his grandparents. And he was also pining quite acutely for a house with a blue door in Sydney and for someone named Dave whom you declined to talk about. Other than to tell me that Dave was not his father."

"What a sneak you are."

"Let me talk to Adam."

"For heaven's sake, Jason, it's the middle of the night. Adam's asleep."

"No I'm not, mummy. Can I talk to Uncle Jason?"

Emily raised her eyebrows in mock anger and handed him the receiver, bending over to kiss the top of his tousled head.

Yes, she heard him say. Oh yes, that would be super, Uncle Jason. Just for a little visit, yes. Okay, here's mummy.

"Boston or New York?" Jason asked.

"What?"

"Where do you want to be met?"

"What did you say to Adam?"

"I knew he'd want to come. Where will I meet you?"

"Oh, Boston, I suppose. If I can get a direct flight."

"If you can get a Thursday flight, come to New York. That way we can all spend Friday at my place and then drive up to Ashville on Saturday afternoon. Tory will be with us from the middle of this week. I figure she needs a debriefing period—as it were—before father is sprung upon her. We felt we could cope for a few days."

"We?"

"Ruth and myself."

"Oh." Emily had almost come to believe that Ruth did not exist, that she was a necessary fictional background to make affairs illicit and possible. "You really live with her?"

"Quite happily."

"She's coming to Ashville?"

"Probably not. It would be pointless, I think. The family has nothing to do with her."

"Hmm. I would have thought..."

"New York then? Thursday. Call me with the flight number."

"Oh Adam," Emily said as she hung up. "We seem to be committed to it. You capitulated."

She often spoke to him as though he were an adult and a co-planner of their lives. He waited for her to translate.

"I thought you didn't want to go," she said.

"I didn't want to miss Verulamium. And I thought, I was afraid...we'd never come back here. But Uncle Jason said it was only for a few days."

"Aha. You do like living in London."

"I like my school," he conceded uncertainly, afraid of

entrapment. "But I wish we could go back to Australia."

He said it the way a child says: I wish I could fly to the moon. I wish I had a million dollars. Intense, but aware of powerlessness.

And Emily, against her will, was back there. Refugee from Montreal and Sergei. Foreigner. Drifter in the sun. Awaiting the birth of Adam.

Sydney in that July of 1973 was hardly what she expected – a city dignified as an Empire dowager with secret slatternly ways. On mornings when she should have been practising, Emily spent hours on the harbor ferries, traveling through blueness, letting the child ripen in the warmth. The sun fondled her like a lover. And this was supposed to be winter!

At the Taronga Park dock she would leave the ferry and simply walk a quarter of a mile and back along the road, filling in time until the boat returned.

Perhaps it was the pregnancy, perhaps the eucalypt-sharp air, perhaps the sun. Contentment was everywhere, a profound physical fact. She walked with one hand on her belly, and was able to think of Sergei with gratitude, with affection, without anguish. Almost.

I will not need men any more, she decided. She had leaned into the very flume of obsession (a siren song, deadly) and had careened on as unscathed as Ulysses.

Not like mother.

Unbidden that image arose (it had floated up in dreams recently, because of the baby, she supposed): the delicate figure, intense with otherness, caged behind the French windows of the old house. She thought also of Anna in Montreal.

But she, Emily, had escaped.

When the ferry slapped softly against the dock timbers she would commit herself again to the harbor, tranquil cradle, and glide back toward the skyscrapers and Circular Quay. The Opera House arches, white and glistering as Fabergé eggshells, soared into lapis lazuli.

When it opens in a few months' time, she thought, I will be

playing there. People on the ferry boats will hear the applause drifting out over the water. This is the lucky country; no entanglement in wars, no civil strife, no dark side; a country still in the innocence of childhood.

"Utter rubbish, I'm afraid," Ian said, handing her a beer under the shade of his mango tree in Mosman. To the assembled company strewn about his lawn he announced: "Emily thinks we're an innocent country."

A breeze of tolerant derision wisped through two dozen people, turning heads, stirring languid limbs. Such an extravagance of golden flesh and sun-bleached hair, Emily thought. How casually Australians take their bodies. As they take their sun. With an easy gluttonous indifference.

"Innocent!" Someone laughed. "Wishful bloody thinking, sweetheart."

"Once upon a time," Ian said, "some Chinamen were strung up in these trees like flypapers for living too cheaply when the gold gave out and doing the Aussie worker in. I could point to many contemporary blots."

"However, since he likes his view of the harbor and his ever escalating equity in this piece of real estate," a woman said sardonically, "he'll refrain, for decency's sake. Besides, we all have hope that Whitlam will save our national soul, and Ian'll vote Labor with the rest of us. But that's as far as it goes, right, Ian?"

"Denny, darling, since you're making so free with my booze and my steaks, why don't you go jump in the harbor and leave me to dazzle Emily with my jaded innocence?"

"Subtle, aren't they?" Denny demanded. "You'll find the men are a decade behind North America. Especially the intellectuals. Don't contradict them, whatever you do."

"Try to ignore her," Ian said sagely. "She writes strident poetry but we love her because she has such gorgeous breasts. She spent a semester at Iowa (as feminist in residence, I think) which is why she's an authority on the American male."

"Fuck off," Denny told him amiably. "Actually, Emily, if you can allow for Neanderthal imagery and symbol systems, the Australian male is tolerable. Shall I treat you to my insightful glossary on this particular collection of painters, poets, musicians, intellectuals, and other misfits all pining for London or New York?"

"London if they haven't been fully appreciated yet," one of the men said, a shaggily bearded satyr, brown as desert sands, shambling over to them barefoot. "Critically speaking, that is. New York if they're past that stage and just want to make money."

"This is Deakin," Denny explained. "History prof. Haggard from churning out papers to present at overseas conferences so that the world will remember his existence and his Oxford D.Phil. And will offer him a professorship in California which has higher salaries and gentler tax brackets."

Ignoring her, Deakin said: "What you are going to have to realize from the start, Emily, is that you don't have a hope of being taken seriously here while you're so undilutedly American. You can't expect to get anywhere in Australia until you've suffered through a couple of winters in a poorly heated London flat. There's just no evidence of artistic integrity."

"Deak's hot new scheme for an expenses-paid trip to Denver, Colorado," one of the women said. She wore very short shorts and a halter top and tossed her long chestnut hair like a colt. "A Social History of the Colonial Inferiority Complex: Some Cultural Implications. Grateful acknowledgments to the Australia Council who made this trip possible. Annotations, pomposity, and bullshit courtesy of Deakin Frazer."

"Come here, Heather," Deak said sternly, frowning at her from under his bushy eyebrows.

"Make me."

"With pleasure."

He scooped her up and slung her over his shoulder like a sack of wheat; she hammered on his back with her fists; they rolled in the grass together, laughing.

Emily was entranced. It is the sun, she thought again. It is a lubricant; it gives a perspective of mirth to everything; it coats their faint bitterness with nonchalance. She wondered if it were possible for anyone to maintain outrage or moral purpose or even the selfish restlessness of ambition in Sydney.

Tranquility must surely do everyone in.

"True. It's like molasses." She was startled. Had she been thinking aloud then? "Like trying to run in a dream."

What she noticed, apart from the inevitable glow of tanned flesh that assaults the senses of newcomers, were his eyes, the skin around them weathered like a network of dried riverbeds.

"I'm Dave," he said.

"It's the sun." Emily was eager to explain, to give him the benefit of an outsider's clear-sightedness. "You take it for granted. You can't imagine what a difference it makes. And the sheer clarity of sky. You must grow up with the goodwill of the universe as a certainty in your bones."

"That's just Mosman, lush with shade and well-watered gardens. I would only need to drive you out into the southwestern suburbs to see grit and irritation. I could take you out to my property west of the Blue Mountains and you could see dry waterholes and the carcasses of sheep and bushfire scars. I grew up there and I never thought of the land as well-intentioned. I guess I thought of her...." He trailed into silence, seeing the shimmer of heatwaves over scrubby spinifex grasses. "She's one tough seductive lady. She's a bitch I'm in love with. It's a thrill to do battle with her because she never lets up."

"Oh!" I am fascinated by men with obsessions, Emily thought. I see the tongues of fire over their heads and am instantly bewitched. "I'm partial to bitches. I hope you'll introduce me."

"Any time. First the southwestern suburbs," Dave said. "Brown grass and red dust. Shall we go?"

Driving across the Harbour Bridge, inevitably he asked her: "What do you think of our white elephant?"

"Your white elephant?"

"Our hundred-million-dollar idiot child" – indicating it with a nod of his head.

"Oh, the Opera House! I think it's breathtaking! Dazzling!"

"Do you really?" He seemed pleased. "To tell you the secret truth, I'm rather crazy about it myself. Though it's quite unfashionable to admit that. In our circle, anyway."

"Why?"

"Oh I don't know. Showing off embarrasses Australians.

We leave that to the Americans; you know: world's greatest this or that. We go the other way. You're supposed to say witty disparaging things. Like: It reminds me of an untidily sliced apple."

She laughed. "Now that you mention it..."

"Or a highly successful cement works."

"Oh cruel. How about a bevy of paper planes?"

"Hey!" he said sternly. "*You* can't say nasty things, only us. Those are the rules. You're a bloody Yank and it would be filthy cheek on your part!"

"Well, since I do think it's gorgeous...."

"You'll be playing there by September probably."

I'll be five months pregnant, she thought. I'll play for the opening, but will they make me take leave soon after?

"Before you," he said theatrically, in the overly mellow voice of a documentary narrator, "are the rusting iron roofs and shriveled lawns of suburbia. Behind that peeling paint, the world's most bored and unhappy women await the return of pot-bellied husbands who are even now emptying their pay envelopes in the six o'clock swill of every corner pub in Sydney."

"You seem determined to make me despise the place."

"I thought I already explained my coded comments. This is an absolutely dreadful country except for Gough Whitlam and Bob Hawke and Patrick White and Test cricket. And Joan Sutherland and Co., who of course don't count, having fled. It's parochial, isolated, sun-blasted, and full of beer-punchy Philistines. I love it with a bigot's passion and I don't want you saying anything unpleasant about it. We'll swing east and I'll show you my house. It has a view of the Pacific, but it's not too far from the airport. I keep a small plane there for getting out to Kurrajong."

"Which is?"

"My station out near Bathurst."

"I know you're not a musician. Are you an artist or a professor?"

"None of the above. I don't quite belong. But we all went to university together and we keep in touch. Besides they're all clients of mine, not all of them paying ones."

"What do you do?"

"I'm a lawyer. Partner in a Sydney firm. And a gentleman farmer on a modest scale. Benefactor of the arts. That means I give free legal advice to impoverished writers and painters I was an undergraduate with."

"It's an interesting group."

"We're all scholarship kids. Amazing country when you think of it. Anti-intellectual to the core, and yet there's a pack of us. I was the golden boy of Bathurst High who won a university fellowship. My father sheared sheep for station owners all over western New South Wales and never had two sixpenny bits to rub together. I managed to buy Kurrajong in time for him to die on it."

Kurrajong.

If it had not been for Tory's letters, Emily thought. If the past had not crowded her, if she had not been pregnant, if she had not retreated to Kurrajong. If she had never taken refuge in the town house in Sydney.

If extrication were as simple as the process of hopeless entanglement with Dave had been.

"Oh Adam," she said, holding him tightly, remembering his birth, the tiny body cradled between the crook of her elbow and the palm of her hand, the sense of awe (a life, a responsibility). Dave, as proud as though he were the father, bending over both of them, telling her:

"I'll call your parents."

"No!"

"But Emily, surely...?"

"No. It's not their affair. It has nothing to do with them. I don't want them to know."

I do not, she could not quite have articulated, want this occasion sullied by my father's judgments, by the things he will not be able to stop himself from saying.

There had been more than shock in Dave's eyes. She had perceived a kind of stunned fear, as of something more awful than he was able to understand. He had stroked her hair with one hand and the baby's down-soft head with the other, waiting for her to reconsider. Not able to believe she meant it.

She had seen the same gaunt look of loss in his eyes five years later.

"You can't dispense with your parents like that, Emily. You can't dispense with me like this. You can't do it to Adam. He has a right to all of us. I have a right to him. I have a right to meet your family and they have a right to know about me. You can't snap your fingers and extinguish people."

But I can, Emily had thought then. I have to.

She had changed her flight reservations secretly, leaving for England several days earlier than Dave was expecting. No one had seen her off from Sydney airport, no one had met her in London.

But Adam still mourned, three years later, for Australia and Dave. He said it again, his voice uninflected by hope: "I wish we could go back."

"Everyone has to move on, Adam." She snapped her fingers to disperse his memories. "Time itself moves on."

IV Edward

In moonlight the flakes of peeling paint jut out against the light like a cluster of batwings. I possess it then. Alone at my window, pacing through a litter of memories like an unquiet ghost, I pass through its matted tresses of honeysuckle and stalk its benches like a tomcat. Under the weightless pads of my feet, the wood is soft and rotten, smelling of sugared vinegar or overripe oranges. I pace, I pace, snarling into its eight niches, sniffing out the past. The tiger in the tiger pit is not more irritable than I.

By day it is merely shabby, listing toward the southwest plane of its octagon. In daylight it is violated by squirrels and small children. Sunlight, the great mocker, leers in at my window where I sit helpless, chained to my chair, manacled to my unedited and unacceptable life. I watch the smothering mutations of the honeysuckle.

Since the thaw the entire structure has slumped a little more into its southwest footing. I monitor this decline with avid interest, with far more precision than that sapling of an intern takes over my heart charts. I would like to think that on the day of my death the foundation will give way with an organic moan, will offer itself up to the honeysuckle in vegetable submission. My personal icon.

I remember the first day I saw it.

I remember the instant of lust, the precise moment of obsession, the determination to be offered this hitherto unappealing position. I would become the principal of a country high school, I would live in this schoolmaster's house. How I coveted that skeletal tribute to graciousness, not even knowing what it was called. Resolutely I looked away from it, feigned a lack of interest, afraid the board members would detect the beating pulse of my motivation.

It has always been a problem, this tendency to fixate on details. For example, the minutiae of love. Insanity. I tripped over details too fine for an unfevered eye. Bessie, that first time I saw her....

But this requires a detached perspective....

One Sunday afternoon in Boston in his prehistory, his apple-tree days, young Edward Carpenter stands diffidently outside an imposing house, the scholarship boy from the mill town who has scrabbled his way into respectability via earnest years at Harvard, via chalky days of teaching at Cambridge Latin. He has made passing acquaintance with the families of several of his students, he has been invited to a number of terrifyingly stuffy afternoon teas to which he has always gone although knowing his presence to be a symbol of benevolent condescension.

He subjects himself to the sherry, the small talk, the quietly arrogant susurration of silk skirts and silk cravats, the rough edges of his ambition snagging in that seamless web of genteel indifference. He can never belong. The only way to acquire ease here is to inherit it. He is completely *other* to them, pickled like a museum specimen in their immaculate politeness. Their patronage coats his tongue with a fur of bitterness like the taste of a cheap and juvenile sherry.

Through the forest of fathers discussing boardrooms and cigars, he sees a young woman sitting at the piano, playing. She is slender, almost gaunt, with intense cavernous black eyes. An intellectual, a New England version of Virginia Woolf. The type alarms him – with those blackbird eyes casting about for a passionate cause on which to alight. He feels repelled, as by some aberration in nature, yet fascinated.

But then as he watches and listens, she raises her head to look out the window, her hands and body still making music in an abstracted sleepwalking way. Gradually her hands enter the stillness of her vision – some movement of light outside the window? a bird? memories of another time and place? – and rest themselves motionless on the keys. Her lips are slightly parted, her head raised like that of an alert woodland creature, her neck extended. It is white and vulnerable and exposed, unbearably fragile. A vein flutters and twitches like a blemish in finest porcelain. He is mesmerized by it, by that bleating dimple of blue blood against her white skin.

I married her for that. Fifty years of marriage based on the vagaries of capillary activity. It is astonishing how simply and inconsequentially a die is cast. On that very afternoon, at that very moment, I made up my mind. I would have it all – the swan neck, the blue blood, the sherry, the monogrammed napkin rings, the crystal salt-cellars with miniature silver spoons, the children born into thoughtless ease with it all.

If Jason knew, if Emily knew, the cost of their comfortable sarcasm. I gave them that. I gave them the right to be disdainful about propriety, the vantage point from which it is safe to spurn silverware and wedlock and nineteenth-century poetry. If they knew the cost.

I am told that Victoria sometimes throws tantrums, demanding elegance. That she has hurled aluminum salt and pepper shakers across the cafeteria, that the nurses have indulged her with cut-glass ashtrays of salt, providing Q-tips for artful tapping against the finger. This is an obscene parody, typical of the reparations always demanded of me.

Nevertheless. When Adam comes....

If Emily does not bring Adam, this is what I will do: they will have carried me downstairs. (I will not permit Jason; they will have to get the neighbor's son.) When they are all absorbed in the stupid rituals of celebration, I will cross the grounds. Yes, it will be possible with both my canes and the rod of my will. I will stand in the gazebo, I will embrace its spindles and finials and its soft uprights smelling so sweetly of rot and honeysuckle. With a last explosion of the heart, I will pull it down upon my life in a climax vehement as Samson's.

Ever the village schoolteacher, the public performer, the self-dramatist. Watch me, watch me. When I look at myself through Jason's eyes I am embarrassed. I despise my antics.

Reject melodrama then. Edit a little.

Act V, scene v, retake: The old man staggers through the

grounds in solitary pain and sits gasping on the bench, leaning back against the honeysuckle. Around him the indifferent revels proceed, a swirling carousel of inanities. At last he is missed, searched for, keened for. When they find him he is stiff with terminal dignity, his hand clutching his breast, his face contorted in a brave denial of pain. A suitable tragedy, observing the decorums.

I did not even know, that day of the interview in Ashville, what such structures were called. I knew only that it was the equivalent of the blue vein in Bessie's neck, the next rung in my climb.

"There is one of those things in the grounds," I told her, back in Boston. My voice trembled under the strain of its flippant indifference. It was like discussing a woman, a secret mistress, with an interviewing school board official – the irresistible pleasure of the name on one's tongue, the delicious risk. "Like an empty bandstand. Silly things. I don't know what you call them."

I drew a sketch for her.

"Oh," she shrugged, amused. "A gazebo."

I married her for that too: for her amused shrugs and exotic vocabulary, things as unattainable for me as a silver christening mug.

She was not impressed by the gazebo. She saw the whole move as an affliction. I expected her at least to be grateful for clean rural air for the child – Victoria was four at the time and had not yet shown any sign of turning strange – but I should have known better.

Do not expect sensitivity from those who take status for granted. Blessed are they in the land of opportunity who pull themselves up by their own bootstraps, but woe unto those observed doing it. They journey from contempt to contempt within a lifetime, from the polite amusement of in-laws to the embarrassed sarcasm of offspring.

Bessie was never sensitive to my needs, but then she was not, I suppose, particularly aware of her own either. I had seen, I believe, her essence in that arrested moment at the piano. She has spent most of her life outside it, elsewhere. She never showed gratitude though it was certainly due me. (To be fair, she never considered that she had married beneath herself, never flung that at me, though her relatives did. Not in so many words, of course, but by a lift of the eyebrow, an infinitesimal grimace at the corners of lips.) It was due me, her gratitude, because of what I saved her from – the life of a genteel Radcliffe-educated New England spinster. (I am not referring to her age – she was only twenty when we married – but to that air of over-intelligent quaintness.) You can see them any day in Copley Square, their family monies eaten up by inflation and taxes, their teaching pensions woefully inadequate, their sharp intelligent faces and sparrow hawk eyes daring you to snicker as they spread newsprint with fastidious care on the steps of Trinity Church and bring forth their picnic lunch of one orange and one styrofoam cupful of soup. You can see them any day on Beacon Street and Marlborough Street, hobbling along with their canes and their tattered pride, muttering to themselves about A.N. Whitehead – all the brilliant Bessies who did not get married to gauchly aspiring young men; the Bessies whose beauty was ambiguous and was easily mistaken for homeliness when they were not animated by the discussion of an idea.

"Ashville," she had said, as though I had mentioned some disease. "It's so isolated, Edward."

She meant: How will I sustain the loss of Boston?

It was typically inappropriate that she should think of it in that small self-preoccupied way at a time when war was tearing through Europe like a shredding machine. Who knew what was going to happen in the next few years? Those of us with a sense of history saw apocalypse around the corner. Bessie's people, the people of the afternoon teas and grand pianos, saw inconvenience.

It was 1940. I remember waking one morning and asking myself suddenly: Will I die in the country of my birth? I remember holding one arm up against the early light and wondering: Will I die in one piece, all my limbs still attached?

But Bessie cared only for the loss of Boston.

Victoria ran in from the garden, I recall, prattling, "Daddy, daddy," a flawless child she still was, her black curls bouncing. (Interesting that she should have Bessie's coloring, the dark mad strain in full bloom, I suppose. Jason and Emily are fair like me, though there the resemblance ends.) She was greedy as a puppy for affection, wanting kissing and hugging, a basic weakness in her nature even then, though we did not realize it. My impulse was to take her in my arms and kiss her ravenously – the delicious peaches of her cheeks, the little cushions of her buttocks in my hands. But I have never indulged myself in that way.

I gave her a pat on the head, restraining her, holding her away a little with my hands. They need to be taught that.

Bessie, however, fondled the child in a way that was quite distressing to me. She was always cavalier about propriety, being so steeped in it. For a well-bred woman, my wife several times shocked me in the early years. On our wedding night, for instance, when I discovered how misleading the discreet flutter of an aristocratic vein could be. Perhaps she thought it would please me, that vulgar energy. I never spoke of this but was pleased that in time she became a lady again, white and still and intoxicating.

Victoria was burrowing herself into the space between Bessie's thighs.

"Don't spoil the child," I said angrily.

She went on stroking Tory's cheek, caressing her hair, staring at me out of her black eyes. I would say, looking back, that something happened within Bessie on that day, but she was always unreadable. From one perspective, something snapped, I suppose. From another, perhaps, she simply came to terms with reality, acknowledged me as the rightful director of our fate.

I would say she never forgave me for the move to Ashville. In another sense I would say that everything ceased to matter to her. She was docile. She began to become stupid. She lived permanently within the ambience of that abstraction I had first seen on a Sunday afternoon in a Boston living room, books and music walling in her life like fortifications. A solitary impregnable tower. And always, and still, when I see her poised in that fragile Patrician fog of distraction, like a dove suspended in flight, my blood rises. And in the passive aloof way she has gone on submitting for these fifty years to my fever of possession, my frenzy has been reborn over and over again. To possess the unpossessable. That is why I married her. Married into them. To ruffle their calm.

None of this is true. None of it. The medication makes me maudlin. I married a plain girl out of pity, a proud plain girl, gaunt as fencing wire, who came to me on our wedding night with a gauche vitality hoping to please. I was offered a promotion, a schoolhouse, and gracious living. Away from the city her bogus intellectual interests withered. She was bookish but withdrawn, eccentric. An ordinary uninteresting vegetating country housewife and mother.

There followed disturbances which require editing, which require a certain distance, which require dispassionate narration.

V Adam

Cobwebs of a gray June mist that was almost rain floated down on the excavated layers of Roman Britain and on the neatly turned out schoolboys spilling from a chartered bus like lava over their own past. So delightfully proper the boys looked in gray flannels and white shirts and light summer blazers, that several ritual-hungry visitors from Illinois were moved to preserve the charming sight on Polaroid film. Two by two, filing through ancient history, the boys marched down to the stone-tiered amphitheater and into the greedy lenses and on to the rec room movie screens of middle America. As a final flourish one camera took in the little knot of chaperoning parents who huddled in weatherproof jackets at the rear. A nice touch, thought the photographer. After drinks one fall evening, he would show his neighbors in Evanston, Illinois, a spliced and fast-paced distillation of Europe. They would idle with swizzle sticks and ideas, speculating on the degree of damage which uniforms and regimentation and military drill inflicted on the schoolboy psyche. Probably substantial, they would conclude; only consider the state of Britain's economy and the attitude of the British worker. No individual initiative, no dynamism. And yet they would feel a certain wistfulness; would ply grandchildren with flannel blazers complete with embroidered pockets (the real thing!); would rise at inconvenient hours to observe royal occasions on television; would preserve the neat crocodile of boys forever coiling their way out of Kodak microframes and into the crumbling grass-glutted amphitheater.

"Hey, Carpenter," murmured the fair-haired boy who was Adam's partner in the crocodile. "I dare you to ask Price if we can have a treasure hunt for gladiator bones."

Adam's mind skimmed through an extensive and recently

garnered repertoire of Imperial trivia: the papier-mâché model of a walled city with its forum and theater, its villas and baths; the colored chart of gladiatorial weapons; the re-enacted conquest of 55 B.C. (Adam had not been cast as Julius Caesar or any of his bare-legged mini-skirted soldiers, but as a Briton daubed in woad.)

"I dare you back, Snelby," he said coolly. He knew how to play this battle of wits. Never flinch, and always go one better. "I'll do it if you ask him what Roman loos were like."

"Done!" A snicker of delight. "That's a good one. My dad would like that."

Adam had seen Snelby's father on television from time to time, speaking in clipped tones on important matters. It was difficult to imagine his having an opinion on Roman loos.

"Your father an Oxford or a Cambridge man, Carpenter? Which?"

Adam looked thoughtfully at his feet for several seconds and then said carefully: "Can't you guess?"

"Cambridge. I knew it! Was he a sporting man too?"

"He won lots of sporting awards. He's fantastic at surfing and mountain climbing."

"*Surfing*! Where does he go surfing?"

"Oh, all over. In the Pacific."

"In the Pacific! Gosh, what is he? I mean, what does he do?"

"He's a lawyer." Also a weekend sheep farmer, but it might be better not to mention that.

"Is his practice in London? I mean, when does he get to the Pacific?"

"It's hard to explain," Adam fenced. "He's away a lot."

"For the government?"

"Sort of."

"I say, he's not in the Secret Service, is he?"

Adam smiled, but said nothing.

Snelby was impressed. "Of course, you're not allowed to tell, I know. Which college?"

"Pardon?"

"At Cambridge. Which college?"

"Ah.... Can't you tell?"

"King's too! That means we'll go there together! I say, can I meet your father some day?"

"Well, uh.... Right now he's in Australia."

"That's why you had that awful accent. You travel around with him, lucky devil! Is it very hush-hush?"

"I really don't...Snelby, I should be..."

"You can count on me. Absolutely. You don't need to say another thing. I won't breathe a word. Gosh, your mother must have to be brave." Craning back to see where Emily was. "She's very beautiful, your mother. Of course, I know Secret Service men always have beautiful women. Like James Bond."

They had reached the amphitheater into which a breeze blew the thin rain in reams of the sheerest chiffon. From the wet grass beneath his feet, Adam fancied he heard the sighing of legionnaires worn out in foreign service, their sighs stretching out across Gaul, their dreams touching the lonely sons growing up without them in Rome. He wondered what Dave would be doing at this moment.

Rain always made him think of Dave. So did the sun; so did the beach. Because they were all so startlingly different, so absolutely unlike anything over there. After months of bleak drizzle when he had first arrived in London, a master had said to him: "I suppose you're sick of this rain, Carpenter? After Sydney?"

"Rain?" Bewilderment. "Is this rain, sir?"

The master had laughed. "A good line, Carpenter. A good line. Not bad for a wild colonial boy."

But Adam had been genuinely surprised, thinking of the lashing fury of thunderstorms, and of southerly busters, and of cyclones hurling themselves in off the Pacific. He had not seen or felt anything that he recognized as rain.

Australia existed for him as a series of intensely remembered but permanently lost sensations. He grieved for them as for the loss of paradise. He would be walking over the shingle at Brighton in his rubber-soled shoes to where the weary Channel lapped against the gray stones, and he would feel affronted, as though words themselves were not reliable. He would stare at this sleeve of the Atlantic with disgust and think "ocean," and the surf below Dave's Sydney house would crash over powdered golden sands and through his nerve-ends and he would remember the feel of Dave's hairy chest. His arms would be tightly around Dave's neck and together they would brace themselves against the will of the breaker, would swoop up, up its glassy wall, ducking under the foaming crest, coasting down the gentle green valley on the far side. If the wave were particularly high, Dave would say to him, laughing: "That one came all the way from Fiji, mate."

And once, when a wave had spun them over and over like flecks of seaweed and had dumped them gasping and spluttering on the sand, Dave had thumped him on the back to get all the sea water out of his lungs and had told him: "*That* one came all the way from South America, mate!"

Mate.

Dave was his best and dearest mate. A father would be a mate you could never lose.

Once, after he and Snelby had both been caned for shooting small paper pellets from an elastic band in class (one of the pellets had hit Higgins on the ear and he had yelped), Snelby whispered to him: "You talk funny, Carpenter, but I think you're all right. You didn't flinch a bit."

From Snelby, who had once held Adam's head under water for some obscure breach of school etiquette, this was high praise. Adam had asked shyly: "Will you be my mate, Snelby?"

"What's a mate?"

Adam had not known how to reply. He could place no further trust in words.

Snelby had simply shaken his head, grinning affectionately. "Peculiar, the way you talk, Carpenter. But I like you. One of the best."

"And here," Mr. Price said, "are the remains of the forum where every important decision for the city would have been made. When imperial messengers arrived from Rome with proclamations from Caesar, this is where they would have been read to the people. And right here, in the center of the forecourt, is the very sundial from which the city kept its time, still keeping the same perfect time from nature. That is to say," he added dryly, "when there is enough sun to read it."

The boys laughed as they crowded around the bronze dial to view the Roman numerals.

"What does it say here?" Mr. Price asked, pointing to an inscription. "Dickinson?"

"*Tempus fugit*, sir."

"Which means, Higgins?"

"Time flies, sir."

"Correct. And it certainly does. Fifteen centuries have passed since the last Roman soldier read the time from this clock. And that was probably just before he leapt into his chariot and headed down the great Roman road to London and then to the port and the ships. He was needed in Gaul and in Rome itself. The Empire was falling apart.

"And yet time stands still too. That road to London still exists. We came over it in the bus today. If we were to dig up a few layers of asphalt, we'd see the very stones the Romans laid down. Their shades are all around us.

"And that's what I want you to learn from this trip. History is a ladder. We stand on the shoulders of other men."

He seemed to be talking at least partly to the little group of parents, several of whom were fathers who had taken the day off from law offices or government posts to accompany their sons. Adam could see that two of the fathers had been paying quite close and gallant attention to his mother. He was used to this. Men always fluttered around her like moths, they always looked at her that way.

Once, on the Harbour ferry, he and Dave had left her standing at the railing and had gone to buy ice creams. When they came back up on deck she had been surrounded by three young men who might have stepped down from billboards advertising suntan lotion. Emily was smiling at all of them in her impartial absent-minded way.

Adam hated the three men instantly. He had tightened his grip on Dave's hand, instinctively afraid that Dave would be upset. But Dave had grinned at him and sighed.

"Don't worry, mate. Only you and her violin stand a chance in her life." His mother, Dave had told him, was like a Blue Wanderer. An odd thing to say, but something Adam had never forgotten. He knew all about the rare butterflies called Blue Wanderers. He had seen one land light as a bird's feather on a bush, its turquoise wings trembling. He knew that a Blue Wanderer could never be kept still.

"...and we'll meet back at the amphitheater in one hour for the picnic lunch," Mr. Price was saying. "Until then you are free to browse in the sections of the museum that interest you most. But I want everyone to look carefully at the restored pictures in the floor tiles and wall paintings. And I want you to study the models of the villa and of the baths, so that you can tell me what aspects of our modern plumbing we owe to the Romans. I want you to look for the present in the past, and for the past in the present."

Dave did that.

Dave had shown him a bora ring up in the Blue Mountains, a circle of magic stones that had once (and perhaps still on summer nights) vibrated to the ghostly sounds of the didjeridoo and the rhythmic stamping of aboriginal tribesmen.

"Those stones have been here since before the first white man came to Australia, Adam," Dave had told him. "And they will probably still be here after the last man of any color has gone up in nuclear smoke."

Did that mean, Adam wondered, that the bora ring had been there before the Romans built Verulamium? He was a little hazy about the sequence of such distant events.

Time.

It was a mystery even greater than the mystery of words.

In the dawn light of his birthdays, he would be wakened by Dave's telephone calls. In Sydney, Dave would tell him, it was black as pitch. Uncle Jason disturbed his midnight sleep to tell him the sun was still shining in New York.

Was Dave, right now, deep in a dream of Adam and Emily? Were the stars winking down on the bora ring? He knew it was winter there, that the stones would be crusted with frost. How could they be so far away, so out of season, out of reach, when he saw them so clearly in his mind that he could have touched them?

Tempus fugit.

He stared at the sundial as a thin ray of sunlight fell across it, marking out the hour close to midday.

He felt giddy, time whirling him around through space and through history like a toy on a string.

Tomorrow he would leave for New York. For a few days, Uncle Jason had said. And yes, he wanted very much to see Uncle Jason and his grandmother again – especially Uncle Jason. He had a sort of hunger for the rough caresses of men, for the smell and texture of tweed jackets when one is crushed against them. He thought he had lost Uncle Jason and his grandmother as he had lost Dave. But would he now lose Snelby and Mr. Price? Would his mother really bring him back? He thought of the Blue Wanderer and could not be sure.

Was there a place in history where he could just be still for a little while?

He put his arms around the sundial as though anchoring himself to something that had kept its moorings in the mad tidal flux of years, a still point at the eye of the reeling storm of history.

"What is it, Carpenter?" Mr. Price asked in a kindly way. "Is something bothering you?"

"Oh! No, sir."

"If you don't hurry up and study the museum model of the baths, you won't be able to tell me about the plumbing in school tomorrow, will you?"

"I won't be there, sir. My mother is going to speak to you about it today. We're flying to New York tomorrow and I'll be away for a week."

"New York! Goodness me, Carpenter, what a lucky fellow you are, traveling around the world with a famous mother!"

"Yes, sir."

"I keep forgetting you are actually an American. You sounded so very Australian when you came to us. I suppose you've been to the States many times for your mother's concerts?"

"I've never been there yet, sir. I'm not an American, really, although my mother is. I'm a citizen of the world."

"A citizen of the world!" Mr. Price raised a startled and amused eyebrow. "Is that so, Carpenter?"

"Yes, sir. You see I was conceived in Canada and born in Australia and now I am being educated in England."

"I see. Yes. Quite, ah, quite cosmopolitan, Carpenter. Your ...ah...your mother...won't she be upset if you describe yourself like this?"

"Sir?"

"I mean, you know...the bit about Canada?"

Adam was surprised. "But my mother told me that, sir."

"I see. Your mother is...ah, quite a remarkable woman. I have been to some of her concerts, you know. Quite extraordinary."

"Yes, sir."

"I play clarinet myself. Passably, I think. I do hope you're going to introduce me to your mother, Carpenter."

"Oh yes, sir. I will."

"Quite pre-Raphaelite, isn't she?"

"Pardon, sir?"

"Sorry, Carpenter. Just rambling. Here comes your mother now."

Emily was walking in her light unhurried way, her soft skirt lifting and floating gently around her. Her fair hair was shoulder length, a mane of soft and wayward curls that wisped about her forehead and cheeks, always looking just slightly and charmingly in disarray. Her blue eyes, as always, were distant and abstracted, as though – like the sundial – she existed outside of the hurly-burly of time.

She reached them and touched Adam lightly on the shoulder and then moved her hand quickly away, remembering that he had asked her not to do that in public. Snelby would be merciless if he saw it. Her hand fluttered a little like a dove that wants desperately to perch on a forbidden tree.

"Mummy," Adam said. "This is Mr. Price."

She gave him her hand and smiled.

"Adam thinks very highly of you, Mr. Price. I've been looking forward to meeting you."

Mr. Price seemed to have some difficulty catching his breath.

"I've been to your concerts, Mrs. Carpenter," he said,

stammering a little. "I'm an ardent admirer."

"How kind of you. It's not *Mrs.*, actually. Just Emily Carpenter."

"Oh, pardon me, Mrs. . . . ah. . . . I wonder if we might talk a little, while Adam is in the museum. Could we walk through the forum perhaps?"

"Of course."

Adam watched them go. He found that he did not want to move away from the sundial, did not want to disconnect himself from its bluff strength. He traced the engraved furrows of *Tempus fugit* with his index finger. Who had carved it? Who had stood here fifteen centuries ago? Who had stood here since?

There was just enough sunlight for him to see that the shadow of the marker had moved a little around the circular dial. Day after day, year after year, century after century, it had moved around the same circle and come back to where it had started from.

Time itself moves on, his mother had said, meaning he could never go back to Australia, never see Dave again. Time itself moves on, moves on, moves on.

Not *on*, he thought with sudden excitement. But *around and back*!

The realization came to him like an epiphany. The past was not gone, not lost. The Roman roads, the bora rings, they were all still with him.

And Dave.

Dave who phoned him on his birthdays and at Christmas, and from across time and space whispered into his ear: "Whatever happens, mate, we'll always have each other. Don't forget that. Always."

Tomorrow he would fly to New York. He could hardly wait. He had been so careful not to let Uncle Jason and his grandmother matter, not to let himself miss them. Now he would meet his Aunt Tory and his grandfather too. There was more past in his future, time and history rolling over and over on themselves, an acrobatic display for his special private pleasure.

He felt certain now that Dave would somersault into a

London or a New York morning. It could happen any old time. They would slither through present and past and future like gubbies through the creeks of New South Wales. And together they would weave a magic net for the Blue Wanderer – not to kidnap her; just to keep her still for a little while.

He hugged the sundial to himself and touched his lips against its cool bronze face in an ecstatic kiss.

Then he looked quickly back over his shoulder in case Snelby was anywhere about.

VI Elizabeth

Dear Dave, she writes, *The problem is*, and then looks out across the lawn, forgetting what she was going to say, wondering: what does he see from his window in Sydney?

Coevality. The notion absorbs her. What is Emily doing at this instant, as my pen is poised above paper? From the moon, say, could one tell London from Ashville from Sydney? When I think of Emily and Dave in conjunction, does something happen in the ether where thought waves bounce around like ping-pong balls?

Napoleon materializes from the grab-bag of her mind. He wears a cocked hat and tight tights and a hand on his breast. He bows and pontificates: Allow me a suggestion. I understand this obsession with time and space and simultaneity. I imposed my own grammar texts on an entire nation so that I could pull out my timepiece and say: Every twelve-year-old in France is doing exercise III on page forty.

Insane, Elizabeth tells him, but magnificent in its own way. Not incomprehensible.

Thank you, he says. The passion for order.

For harmony, Elizabeth corrects, for wholeness.

She puts down her pen and crosses to the piano. She begins to play Handel's *Water Music*. She sees the River Thames and the Greenwich boat rocking gently at the Westminster pier. She and Adam find seats by the rail on the front deck. It matters to neither of them that everyone else is huddled inside against the rain and the bleakness.

Yesterday he was seven. She looks at him and holds his hand and knows that all things are possible. The way spring makes churlish old misanthropes smile at their neighbors in spite of themselves: that was how it was with a grandchild.

She knows if she can just get Edward and Adam into the same room together....

She stops playing and leans on the keyboard. Frowns. What is the word she's trying to think of? *Catalysis*? She goes to the bookshelf and takes down a volume of the encyclopedia. But the Cs waylay her utterly.

Carthage. A city founded in the ninth century B.C. by Dido of passionate memory. And what has Elizabeth ever suspected of the glories, the rises and falls of that fabled place? Defeat at the hands of Gelon of Syracuse in 480 B.C. But then Hannibal, great general, with his convoys of elephants and troops, soars with victory in his wings. Elizabeth closes her eyes and sees the elephants humping over the Alps, their bewildered trunks groping delicately, inquiringly, sensuously in the snow, causing astonished Swiss dairy maids to have lascivious thoughts.

She reads of *Casimir*, duke of Cracow, 1177-1194, and of *Castor and Pollux* and of *Castruccio Castracani*, leader of the Ghibellines in thirteenth-century Italy. Dante gave him a spot in the *Inferno*, she has not read Dante for years, she makes a mental note to do so again. There are glowing pages of *Catalan* art (fifteenth century) and the history of *catalepsy* to be absorbed before she reaches *catalysis*, remembering.

Yes. She was right. It was the word. If she brings them together, Adam and Edward, the chemical reaction will take care of itself. She won't need to do anything else.

She goes back to Handel's *Water Music*. She is on the Thames again. Adam has made this trip before, with his school. See, he points out for her, as they glide past the graceful Norman towers. That's the Traitor's Gate. And Sir Walter Raleigh was in that tower there.

But it was in Greenwich, in the old Royal Observatory, as they dallied among astrolabes, that he said: "Dave would love this. I wish Dave could be here."

"Who is Dave?" she asked him.

"Dave's my father. Sort of. He's not really my father, but he's my real father."

Elizabeth loves the illicit and the passionate as much as Adam does. She seduces him. He tells her everything. About the shearing and the wool sales and the law office and the Blue Wanderer and the time Dave didn't come to the airport to say goodbye. But Dave calls on his birthdays and at Christmas, and yes he does have Dave's address.

She wrote her first letter as soon as she got back to Ashville. He replied, she wrote again. She kept all his letters in a drawer in Emily's old room. About some things, she felt superstition couldn't hurt.

She was still playing the *Water Music*. If she were a better planner, she might have been able to orchestrate Dave's presence at the reunion. Yet what could she have done when she still didn't know for certain if Emily would come? Nevertheless, there would probably have been a way. And then: catalysis again. Simply bring them together, she is certain, and these senseless barriers Emily has erected against her own happiness will crumble.

Is Elizabeth a meddler? Does she have the right? She considers the question seriously.

She is in Emily's minuscule kitchen again, saying with careful lightness: "Adam seems to miss Dave a lot."

It was as though she had injected agitation. She sees want in the tremor of Emily's hand and the quaver of a facial muscle. Elizabeth thinks of childhood anxieties and school heartaches. Of one of the earliest music competitions, when Emily, still just a child, faltered in the difficult second movement of a sonata, missed a phrase, came to a dead stop. Elizabeth, accompanying, marked time, sidling around the problem passage, giving Emily cues, waiting for her to pick up and go on. But Emily was rigid with stage fright. There were little stirrings and rustlings of sympathy from audience and judges.

"Emily," Elizabeth called softly. And woodenly the child turned, her white face streaked with tears. "We'll start the movement again," Elizabeth whispered. "Face me as you play."

Profile to the judges, Emily began again, a perfect performance.

The trouble one has with one's youngest, Elizabeth thinks, is the difficulty of accepting she has outgrown your power to protect. She wanted to take her daughter in her arms, to say. "There, there, let me fix it."

"Why," she began to ask, "when Dave seems to both you and Adam..."

But Emily cut her off. "One wasted musician in the family is enough. I don't want nooses around my neck."

Elizabeth does not consider her life a wasted one. She tries to absorb the idea that she has somehow imposed solitude on Emily, and willful unhappiness. She is unable to say anything. She goes home and writes to Australia.

> *Dear Dave:*
> *It is possibly quite improper of me to send this letter. I am, however, moved to do so by the enthusiasm of my grandson, Adam.*
>
> *I wish simply to thank you for the way in which you were, and are, his father. He thinks of you constantly. It is clear that you have given him a rich store of love on which to draw. I cannot thank you sufficiently.*
>
> *I have reason to believe that Emily misses you as much as Adam does. I cannot know, of course, how events have affected you. But if, as I suspect from your phone calls to Adam, these connections still matter, I wish you would consider visiting them in England.*

Dave answered promptly. He was overjoyed to receive her letter, to meet her as it were. He had, in fact, felt connected to the family for years. He was especially grateful for news of Adam whom he missed more than he could say. As for Emily, he would never get over her. And yet he had feared from the start that she would never stay anywhere long. Besides, she had told him that she was involved with someone else. There was nothing he could do. Certainly he could not go to England, he would never impose.

There is no one else, Elizabeth wrote. *Emily must have lied in self-defense. Please go to England.*

One cannot coerce, he replied.

It was mad the way people balked at their own happiness.

She should have planned better, should have arranged for Dave to be at this reunion, for Emily to be caught off guard. The problem was her precarious grip on time. It was too late now to do anything.

She went back to her letter. *Dear Dave*, it said. *The problem is....* She wrote:

> *The problem is my precarious grip on time. I should have brought you together, should have thought this all out earlier. In any case, I want you to know that I am hoping to have Emily and Adam here on the weekend for a family reunion. If it happens, it will be significant, considering all the vowing never to set eyes on, et cetera, that has gone on. (I told you what happened in New York.) I rather expect something (I don't quite know what) to happen. (If this letter strikes you as a little ludicrous, put it down to an old woman's wistful belief in hocus-pocus and magic.) Anyway, I thought you should know.*

A rare practicality inspired her. The problem of time: Emily would (if all went well) be here in a few days; letters took over a week to reach Australia.

She called Western Union and dictated it as a telegram.

The clerk giggled nervously. "I think that's the longest cable I've ever taken. Are you sure you want to send the whole thing? You could cut it a bit."

"You're right," Elizabeth said. "Omit the *Dear Dave*. It's unnecessary, isn't it?"

VII Edward

Sometimes they still eddy through cracks of memory. They are lingering smells: the machine oil slick of a mill town; the sodden whiskey stink of defeat; mother's perfume of soap suds and fear. But I washed my hands of them. I shook the dust of childhood from my shoes. I left. And it was as though that time had never been. It was prehistory, the incunabula of my life.

Then came the events of college and marriage and the birth of my first child.

This was all Advent: life before Marta.

I remember waiting for the doorbell to ring....

Let me illustrate. At an airport, say, a man waits for a flight that is bringing his wife and children home. There is a somber announcement: disaster; an air collision; no survivors.

At the takeoff point another man in another transit lounge, having missed that very flight, has been fuming over his beer, cursing a slow taxi driver, rehearsing apologies to his corporate overlords. There is an announcement.... His hand trembles. He orders another beer.

Afterwards it seems to both men that they already knew, that the waiting was febrile with extraordinary premonitions.

Even so I remember waiting for the doorbell to ring. Knowing nothing, blandly expectant, and yet in retrospect surely conscious that the quality of life was about to change forever.

It is important to reconstruct objectively, it is important to conduct research from different perspectives, looking for clues. Experiment number one, then.

He was waiting for the doorbell to ring.

Mrs. Weatherby, had she been able to speak freely from the depths of the sofa, might have remarked to her sister, Miss Constance Simcoe, that Edward Carpenter was such a *competent* young man.

"And so handsome," Miss Constance might well have murmured in response, watching the light burnish his fair hair with reddish gold.

"Really, Constance, I don't think that is a fitting remark when we are both on the school board. Pedagogical excellence, that is our concern."

Edward Carpenter, however, was unaware of their admiration; and he was, as he clenched his hands and waited for the doorbell, as extremely nervous as he was tentatively proud of himself. He moved the heavy drapes a little, partly in order to observe whether his hand was visibly trembling, partly to ensure that one edge of the drapes made a pleasing off-center perpendicular to the sofa. He grimaced at the clutter of music on the piano and when Mrs. Weatherby and Miss Simcoe moved out on to the terrace with his wife, scooped everything up and jammed it below the hinged lid of the piano stool, paused, riffled through the books and selected one. Schubert. He flipped through it until he found a page suitably dense with demi-semi-quavers and then propped it open above the keyboard.

It was as though he had awakened one morning to find himself miraculously poised in the middle of a swaying tightrope, no safety net beneath, so many faces watching. Such hierarchies in a small New England town! A wrong step would be disastrous. He was obsessed with correctness and suffered the perpetual anxiety of a soldier crossing a mined field under enemy fire.

In the mornings, as he held his cheeks taut for shaving, he would ask his image: Am I doing it correctly? Should the sideburns be perhaps a quarter of an inch shorter?

And the eyes in the mirror would flash back unease. *We are not certain, we are never certain. You must be more observant.*

His wife was indifferent to correctness, knowing all the rules by heart. This was allowable, a natural law. Only to those who are not sure of the rules is it forbidden to break them. He was therefore afraid of this dinner party, although it had been his suggestion. He had to suggest it. It was the correct thing to do. He was even more afraid when he saw, through the window, two couples arriving simultaneously.

The doorbell rang.

(Who should greet? Should the host? The hostess?)

"Ah," he said, in a scramble with screen door and guests and hands to be shaken. "Allow me to present my wife, Elizabeth. Bessie, my dear, this is Mr. Dalton, chairman of the board of trustees, and Joseph Wilson, my deputy principal. And their wives."

(Oh, *gauche*! Should he not have mentioned the wives first? And by name? Should the entire thing have been the other way around? Should he have introduced *them* to Bessie first?)

Mrs. Wilson – Marta, he had been informed, but he could not possibly say such an extravagant name out loud – was alarmingly incorrect. She was absolutely not what he had been expecting in the spouse of a staff member under his jurisdiction. She wore gold hoop earrings that swung when she turned her head and a dress of unnecessarily bright colors in some flimsy fabric. Edward foresaw disturbances on the respectable and tranquil horizon of secondary education. He glanced warily at Mrs. Dalton and Mrs. Weatherby who seemed to intimate: We regard Mrs. Wilson as an exercise in enlightened though painful toleration. Bessie, on the other hand, they had taken straight to their proper hearts. He was humbly grateful.

As he carved the roast, he surreptitiously observed his deputy principal – an intense-looking man with an air of absent-mindedness – who perhaps had been pondering philosophical questions while dressing for dinner; hence the slightly crumpled jacket that should have been at the cleaners. This was acceptable, even desirably academic. Edward could see that Mrs. Weatherby deferred to Joseph Wilson's opinion. But what could the man have been thinking of, to take such a wife?

It transpired, it drifted to Edward between carving the roast and pouring the wine, that his own wife and Joseph Wilson knew each other distantly, had dim shared childhood and college memories, and mutual acquaintances several times removed. It did not altogether surprise him. Abstractedness. Intensity. It seemed to be as much a part of their kind as the family albums and afternoon teas. What, then, could possibly explain Joseph Wilson's marriage? The only faint hint of rakish propensity that Edward was able to detect was a lock of dark hair falling across his forehead as he leaned toward Bessie to stress a point.

The two were earnestly engaged in a discussion of European affairs as though the outcome of events depended entirely on their deliberations. Was congressional approval of lend-lease aid to Britain sufficient? Would they move to active involvement now that Germany had invaded Russia?

Bessie's face was vibrant with disputation. She still had those pretensions of course – politics and culture. The slow slide into her domestic and interior coma had barely begun. Nevertheless Edward was grateful. Mr. Dalton and Mrs. Weatherby were listening as to oracles. He could not imagine that they would listen to Mrs. Wilson. He could not begin to imagine the effect she must have on some of the older members of the board of trustees – Dr. Richardson, for instance.

"Don't you think so, Mr. Carpenter?" Mrs. Wilson asked him now, catching him unawares, her huge eyes, murky as midnight and witchery, resting earnestly on his face. Her gaze, wholly and undividedly his, implied that no decision on the topic under discussion could possibly be reached until his considered judgment had been given.

He was not used to that sort of attention. He did not go in for that sort of thing.

"I'm afraid I wasn't following the conversation." Self-consciously, hinting at reproach, his vocal cords jamming.

He had to clear his throat. It suddenly occurred to him that Mrs. Wilson could have a whole boardroom full of school trustees groveling at her feet. Not Mrs. Weatherby perhaps, but what resistance could Dr. Richardson offer to those eyes?

Mrs. Wilson raised one eyebrow slightly in lieu of reiterating her question and Mr. Dalton came stumbling in over his own words to rush her with a gallantry of answers. Edward noticed that his own hand was trembling slightly on the tablecloth and he closed it gratefully around the wine bottle beside his plate.

"More wine?" he asked, drawing the mantle of host about himself.

"Thank you, Edward."

He was taken aback. How had they reached first names so abruptly? He did not approve of spurious sociability. He knew it was considered incorrect.

"My pleasure, Mrs. Wilson." He spoke primly, as to an erring child.

"Marta." Looking up at him, smiling lambently. "My name is Marta. That's enough wine, Edward. Thank you so much."

To his embarrassment, he saw that he had filled her glass to an inelegant quarter-inch of the top. He saw Mrs. Weatherby's assessing eye on the glass. His hand accidentally brushed Mrs. Wilson's arm and the wine bottle bridled nervously as he set it down. A dark splash ran on to the lace tablecloth and spread like a burgundy lily opening its petals. Marta traced its outline languidly with an index finger and Edward felt helplessly that a die had been cast.

"We were discussing," she said, "whether Chamberlain could reasonably have been expected to foresee what advantage Hitler would take of the Munich Pact."

Edward had removed his hands, which were refusing to behave calmly, from public view. He clasped them rigidly below the table.

"I mean," Marta went on, her eyes beneath fluttering lashes never wavering in their trustful intensity, "it's so easy for everyone to call him a betrayer of Czechoslovakia *now*. It's as though the international press had perversely decided to ignore the difference between its own foresight and hindsight."

Edward had a sudden glimpse into chaos, a queasy earthquake-like awareness of a great chasm fixed between a peaceful, socially advantageous marriage and a disastrous passion.

"What do you think, Edward?" she persisted gently.

"It is not a distinction," he mumbled, dazed, "in which I have ever previously believed."

"Pardon?"

He felt faint and dizzy, singled out for extraordinary sensations. He felt that perhaps he was capable of great thoughts and daring actions. He felt foolish.

"Forgive me...I'm not following.... Where were we?"

"Foresight and hindsight."

"Oh yes. Quite right. An enormous difference," he assented vehemently, foreseeing tumults and betrayals and surrenders.

"Will we declare war, do you think?"

"Yes. Oh yes, I would say that's inevitable."

And he fancied that Mrs. Weatherby's eye and ear had taken in the truth whole.

But what of Bessie? What of Joseph Wilson?

Sparring with ideas, engrossed in other wars and treaties and deployments, they saw nothing. Throughout that roller-coaster year, and throughout the next summer and fall, as they all careened toward Pearl Harbor, it was the same: his wife and colleague, absorbed, blind, safe in the armchairs of talk, noticed nothing; while he, once so rationally inclined, teetered on the high wire of obsession.

Even on that last chaotic night in the gazebo when pandemonium had stalked their lives, what was Bessie doing? She was discussing with party guests the theaters of war – Europe, Africa, the Pacific – as though assigning grades.

On that night, as he had stumbled from the gazebo in the darkness, heading blindly for the house, he had collided with his wife. Was she not as frantic and distracted as he was? Had she at last realized? How much did she know? he had wondered with terror, fearing a new element in the cataclysmic decisions to be made.

"Edward, have you seen Victoria? She's not in her bed. She's outside somewhere, I saw her run out."

He felt weak with relief. Such a simple and surmountable anxiety. Such a clearly defined task: calling her name into the night, *Tory, Tory*; checking her favorite play places. When they found her, huddled and shivering under the honeysuckle, she seemed dazed, she did not remember anything.

Sleepwalking, presumably.

It was the first inkling that there was something not quite right about Victoria.

And after she was safely asleep again, Bessie had said: "Edward, there's something I have to say."

She knows after all, he had thought with a clutch of panic.

"I'm going to have another baby."

And so of course the decision had been made for him. There had never been any real choice or real chance.

He had always associated Jason with the loss of Marta. Within a few weeks the war had lifted him up like so much effluvia and dropped him in the Pacific. Death everywhere. Disintegration. When his son was born he was in a bloodied bunker and it was weeks before the news reached him.

Yes, a fair account, I think. A fair account, and an honest one, though other versions are no doubt possible. Perhaps I flatter myself, perhaps I overdo the insecurity and innocence. Nothing to be gained at this age, I suppose, by not being ruthless, by trying to keep the past in candlelight. Shall I drag it into the full glare of regret?

Why did I so easily make the wrong choice? That is the question.

Revised editions possible, no doubt, and maybe even beneficial. Try again, begin again. Fast forward in time. Experiment number two: things as they *might* have happened. Should have happened.

"Here he is!" Mrs. Weatherby said as though serving up dessert, the *pièce de résistance*, to the select Sunday afternoon company. "Here he is, our Jason, and just in time for tea."

"And what are they doing in Boston these days?" Dr. Richardson asked, forgetting his question before it was answered and relighting the pipe he constantly forgot he was smoking.

"Dear boy, dear boy, how lovely to see you again. You've been up at the schoolhouse visiting your father and mother? And poor Victoria, of course?"

"Well naturally he has, Constance, what a foolish question."

And Jason, dryly: "Oh yes. Father and I have had our obligatory battle."

"You are too hard on him, Jason." Mrs. Weatherby observed him thoughtfully as the small talk ricocheted inanely back and forth. With casual brightness she invited him to inspect her oriental poppies in full raucous bloom beyond the terrace.

And then she would tell him, feeling it was time.

"You should know this, Jason. It may help to explain. You've tended, I think, to blame your father but you are wrong. You cannot know the struggle he has had. I knew him from the first, you know, I miss nothing. He was raw when he first came here, of course. Quite raw."

(*Yes, admit it, she would have thought that.*)

"Born, as we say, on the wrong side of the tracks. But a man cannot be held responsible for his birth, Jason, and it was given to your father to recognize pearls when they were cast before him. You are too hard on him."

Mrs. Weatherby walked to one end of the terrace where the lilacs tossed their cones of blossom lightly against the cement balustrade every time a breeze caught them. She buried her lined but still imposing face in the scented boughs as though conferring with the forces of delicacy.

"Yes," she said. "Yes. I will tell you. Though you must keep it in the strictest confidence. A temptation of the cruder sort was thrown in your father's way. Oh I know, Jason, you do not think your father capable of passion – the young never expect it of their parents – but I can assure you.... They were kin in a way – both out of place and lost – base blood calling out to base blood, I suppose you might say."

(*Oh, this is the relentless courage of old age. She must have seen Marta that way.*)

"She was educated and ambitious and so was he, and I can assure you, Jason, that the air around them was charged, positively charged.

"But he knew it would never do, you see. He knew what there was to lose. His will power was extraordinary, his sacrifice magnificent. And he did it for you, Jason. For you. You must look at him through different eyes."

Oh such waste, such waste. To have opted for the good

opinion of Mrs. Weatherby. To have chosen for Jason's respectability. I shall go mad.

But somebody should explain to Jason. I deserve that somebody should explain. And to Emily. Surely she will not be so heartless as to leave Adam behind? Somebody should explain to her.

VIII Victoria

On the ward they were making apple people. First the fruit was peeled, then the faces carved – any sort of crude holes for eyes, nose, and mouth would do – then the entire apple-head was dunked in lemon juice. After a few days on a sunny windowsill, the heads would wither into a genuine and miraculous old age with pinched cheeks and sunken grin and wrinkled brow. The women on the ward would begin to recognize people they knew – their grandparents, their parents, other patients, themselves.

"This one is my father," Victoria said.

"Why do you say that, Miss Carpenter?" asked the young arts-and-crafts volunteer.

"The prying nose, see? Long and sharp as an eagle's beak. And these X-ray eyes, a bird of prey. Quoth the raven, nevermore."

"So." The volunteer skewered the apple head to a stuffed doll's body. "What sort of clothes do we need for your father? How about these denim coveralls? And a pipe for his mouth."

"No, no! Don't put those coveralls on him. He'll be very angry. We have to have a gray suit."

Together they began to rummage through the carton of dolls' clothing.

"Miss Carpenter, dear," called a nurse from the doorway. "Time for you to see Dr. Blackburn."

"Oh, what a shame. We'll have to finish your father tomorrow. I'll find a suit while you're gone and put it in your workbox."

The volunteer handed the undressed doll to Victoria who dropped it, agitated.

"Cover him, cover him!" she begged.

She spread her hands over her face and huddled herself into

a small bundle that began rocking itself back and forth.

"Come on, Miss Carpenter, I'll take you to Dr. Blackburn."

Victoria, rocking and whimpering like a child, ignored her. The volunteer put her hands under the patient's armpits from behind, and raised her to a standing position. Ballasted with flesh – a side effect of medication – Miss Carpenter was half guided, half propelled, like a galleon tacking against the wind, toward Dr. Blackburn's office.

Sometimes Victoria swam, sometimes she flew. In either case, the motion was a tranquil swaying one which she could sustain by minimal muscular contractions in arms and legs. Consequently her movements were invisible to an observer. She could circle him with the languid gracefulness of a porpoise in its aquarium, and he would never realize. Or she could glide around and over him, coasting on banks of air.

On some days the air would cloud quite abruptly with a smog of minute glass splinters. It would rake across her tongue and through her nostrils and into her lungs, ripping and tearing at her as it went. She would spit blood, although the nurses never believed her. It was willful of them, of course. Ignore the mess and you won't have to clean it up. She knew their little game. She had written letters to Jason and Emily, complaining, but no one answered.

Poetry helped:

the glass shards,
the razor blades, are full of eyes.
My life crammed with eyes, surfeited
with calibrated eyes, every tic
of thought watched and charted; yet blind
every one of them unseeing
when the bleeding starts

The nurses – Philistines – ignored her poetry and the spits of blood. On such days there was nothing for it but to escape from air altogether, to flow into her other medium of water. And today was a swimming day.

She trod water, breathing by her other system, her secret gills. The water was green and murky and restful. No one could be seen too clearly, an added benefit. There were other days when the water was too clear for privacy and she would have to hide behind seaweed, but today was satisfactorily opaque. She relaxed within the greenness, buoyant and at peace.

Aqueous eyes peered at her like floating moons and she let herself ride motionless on the swell, curious. It was Dr. Blackburn's face, a kind one. She saw his gills working, his mouth opening and closing. He did not realize that the waves distorted all sound, that it was futile to speak.

She circled him, rubbing scales, to show that only touch communicated – or certain vibratory patterns set up by fin rhythms and telegraphed direct to receptive minds. He understood. Together they swam through caverns to a large concourse of waters where the waves were crystal clear and full of bodies and she wanted to dart back to murkier rock crevices when she saw suddenly someone she had lost a lifetime ago – her little brother, ludicrously magnified by the crazy lens of ocean.

She surfaced gasping and the air was soft and clean as childhood. She ran and stumbled up the beach, laughing, and gathered him into her arms.

"Oh Jason," she sobbed. "Oh Jason, Jason! How you've grown!"

Dr. Blackburn said, "Your brother has come to take you home for a few days."

"Don't you remember?" Jason asked. "We're going to see mother and Emily."

He was never prepared for Tory. Never. Every time the shock was greater. There did not seem to be any way to protect himself from it.

Submitting to the soft swallowing pillows of flesh, he felt the past shambling over him like a drunken elephant, ponderous, random.

IX Elizabeth

The nice thing about a power mower, she thinks, is the illusion of strength it gives to these old arms and legs.

Also she loves the tang of the cut grass and the knowledge that it is still growing even as she is cutting it. In three days it will have to be mown all over again. And again. And again. Such pleasing confirmation that living things need never be daunted, that hope is instinctual. She always feels like saying: Good for you, grass!

She has to be careful not to let Edward see her from the window. For the swath of lawn in his view she has to pay the neighbor's son – if she remembers to stop mowing in time, and if she remembers to ask the boy. As far as Edward knows, the neighbor's son mows it all. And it is, really, wickedly self-indulgent of her to sin in secret like this, but she cannot bear to give it up.

Edward is enraged by evidence of the agility of others. How he hates aging, she sighs. And wonders: if my heart wavers, if my sight (which is deteriorating) blinks out, if my body is shackled to a chair, will I be as splenetic as he is?

She truly does not think so. She thinks she will continue to shake the marrow from each day, that she will say to her body: Try to defeat me, old bag-of-bones. She thinks the thrill of outwitting the daily diminishments will continue to absorb her. She expects she will do what she does now, on impossibly arthritic mornings. First the testing and flexing of wrists, shoulder blades, ankles. Can she get out of bed? Will her ankles hold up on the steps? On a day when the answer is no, she starts with rubbing and moves on to her own brand of isometric exercises. Just enough to coax rudimentary life into the joints. And then the experimentation: how many ways to get a bathrobe on, to get to the bathroom, when the limbs are as uncooperative as chair legs?

It's a serious game, demanding more concentration than chess or bridge. So far she holds a trump (playable after the first skirmishes of pain and gritted teeth). Her body cannot resist the pummeling of a hot shower. It softens. It yields.

She rewards it by mowing the lawn, a sensuous business. Now she is roiling like a skiff between delphiniums and poppies, grass flying like spume, settling on her hair and arms and legs. (She never uses the grass-catcher, she likes raking too much.)

By the back fence, matted with blackberry runners and Virginia creeper and assorted flowering and fruit-bearing vines, she accidentally shears off a trailer of honeysuckle and the air is heavy with chopped fragrance. The vine is caught in the blades like a piece of string and she turns off the motor to pull it out.

She thinks of Victoria. The honeysuckle always reminds her of Victoria. Just a little short of breath, she sits on the grass and rests, her back against the mower. Twisting the ravaged cord of honeysuckle in figure eights around her thumb and fingers. Why should it smell of Tory?

The bruising perhaps. The damaging.

At Tory's birth....

There is, Elizabeth supposes, nothing quite like the birth cry of a first-born. One of those moments when the meaning of life shimmers clear as a dewdrop in the mind.

She remembers Edward standing at the bedside watching Tory sucking at her breast. She remembers that she thought of tales of mythical transformation: beautiful young men turning into fauns, children into unicorns. There was about him some quality of awe that made one think of wild deer. Or of stranger creatures, fey and otherworldly.

The hush of his features: could I have set this in motion? Could I have stirred in the night and cast this life upon the waters? Tory's black curls still sticky with birth fluid, her fingers and nails – the work of an incomparable miniaturist – the fine whorl of her ear, the little slurping animal sounds, the blind and voracious sucking, the mad energy of her lips and cheek muscles – he watched it all in a trance, his being vibrating like a drumskin. His right hand, his knotted mill-town fingers, advanced in worship. He stroked Tory's head, her ear, the line of the cheekbone, her lips, the pink-brown circle around Elizabeth's nipple, her breast.

She remembers that. She can feel it still, the touch of almost fifty years ago. She had murmured to him, mother and seducer, newborn love merging with old. And his hand had clenched and taken refuge behind his coat lapels, a guilty thing. It was as though he had been caught fingering his own mother's private parts.

Oh Edward, she sighed, she grieved. If she could have taken him in her arms and given him her other breast to suck.

Elizabeth sighs and runs her fingers over her sun-warm arms. Tissue over bone. Its hour is coming, she thinks. The bone hibernates from birth, biding its time, rearing its implacable form closer and closer to the surface, awaiting the last great spring of death. She buries her fingers in the cut grass, massaging earth, and rubs the tang of summer into her arms; reaches under her cotton top and anoints her breasts. There is juice in her yet.

Poor Edward, she sighs, so afraid of the flesh. His great shame: in the beginning, now, and world without end, amen. How she had mistaken the ragged energy spilling from him in her parents' drawing room. And perhaps Tory confirmed something for him: the hugger-mugger of copulation and begetting.

They had watched her, their first-born, grow into imperfection.

But Elizabeth cherishes flawed things. It seems to her that their beauty is somehow ethereal because more vulnerable. She has given succor to cats without tails and dogs without ears. Her window ledges are cluttered with relics from antique auctions: blood-red crystal pitchers with chipped lips, milk-glass with hairline cracks, porcelain cups without handles. Anthropomorphic things. She endows them with tragic histories and grieving memories and present contentment.

She thinks: When Tory comes, we'll sit here in the crushed grass and thread flowers and sing songs.

But the shredded length of honeysuckle disturbs her. Her mind veers away from the act of injury itself. The moment of damage cannot be redeemed into art. There are two black holes in the past, two different nights of harm.

Elizabeth is agitated now, brushing two images from her eyes with nervous hands. Tory as a sleepy child, Tory on her seventeenth birthday. Elizabeth is on her feet now, pulling at the cord of the mower. Tory in a white nightgown, a frightened child, is sliding down the banister of the handle. Elizabeth pulls the cord sharply, the motor growls and stops. She pulls again, swearing at it softly, beseeching it for its roar of white noise. She pulls again. Perverse, the motor hunches like a sulky cat and ignores her. She looks across the lawn and the gazebo is full of Japanese lanterns and party revelry, and in the doorway, Tory at seventeen....

Elizabeth is crying now, and digging with her bare hands in the nearest patch of garden. Tending things. Removing weeds. Binding up.

It is not enough.

She rubs her hands jerkily in the grass to clean them and runs across the lawn into the house. She needs the piano.

She plays for a long time and when she lifts her head and looks out through the French windows, the gazebo is softly blurred like a pagoda in a Monet painting of the gardens at Giverny.

She plays a dance. In the dance Tory, today's Tory, large and graceful, circles the gazebo with languid and delicate steps, and honeysuckle is braided through her hair.

X Edward

So.

It is possible that there was something slightly coarse about Marta. It is possible that the sort of gypsy musk she gave off aroused my earliest crudest boyhood memories – the smell of cats mating in alleyways, the pungent furtiveness of mill-hands and girls from the spinning rooms groping in the hedges at the back of factories.

It is possible. I am trying to be dispassionate. No doubt Mrs. Weatherby saw Marta as... well, gauche – always having confidence I would rise above my lower instincts.

It is also possible that there was something of the hermit in me (cooped in too long by discipline and cerebration, by a fear of poverty and a fear of taking a wrong step, by a fearful memory of father coming in late smelling of whiskey and other women); and something of the temptress in Marta.

But to be honest, to be quite simply honest, I believe it was beyond explanations, beyond a need for justification. A cataclysm of nature. Of the order of Paolo and Francesca, Antony and Cleopatra, Anna Karenina and Vronsky – doomed as such passions always are. I do not think I am exaggerating. I am too old to deceive myself.

This is how it was.

After that first dinner party I became aware of her in the uncanny almost psychic way of one who loves totally and helplessly; the way of the fly, trapped but tranquilized, watching the slow ballet of the beautiful deadly spider. I knew without looking when she had entered a room by a certain displacement of breathing air, a change in blood pressure. I knew by an abrupt sensation of vacuum if she left town for a day. I knew when I was about to see her. I would be walking along a street thinking of anything or nothing and my hands would sashay into an unaccountable jitterbug routine of such flamboyance that I would have to push them deep into my pockets. Marta! I would think. And indeed she would appear, just turning the corner ahead, just walking through the park with her little daughter, just coming out of someone's front door.

Oh *rage! rage! against the dying of the light.*

To have lived like that.

To have come to this.

See how the squirrels mock me. See them chattering over a hoard of stolen tulip bulbs, desecrating the gazebo with their feverish chewing and spitting.

I will smash out the screen, I will throw myself into the lilacs, I will scream, I will go mad.

"Bessie!!"

Here she shuffles, here she blows.

In torment, one finds ease only in causing pain. When cornered, one must lash out.

"Where are the Wilsons?" I bellow, as though she has stupidly mislaid them along with my clean underwear and socks. (She does that, she does that, damned abstracted woman.) "Whatever happened to them after the war?" My eyes glare: you have willfully withheld this information all these years. (She has, she has, to try me.)

Why am I doing this? We know what happened. We know that Joseph was killed in New Guinea, that Marta moved to New York. I repress this knowledge. I have forgotten it daily for half a lifetime. Did she remarry? Is she still in New York? It would be madness to inquire. Like a reformed alcoholic, I censor out all knowledge of her life. Otherwise, how would the tissue of duty hold me?

God. Oh god. Still when Bessie does that, still after fifty years, when she goes into that birdlike suspension, her breath trapped in her throat, her veins bleating in her neck, I still want her. What mockery when my systems go on strike more often than the teamsters, when I have this tin box stitched into my left chest, when my useless legs wilt over the chair edge, what mockery that the wanton and adolescent blood, too stupid to know it is old, goes thumping around my genitals.

God. She is white as a saint piled around with fagots, her lacerated eyes have known all along. How brutish I am. From the mud of a mill town I came, to mud I shall return. If I shout at her again, she will shatter like fine crystal.

"And the Roxtons," I grumble. "And Feder, that young teacher who was shipped to Africa? And the Stanton girl that went into the nursing corps?" Playing it up now, the delirious old man rambling in the garbage of his past. "What happened to all those people we lost track of after the war?"

"Ah Edward," she says, her lost voice fluttering back to her from limbo. It is trembling, her hands are trembling. "Who knows where the time goes?"

(*Elizabeth*)

Liz, he was saying. *Oh Liz, oh my god.*

And then chaos....

Elizabeth puts a hand out to steady herself, clasps a chair back. She strains to remember something. How much later was it – a week? a month? – when Marta, measuring her as a duelist might measure a rival, said levelly: "My baby's due after Christmas."

And Elizabeth, going for the main artery: "So is mine." She had been going to say more, to throw shrapnel, but Marta had turned white and had leaned back against...her car door? a tree in the park?

"What a savage bitch you are, Elizabeth," she said. Then she began to cry silently and helplessly.

"Oh Marta."

They had almost embraced.

All that time gone, all that time. Who knew where it went?

◆◆◆

"Ah Edward," she says. "Who knows where the time goes?"

"My cushions," I mumble, growling a little, wanting to

make amends, to give her a chance to offer comfort. (I am not, after all, so very barbaric. I have gone on letting her love me.) "My back...my cushions have slipped...."

She plumps them, she rubs my back. Gruffly I stroke her forearm with my fingers and she is startled. I feel the tiny tremor, as of butterfly wings almost still on a bough. She is standing behind my chair, she bends over and kisses the nape of my neck. My blood crashes about, my eyes water, for an instant I feel: it has been a warm and comfortable marriage. But then I think of drooling Victoria, of Jason bristling with pedantry and contempt, of Emily, my freewheeling slut. My irritation rises, as constant and internal as phlegm.

"Isn't it hot enough," I snarl, "without having a body all over me like a blanket?" (I wish I would not talk like this. I wish she would not provoke me to this extreme.) "Cooped up in the house" – by way of extenuation – "without a breath of fresh air."

"Shall I turn on the fan?" she asks. "Or would you like to be taken into the garden?"

Out in the garden! To sit in the gazebo! How my foolish blood jangles about again. But she knows I will not submit to that utter circus, the neighbors' sons called in, the cheap adolescent cheeriness, the easy strength with which they hoist my weightless torso into the hammock of their hands. Never.

It is perverse of her to ask and I do not deign to answer. She ought to be able to read my mind. She has had fifty years' practice. I wait for her to bring the fan. She continues to stand, pretending not to know what I want, pretending to listen for my answer. We will see who wins this battle of wills.

Two minutes and she has not moved. How can I hope to compete with the sanitized stillness, the perpetual abstraction of her dreamtime?

"Well?" I rage. "Will I have a fan by September, do you think?"

See her startle! She had forgotten I was here. Back with the Wilsons, exploring that pain, sliding back into that white shock. I want her gone before I see that in her again, before the ceaseless tide of guilt and brutishness returns to swamp me.

"Leave me, leave me. For god's sake, leave me be, woman!"

Gone. I won't willingly cause her pain. She looked that way, I recall – that *winded* bruised way of frightening stillness – the night it ended, the night Marta and I came together in the gazebo like worlds on fire, the night we parted. It was a party, we must have been observed, must have been missed. How did it begin? Scotch. I remember the taste of Scotch. I remember Marta's flesh cool as honeydew melon. Bessie's face – like bones bleached on a shoreline, gaunt, motionless, deathly pale. People everywhere like shadows moving in, it must have been a party....

There had been a party. Twenty to thirty people perhaps, the mood one of determined revelry stretched tight as a membrane over the universal anxiety. The talk in that summer of 1942 was all of the war. Would the tide be turned against Japan? They all drank a great deal and danced and talked endlessly. There were, of course, more women than men, and most of the men were in uniform.

Not Edward yet, and not Joseph Wilson, selective service priorities valuing teachers.

Standing by the French windows drinking Scotch, the fire slithering down his throat. Yes, and there were other details clear as yesterday. Clearer. He knew that Marta was watching him from across the room, could feel her gaze on the back of his neck, summer-warm. Desire rampaged through his body like a tidal wave.

Something would happen soon, he knew. Before the end of the summer, something irrevocable would happen. It was as inevitable as a thunderstorm after days of steamy torpor. His dammed-up passion would roar across the retaining wall of his caution, smashing propriety like matchwood, foaming and spuming into magnificent chaos.

He knew it was the same with Marta. It was as though nothing else, not even the war, was real for either of them. In a crowded room, on a downtown sidewalk, he performed for her alone, she for him. He was like an organ-grinder's monkey, going through rehearsed actions and speeches. Look at me, look at me! "*The purple testament of bleeding war,*" he murmured at one gathering half aloud, playing a role of abstracted reverie, being poetic for *her*. And Marta, in a soft aside, as though no one else was on stage, had said: "Oh yes! *Richard II*. How apposite, Edward."

When he and Bessie arrived at a concert, a party, a school function, his eyes would sweep the assembled people until they met Marta's questing for him. Color would branch in her cheeks like a spill of red ink on blotting paper and she would look away. And yet nothing, not a single verbal innuendo, not a touch of endearment, had ever passed between them. Their daughters, Victoria and Sonia, played together on swings and slides while they, fond parents merely, stood talking in public: Do let Tory stay for supper, Sonia loves to have her.... Have you bought Sonia a copy of the new illustrated *Grimm's Fairy Tales*? Never an improper word. They were like chaste medieval lovers sleeping with a sword between their bodies.

The question was, however, how much had Bessie noticed? What did Joseph Wilson know? Possibly everything. Was it possible to hide such feelings? He did not dare even pronounce her name. He could not even allude to the Wilsons for fear the air around him would catch fire.

Yes, he was standing at the French windows drinking Scotch. He was conscious of Marta's glances creeping over his back like ivy, massing themselves around his neck and shoulders, looping and trailing around his heart, strangling his genitals with painful want.

And suddenly, through this thicket of desire, there came as it were a wrenching hand, tearing away fistfuls of protective dreams.

It was Joseph Wilson's voice, after the ritual throat-clearing that precedes self-conscious announcements. Going, he said. Next week...just had word. Hadn't even had time to discuss it with Edward...somewhere in the Pacific...couldn't give details naturally.

A flowing in of people, a static of talk. Champagne corks popping. But Edward sees two faces: Marta's, Bessie's. Both white. Marta's eyes on Bessie, Bessie's on Marta.

Bessie realizes, he thought. What she is looking at so starkly is the almost immediate future, the last barrier down. She is afraid of abandonment. In his heart he cries for her, for his own ungovernable passion, for what he knows he is powerless to prevent.

Bessie's eyes shift to Joseph. Why does she stare at him so fixedly? She pities him as she pities herself – for this blow of fate, for his having to exit and concede the fight.

And Marta, so immobile, so porcelain pale? She feels, Edward decides, as I do, the awesomeness of the inevitable, the weight of destiny, the blood of chaos on our hands.

And here was another detail, ballooning large in memory: Joseph was looking at him, his eyes acknowledging something, saying something, waiting for something. For what? And then Joseph's eyes move, not to his lost wife Marta, but to Bessie. Why? An instant shared perhaps: be brave! Edward wonders: have they discussed the matter?

And then Joseph's eyes are back on Edward. Everyone's eyes are on Edward. What are they waiting for? His hands feel cold and slick as ice. Will they suddenly turn on him, stone him to death? But of course it is a speech they want. Some sort of formal acknowledgment from the principal to his brave young deputy marching off to battle.

Edward clears his throat and says the required things. Stuff this country is made of. Making the world safe for democracy. The men in the jungles. That sort of thing.

Applause and clinking glasses. He leaves them all milling around Joseph. He opens the French windows and walks out into the garden. He sits in the gazebo.

Time passes, he supposes. Guests leave. He hears car engines spitting and stuttering and swearing into the quiet night, an echo of machine-gun fire.

Time passes. And yet time stops. He does not recollect thinking anything at all. Just waiting.

And finally he sees Marta approaching the gazebo from the house. He watches her, scarcely able to breathe.

But at the periphery of his vision, blurred and out of focus, he sees movement. Background only, an insignificant detail, yet strangely disturbing. Through the lighted upstairs window at the stair landing, he can see Victoria, sleepy six-year-old in her nightgown. She has had a bad dream perhaps, she wants milk and cookies, she is looking for mommy and daddy. Hesitant and wistful, she leans the upper half of her body over the sill, stares into the night. Her vulnerability pierces him like a spear. What will happen to her now? He is filled with the impulse to stride into the house and gather her into his arms and carry her back up to bed.

But Marta is entering the gazebo, obliterating background. And the war like a hurricane obliterating everything, himself blown into uniform in a matter of weeks and the future to God knew where.

XI Jason

Jason's dreams were as disordered as his days were precise. In dreams he was always trapped in small spaces choked with clutter – attics, chicken coops, cellars, closets. Cobwebs would threaten to engulf him, dusting his face and arms with their light malignant caress. He would thrash around in darkness, knocking over old suitcases, showering himself with mothballs and the molt of ancient eiderdowns and cascades of sepia photographs.

Snuffling breathing from low in the eaves of his dream. Owl? Bats? Frantic, he clambered over packing cases, feeling for a gable, a skylight, a vent. The breathing became louder, there was a shuddering sigh, a cobweb settled around his face like a shroud. In terror he smashed his fists against the low roof and the weak tiles clattered into the night. He cranked his arms rhythmically against the air, gravity shrank away from him like an exorcised demon, his feet rose above the packing cases, an arcane and potent childhood fantasy winging to his rescue. He gulped in the free oxygen beyond the tiles, soared out over the eavestroughing. Steady now, palming the air with regular beats, his legs held taut and together, acting as a rudder. He eased himself earthwards.

Sweating, almost drowning in sweat, he touched down in his bed and jolted into wakefulness to find the sheets tangled around his feet. He could still hear the noisy sigh-strewn breathing. His dreams, he thought, were nothing if not functional, incorporating local sound like an artist working with flotsam.

It was not Ruth. Her sleep in the twin bed at the far side of the room was neat and antiseptic as always. This shuddering was more wanton, uninhibited, lumbering across the hallway. Victoria, he remembered, and lay listening. Like brackish water raking its way across siltweed, her night-breath foamed and staggered in and out of her body.

Jason found it unbearable. He extricated his legs from the ropework of bedding and crossed the hallway. Shadowy light in her room: the refracted nimbus of a street lamp. Tory's slack and dimpled torso presented itself in shocking nakedness, a kind of bitter parody of a Renoir, the amplitude there, but not the sense of inviting ripeness. A large woman, forty-six years old, yellowing with defeat and age. Her nightgown was twisted up across her breasts, a balled-up wad of fabric clutched in one hand and held to her mouth. She sucked it noisily, moaning and heaving herself about, her large thighs scissoring toward Jason and trapping his eyes in an unruly mat of pubic hair.

He recoiled as though spat upon flinging his hands over his eyes, propping himself against the wall in the hallway. He thought he might vomit. Certainly his legs could not support him and he slid his back down the wall until he was sitting on the carpet. It was the travesty that was unendurable, that muffling disguise she ingested with her medication. He could still remember her at sixteen, willowy, with skittish eyes, her body unstill as a colt's. Astonishingly beautiful. He could not cope with this sordid metamorphosis. He needed a strong drink.

In his study he poured himself a double Scotch and then locked the door. It was not really necessary, Ruth knew better than to intrude on his moods. *She* called them "his moods." I am, he thought, a bastard to live with. But considering everything, I do the best I can.

Three of his study walls were lined from floor to ceiling with books. He sat on the carpet and pulled from a bottom shelf the four substantial volumes of *The Encyclopedia of Philosophy*, extracting from the space behind them a shoebox which bulged at the seams, its weakened corners several times fortified by layers of masking tape. With the excitement of a child creeping downstairs around midnight on Christmas Eve, he took off the lid and stared into the rummage of his past. What, he wondered by professional habit, did this furtive poring over hoarded scraps of history release in his brain?

And to what extent was he addicted to his own neurochemical juices? He was more ashamed of his sentimentality than of his dream-belief in flying. If he had to choose, he would rather be seen flapping his arms in bed then be caught looking through this memorabilia, this testament of vulnerability to the past.

He overturned the box and sat staring at the pyramid of photographs, cards, old theater programs, letters, and envelopes stuffed with sub-categories of all of the above. He felt as though he had simultaneously ingested valium and amphetamines: a manic *frisson* of pleasure zipped around like mercury over a layer of almost infantile peace. Part of the cabalistic thrill came from the clutter of the contents.

Jason was fascinated by clutter in the way a teenage boy is fascinated by a brothel. He admired tremendously people who could live in disarray. He felt that they were of a superior order, akin to Albert Schweitzer or Mother Teresa. This was partly a legacy from graduate school in the sixties, the heyday of Cambridge, Massachusetts, when living in clutter was a necessary political statement. He had tried very hard to live that way.

At the time he had still been married to Nina, but things were going badly, and he was having an affair with a girl named Natalie who lived in a state of clutter so absolute that one could only assume she was gifted with a sort of divine countercultural infallibility. It was Jason's perception that a direct relationship existed between clutter and love – love, that is, as nonexclusive communion, as earthy regenerative force. Natalie's love spilled over as copiously as did her table tops with mounds of books and dishes and left-wing political pamphlets and items of clothing and plates of dried spaghetti. She took in stray dogs and cats along with the many roaming friends and relatives of former boyfriends and the various construction workers and Boston dock hands whom she was busy politicizing.

Sometimes, coming in late after a night course (it was his teaching assistantship year) before heading back home to Nina, Jason would have to step gingerly over various human humps in sleeping bags to get to Natalie's room. Natalie was the only person he knew who had a brick-and-board bed. In those days, everyone had discovered brick-and-board shelving for books (though he and Nina, living outside of Cambridge, had custom-built floor-to-ceiling oak) but the bed was a refinement on student thrift. It gave a certain piquancy to love-making. On their unsteady brick foundation, the five planks shifted and slid beneath the foam mattress, dragging at an assortment of mismatched bedding garnered from the local goodwill store. During erotic activity the boards made percussive comments and the bricks would sway uneasily and the foam mattress would dip into little hammocks of surprise only to pleat itself with a gasp of expelled air as the planks collided together again with seemingly vicious intent. There were times when Jason felt that the bed itself was an instrument of feminist polemic, dangerous to appendages.

But this was unlikely: even Natalie's ideology was cluttered, subject to caprice and contradiction. She was impossible. She was delightful. She of the madonna face and ingenuous concerns, who used the word "bullshit" in graduate seminars as though it were a seal of academic insight and conviction; she who spoke so fiercely and frequently about sexist oppression, but cooked up meals like some Salvation Army earth mother for the crowd of workmen and students who randomly slept at her place.

Jason felt utterly at peace in her chaotic house during the three or four hours a day he spent there. When he went home to the little Renaissance haven that Nina kept for him, with its Rubens and Rembrandt reproductions framed in old gold, with its mandolin gracefully placed on top of an antique trunk in one corner of the living room, with its butcher block kitchen table where Nina waited for him with hot chocolate, he would feel tense and constricted and ashamed. Hypocrite! Even at the time he knew it, being passionately fond of some of the beautiful things Nina collected. Especially of a carved wooden figure she had given him. It was sensuous to the touch, its head and body cowled in grief. An Old Testament prophet perhaps. Or a woman sustaining a great loss. It was a sacred object to him, a symbol of Nina whom he loved so ineffectually and destructively.

After he left Nina and moved in with Natalie, he discovered

that he was not capable of living with her absolute clutter round the clock. In less than a month he got a small apartment for himself and only visited Natalie in the evenings and for part of the night, as before. Of course he had to give a political reason: he said his presence was interfering with her *conscientization* of the workers; he said he needed more space for his own project, a series of articles showing how therapy had been co-opted by forces of oppression, how industrial psychologists were being used by management to defuse worker dissatisfaction. They were all very busy changing the world and love was a secondary thing.

In his own apartment, Jason tried very diligently to cultivate a certain amount of clutter. He built brick-and-board shelving for his books. He taped to his walls stark graphics of workers' fists and the silk-screened sayings of Pablo Neruda and Simon Bolivar. He made a determined effort to leave his bed unmade and his dishes unwashed and his books scattered over the floor. He was delighted to have his parents visit during this stage. His father's disgust so pleased him that he was able to persist with the disorder for several more weeks.

Unfortunately the mess interfered with his ability to study and write. And then it distressed him to see the beautiful wooden figure (which he had salvaged from his marriage) slumming it on a packing crate. He began to browse in Boston's antique shops. Just for interest. When he saw a weathered oaken chest he felt that he owed it to Nina to buy a fitting pedestal for the carving. But then the posters on the wall looked tacky and the floor looked excessively bare. He bought a white flokati rug and a couple of small watercolors and a lithograph of an interesting androgynous face. He replaced the director's chairs with a sofa covered in textured off-white Haitian cotton and sat in it listening to Mozart on his stereo. He looked about him and accepted the fact of his bourgeois unregeneracy, and yet he loved to escape for several hours to Natalie's house of pandemonium.

Natalie. He thought of her messy life with affection, riffling now through the contents of his shoebox looking for signs of her. Here she was. A playbill for *Mother Courage*, put on at the Loeb. An excellent production, the Kurt Weill music stridently passionate. Romanticized bourgeois bullshit, Natalie had said. Brecht had committed the sins of cleverness and artifice. By then only Mao was still pure as far as she was concerned and that changed with the table-tennis tour and Nixon's smiling of pure smarm from the Great Wall of China.

But it was not Natalie he was searching for tonight. He shuffled through the pyramid of papers and found an envelope labeled *Victoria*. The photographs were not in any sort of order and some of them dated from before he was born. The first one, in black and white, must have been taken at his grandparents' home in Boston. Both his parents were kneeling on the lawn, arms open, and Victoria was taking what were probably her first steps from her mother's arms to her father's. His mother was facing the camera almost full on, her lips parted, all her concentration on the unsteady laughing child. She would have been in her twenties. She was not ever beautiful, Jason supposed, by any of the standard assessments, but she had one of those unusual faces that delight sculptors and that can beguile with such mobility of expression that the watcher is tricked into adoration.

Tory's beauty was of a different order. Had been. Unambiguous. In the twelfth century, Jason thought, she would have been considered a faery child. A white witch's foundling, of a beauty so stunning that people were almost afraid to look. No one would have been surprised by what happened.

In the photograph, he could see only the back of his father's head and a quarter profile of cheek, brow, and nose, but that constant inner dynamo of rage and dissatisfaction was unmistakable. Jason could read it in the soles of his father's shoes, in the savage thrust of toes into the turf of the in-laws' lawn, in the jut of the thighs, in the backs of the hands waiting to receive Victoria.

What had he been thinking? Had he been bursting with the excitement of his tiny daughter's achievement? Ready to cry out with irritation if she fell? Both, probably. From as early as he could remember, Jason had had an image of his father clanking along in invisible armor, with steel guts and an overwound inner spring.

The next picture startled him. It was in color. Tory, at about sixteen, was holding hands with some lanky young man and gazing soulfully into his eyes. Jason felt as though a switch had been tripped in his mind, that there was something at the edge of his memory, something bale. His hands were trembling and he took a quick mouthful of Scotch. He had a strong sense that he did not want to look at that photograph any longer, and shoved it hastily back into the envelope.

He pulled out another picture. Black and white again. Tory, about seven or eight years of age, playing mother. She was seated in an armchair with a real baby in her arms, bending over it adoringly. Jason realized with a shock that the baby was himself. For a long time he stared at the wall through tears. Such good care she had taken of him. He had been unable to help her.

Here was another. This time he and Tory and their father were crowded into one of the seats of a Ferris wheel. Yes, he remembered that day. The picture had been taken by one of those photographers who roam around fairgrounds snapping their shutters every time someone moves.

I remember the man with the camera, Jason thought. I remember that ride.

Father is sitting between us. Tory's eyes are huge with nervous excitement. She did not want to come on the Ferris wheel. She was always frightened, jumping at shadows. I was only four, so she must have been eleven, yet I was braver than she was. My eyes are glittering with pleasure.

I remember that the second time we went over the top Tory gave a sharp cry and a thin stream of vomit, dyed dark pink with cotton candy, arced out from her lips like a reddened rainbow. Fascinated I watched it fall, slurping its way across the awnings of seats below us on the wheel, losing itself far under.

Why ever did Tory, so gray with terror, not stay with those little puppets of people on the ground? Why did she not stay with mother? Because – I remember now – mother was away in Boston or New York. I forget which. Visiting relatives whom father didn't like, I think. Or maybe old friends from Radcliffe. And I remember that Tory was even more afraid of being alone on the ground than of being with us in the sky.

Father would be so utterly different when mother was away, taking us to movies or to parks, telling us bedtime stories.

Consider that day. He did not rage at Victoria. I waited for him to shake her roughly as the wheel careened down and under and up again, to tell her irritably that she was a big girl now. But he took her in his arms, he pushed her head gently against his shoulder, he wiped her ghastly blotched mouth with his handkerchief, he did not even flinch when more pink vomit gurgled from between her lips and down his shirt front.

I was dumbfounded.

Poor darling, he kept saying. Poor darling.

When the ride stopped, Tory was white as new porch paint but she had her arms around father's neck. He carried her, I remember. She was eleven – a slight eleven, it is true – and he carried her, while I tagged along hanging on to his coat sleeve, amazed.

I loved him at that moment. I remember it distinctly because it was so unusual. Most of the time I was afraid of him until I began to hate him.

When he sent me away to boarding school (so you'll be well prepared for Harvard, he said) how old was I? Seven? Eight? About Adam's age. More terrified than Tory on the Ferris wheel, though not showing it of course. But he never offered me his handkerchief or his shoulder. I wrote to mother almost every day, but I never wrote to father. What is it that I can't forgive? Not boarding school itself. I came to love that school. Why, when it would have been so simple, did I never add "and father" to my letters?

What was it stretched like barbed wire between him and his father?

Staring down into the funnel of his past Jason focussed on departures. On saying goodbye. On sensing damage to the women in his life: his mother, his sister.

He thought: I fear being responsible for women. I fear leave-taking the way other people fear death.

He was in his new school blazer, his mother was holding him at arm's length surveying him proudly, sadly. September was just brushing the garden with brilliant decay.

"Jason." She couldn't say anything else. She pulled him toward her and held him and ran her fingers up and down the back of his neck as though memorizing him.

"Jason."

And after a long while: "It's very important to him. He has so little." (Yes, Jason knew she had said that. He had always remembered it, wondering what she meant. *He has so little.*) "He thinks it will make everything possible. My brothers went, you see. It's really quite usual." She buried her cheek in his hair. "You must write to me, Jason. I can't bear to lose you totally."

She took his chin in her hand and turned his face up to hers.

"Don't grow away from me, Jason."

And he remembered feeling a love so strong it made him dizzy, and a terror that she was somehow being damaged, that he was part of it, that he had to intervene. He felt, he remembered now, *responsible*.

And with Tory it was even worse.

They had hiding places under the caves of honeysuckle behind the gazebo and there he found her. Just sitting and staring at nothing. She was, perhaps, the loneliest fifteen-year-old in America. She bridled at shadows, she was frightened of everyone. Boys followed her home from school, at a distance, overawed by her beauty. She was too shy to look at them. Though Jason would see her at her bedroom window, watching from behind her curtains, sighing. There was one boy who always lingered near the fence.

Under the honeysuckle, as Jason tried to say goodbye, she cried: "Don't go."

He thought: I'm her only friend.

She held out her arms to him and for a moment he submitted awkwardly. Uneasily. But then it seemed...she was murmuring, wanting to kiss him. He was her baby brother still. Or perhaps the boy she liked to watch through the curtains....

At first he thought she was playing a game and when he realized she was not he was momentarily horrified, then furious.

"You're crazy!" he had shouted at her. "Tory's going loony, Tory's going loony." Taunting and darting about her like a dragonfly. She reached for him and he ran away but she did not chase him. Unseen he crept near again and heard her sobbing. He hated himself. He knew he was responsible. He avoided saying goodbye.

It was easier with Emily, playful toddler. She loved the colored towers he built for her with blocks, she loved to knock them over, triumphantly destructive, squealing with delight. He built her a last tower, she demolished it a last time and became fretful, sensing unhappiness.

It was his father's fault, he perceived, all that grief and loss. His father's fault.

And somehow, obscurely, his own. For which he would not forgive his father.

In the space behind *The Encyclopedia of Philosophy* there were two additional bundles, both wrapped in tissue and tied in string. He had never opened them though he had packed them and moved them with him more times than he could remember: from school back to Ashville, and then to Boston and then through a trail of apartments in New York. He treated them as though they held totemic power.

He reached behind his books and touched the bundles, paused, thought better of it, and left them there. He began to scoop up the other shards of his life and to ram them back into the shoebox.

Over the blather of paper the door creaked. Someone knocking. Jason stiffened with implacable hostility, waiting for Ruth to go. But the sound – scrabbling, more than knocking – continued. With tight lips he reached out, turned the key, opened the door an inch. It was Tory, elephantine with the unchangeable past, huge with shadow. An eclipse of the electric light. Instinctively Jason put his hands up to his head to ward off a landslide of what? Of Tory's memories nudged back to life, perhaps, by this unexpectedness.

She sank down beside him with a little whoosh of released air, her nightgown settling around her like a dejected balloon. Fat lady at the circus, he thought, hardening himself, stuffing a crude and bitter wit into his wounds. In his hands he held the envelope with the photographs of Victoria young and lovely. She reached for it, he jerked it away, she grabbed, they pulled, two children in a sandbox.

God, he thought, yielding. This can't be happening.

"You didn't write to me, Jason," she said mournfully. "All through the term I wrote to you and you never answered."

Time snaked around him like a fun fair ride.

"I did, Tory. I wrote. You've forgotten."

But he had not kept her strange letters, her alarming poems. He had known at the time he was guilty of sacrilege. He had disposed of them as though they were living things, as though he were drowning kittens.

She was staring at the picture of herself and the young man and he watched the pleating of her eyebrows, the effort, the agitation beginning. He remembered her stages of brilliant lucid bitterness, the vitriolic letters that had chased Emily and himself from address to address, the searing lines left on placemats, under pillows:

before birth, when the gills,
still gills, breathe blood, they know.
Unfair. They know it already.
Unjust.

He waited for revelation, for judgment, for atonement.

Nothing.

He watched the energy losing itself like ripples flattening out in a pond. She began to cry silently, a passionless sentimental concourse of the tear ducts. A pantomime of loss. Rag doll in a puppet show, she asked him:

"Where did she go? Where's Tory gone?"

A nursery school game, he thought, wanting to smash something: his inadequate profession; the false god of medication. Reverberations inside his skull: *gone, gone, gone.* Levelled out under drugs, rendered grotesquely amiable, disguised in a costume of flesh, her rages and poetry cured.

What cures we peddle, he thought with horror. He wanted to beat on his own breast.

"Where's Tory gone?" his sister repeated, a child with a

tattered nursery rhyme. "Where's she gone?"

He took her plump clammy not-herself hand and leaned her Halloween costume of shapelessness against himself. He thought of the wood carving when it had stood so wrongly on a packing crate in his old student apartment. (He seemed to be crying for Nina too, for all his failures; she seemed to be drifting waif-like across his vision.)

He said: "Tory, you were beautiful. Everyone remembers. I remember." He tapped his forehead. "You're still here."

"Do you remember the ferry?"

"The ferry?"

"The ferry in New York."

"New York?" It was the first time she had visited him here. He usually went to the clinic, took her for walks.

"We went to the Statue of Liberty. We took you out of school."

He felt a prickle of excitement.

"My god, Tory! You remember that? I'd forgotten it. I'd completely forgotten it. You and mother just showed up one day. I was called into the principal's office and there you were."

"The train," she said, excited. "We went to New York on the train."

It came back to him in gusts like a knowledge of ocean swimming to someone who has spent years inland. There had been an air of wicked hilarity, he remembered. It had been a conspiracy. Father did not know, was not to know. Mother had been going to New York, Tory was supposed to stay with grandparents in Boston, and mother had decided on impulse to collect him from school, to take them both with her.

"Beethoven," Tory said, plucking scenes from the air. "Mother said, 'No, Tory, I'm not crying. It's just Beethoven.'"

He did not remember that. Only the concerts themselves, the splendid hush of the packed hall, the conductor as magician, pulling music from the air with his wand. *Ex nihilo.* Like God saying: Let there by symphonic harmony.

He remembered the art museums – acres and acres of canvases on walls, forests of sculptures, scores of hollow rooms that throbbed with footsteps and heartbeats like a womb.

That was when he became aware that his mother was something quite other than any of them had realized. That in Ashville she lived incognito, in a dormant state; that she had this other life tucked away inside herself. In New York she was the kind of person who said witty things to elevator operators. Taxi drivers flirted with her, gallery owners deferred to her. She sat in concerts like phosphorescence, lit from within. One of the cognoscenti. She frolicked in an almost febrile way with Tory and himself (now, as an adult, he was reminded of the nuns at a hospital with which he was associated; of nuns at a picnic the day after Easter Sunday, an austere Lent behind them) but she also seemed infinitely removed from them.

He had wondered, that time in New York, what kept her attached to them. She was a helium balloon with her string tangled in domestic muddle; if they ever let go, she would fly beyond reach forever and forever. He had held her hand very tightly.

"We got lost," Tory said.

Jason blinked away clouds, shaded his eyes from the rude present, still on the trail of a lost balloon, an impossibly distant bucking dot of color.

"Lost," he confirmed.

Yes. Babes in the woody thickets of culture, forlornly holding hands, they had wandered astray in the Metropolitan Museum of Art. I'll meet you back in this room, their mother had said, because they lingered so long over swords and dagger hilts gaudy with jewels. But which was the room? Hadn't they only turned a corner or two? They had dragged their feet by Etruscan treasures telling each other that *this* was the door. Or maybe that one. She could hardly be far away, just a room further on or further back. They dawdled through Egyptology. In Costumes they forgot her for a while, became anxious again among French and Dutch paintings. The tense face of a Le Nain peasant, perhaps, reminding them. Or Vermeer's *Woman at the Window*: looking for someone, waiting.

The reverent gloom of lighting seemed to be dimming. It was getting late, the crowd thinning out.

"She's probably following us round and round," Jason

said, "and we keep moving away from her. We should stay here."

They sat on a bench facing Gauguin's *Tahiti Women by the Mango Tree.*

"If father finds out. . . ." Tory said.

And he had not known whether she meant the entire trip, the being lost, or the lush coffee-colored breasts offering themselves with blossoms and mangoes. He thought that it would be almost dusk in Central Park and that women might emerge from the shadows with baskets of fruit, their breasts flowering from purple drapery like rare orchids. He imagined that the fruit would be watermelon, soft with juice and sin.

"Let's wait for her in the park," he suggested.

But Tory was appalled.

"She'd never find us. It's dangerous there. I won't let you go. I have to look after you."

He let her do that, hide her panic behind her protective role. The older one, bearing the brunt of life's terrors for him. She must have been sixteen, he must have been nine.

"Soon they'll be closing," he said.

They had to sit outside on the steps, huddled in their coats. Tory's teeth were chattering, not, he thought, from the cold. He wondered if they would join the lost children in Never Never Land with Peter Pan and Wendy. He was sure he could fly like Peter Pan. He wondered if he would manage to pull Tory's weight.

And then their mother was released from a taxi at the foot of the steps and she gusted her way up to them, a darting balloon.

"Oh my darlings!" she gasped, laughing and crying, hugging them to herself. A miraculous rescue. "Oh my darlings! Can you ever forgive me?"

Back at the hotel she explained. Something about the unicorn tapestries. How she always went there next after Renaissance paintings. And she was so used to being at the Met alone, that after they wandered off into forests of armor. . . . "Oh, how could I? I forgot. . . . I thought I was alone . . . I went straight to the Cloisters without even thinking. . . . Oh you poor darling children. But I'll take you tomorrow. You'll understand."

It was all magic to them. They did not expect to follow. When they saw the tapestries, they understood that explanations are always arcane and mysterious. They saw maidens and white horned horses that flew perhaps, or lay down in impossibly flowered fields. They understood that nothing could be clear.

Jason asked: "Do you remember the unicorn tapestries, Tory?"

But the glory had gone from her, the little lightnings of memory extinguished. Gray and slack again, in her medicated present, she oozed into sleep. Jason put a cushion under her head, a rug from an armchair over her. Her breath gurgled like a child's.

He stared at his walls of books. Then with the air of one breaking a curse, he reached for the bundles behind the bottom shelf. He untied them and felt the soft pelt of onionskin, his mother's letters. But he could not read them. Gently he put them aside. His father's letters were fewer and firmer, in envelopes. He opened one. A stiff solitary page of good bond, and also a postcard showing a black-and-white etching of his school. He turned the postcard over. It was stamped and addressed to his father in his father's own handwriting, but the left half of the card was blank of communication. The accompanying letter was in India ink, a genuine nibbed pen, a schoolmaster's hand.

> *My dear boy:*
> *I know that you are extremely busy with school work and sports and I rejoice in the achievements that you have described to your mother. We are very proud of your letters. I do not want you to fritter away time with any such foolishness as writing everything over again to me.*
> *But perhaps you could take two minutes to scribble something on the enclosed card and that will suffice. When you come home we will be able to sit and talk together and discuss literature and politics like two educated gentlemen.*
> *With fondest love, Father.*

After a long time, Jason looked into the other envelopes. There were stamped and pre-addressed cards in all of them. He had never mailed one. Not one. He did not read the other letters. He had an image of himself as implacable. He thought that if he turned out the light and looked at his face reflected back from the dark window, it would be the face of a savage. Or would perhaps be carved from ice. A cruel face.

Dear God, he thought, burying it in his hands. Who is more guilty, him or me?

XII Elizabeth

Elizabeth is standing in Jason's old room. There is dust on the mirror, months of it, a powder of absence. Her ghostly reflection observes her as through a shroud. She winks at it.

Art thou there, truepenny?

She writes in the dust with her index finger: *The British are coming, the British are coming.* Joke, she explains. But you should hear the way Adam talks.

Jason has called and she knows it for certain now. Not that she had permitted herself doubt. A Thursday flight. They are committed to it. Catalysis, catalysis, she sings, brushing away the dust with her sleeve. And the woman in the mirror, unshrouded, smiles smugly: You did it, my dear! Congratulations.

I told you, Elizabeth says. Prospero is my middle name. Just wait for the final act of my Elizabethan opera. The pun her rambling thoughts have stumbled on delights her.

She makes up the bed and places a dish of potpourri on Jason's dresser. Lavender, thyme, and rose petals. *Where the bee sucks, there suck I*, she hums. All from her garden. Dried in bunches hung by the kitchen window and crushed between pieces of muslin in her own hands.

Nevertheless the room smells of Jason.

There is a dream that still haunts her once in a while. It used to come over and over, a nightmare. In the dream, she is taking a taxi through Central Park. Faster, she is begging the driver, but a million things impede. She is frantic, the children are waiting. When at last, at last, the taxi reaches the Metropolitan Museum of Art, the steps are empty. It is past closing time, even the stragglers are gone. The children are nowhere to be found, they are never seen again.

Elizabeth closes her eyes and sees Tory and Jason, lost

waifs. She hugs Jason's bedpost and clasps the children in her arms, weak with relief.

Batten down your life, she warns herself. You're flapping loose in the rigging of time.

In museums, she always goes backwards through history. A conditioned response: after the Renaissance paintings, the fifteenth century. That was why, on that day...she turned from Tintoretto and thought of carved ivories and illuminated manuscripts, the lure of things medieval snared her, the pull of the Cloisters. A logical progression.

(And then the past had interfered. Especially a stolen afternoon before the war. The Tapestries Room.

"Liz, look at the maiden in the fifth fragment."

"What wicked eyes."

"Not as seductive as yours."

She had looked up from her guidebook with dismay: "She's betraying the unicorn."

Despondent, they had pondered betrayal.)

The children were safe in the armory, this must have been backdrop knowledge. Elizabeth did not even remember leaving the museum. She slipped from the moorings of the present, she supposed she took a taxi but it might have been an uptown bus, she forgot time. She sat in a chapter house shipped stone by stone from the twelfth century, she lingered over the ivories, she came to the Tapestries Room. When she saw the maiden with treacherous eyes and the unicorn pensive inside its picket fence, she remembered. Betrayals and captivity and responsibilities.

She remembered the children.

Elizabeth knows the panic all over again. She is promising the taxi driver double to break all speed limits. She is aware that the distance from West 190th Street to 82nd and Fifth is infinite. In the dream Tory and Jason are not on the steps of the museum. They are nowhere to be found.

But Tory had already been damaged.

And Jason?

She remembers the day he left for boarding school. Edward's doing, for complicated reasons. She holds Jason to herself, she does not want him to go, she is so fiercely anguished by his leaving that she knows it is better if he goes.

Elizabeth acknowledges something to the face in the mirror: I always thought of him as mine alone. The solitary pregnancy, the solitary birth.

Solitary Jason.

The face in the mirror accuses solemnly: One may smile and smile and be a villain.

She looks at her hands. They are always covered in blood. She dips them in the bowl of dried petals and rubs them together until her palms are stained with fragrance. She smooths the bedding with her aromatic fingers, strokes the pillow. She takes a palmful of dried petals and herbs and scatters them inside the pillowcase.

From down the hallway comes a sustained crescendo of command and petulance. Something like an enraged cello, Elizabeth thinks, whose player is overly fond of vibrato.

Probably she has forgotten something again. His lunch perhaps. Or his newspaper.

She tucks the perfumed pillow under her arm and goes to Edward's room. An unusual dilemma. She reconstructs it: it seems he has been gesticulating at squirrels again, with one of his canes. He has been vehement, his point has been firmly made, the walking stick is in the garden below, the rip in the screen somewhat larger.

"Oh Edward," she laughs.

But he prefers to intimate that the incident is full of an esoteric dignity.

Elizabeth's shoulders are shaking, she leaves quickly. In the hallway, she hides her laughter in the pillow, goes outside and retrieves his cane.

"Good shot!" she calls up at the window. "It landed upright, like a javelin throw."

But he probably cannot hear her.

She considers re-entering the room with the walking stick carried as a rifle. Presenting arms. She thinks better of this maneuver.

She places the cane with due decorum beside his chair. She

straightens his blanket, ignoring his irritable bridling. She plumps his pillow – then, with a deft movement, switches it with Jason's.

She flashes her Cheshire Cat smile at Edward's mirror, at Jason's mirror, in passing. She sprinkles petals inside Edward's pillow and leaves it on Jason's bed.

She is not superstitious. Not exactly. It is a matter of meeting kind with kind: the workings of damage are so arcane and mysterious, so elusive to the moral eye in the present, so mocking in hindsight.

She is setting a stage.

She demands of herself a well-composed finale.

She leaves Jason's room and goes downstairs to the piano. Ariel's Song from *The Tempest* trips from her fingers. She adds Prospero, confident in the bass notes.

XIII Edward

It's the war we should blame, I suppose, we of the disrupted generation. I never think of those years, a matter of discipline. Sometimes in dreams I smell excrement and the stench of dismembered bodies. I put on lights, I play Mozart, I read Shakespeare aloud. I shrug it off.

When I came back from Guam, Jason was a three-year-old fact, Marta a midsummer night's dream. I never even inquired. What point? The school was waiting for me like a dinner jacket I had temporarily laid aside and I moved back into my life as though I had just stepped out for the newspaper. But certainly there had been changes. No more schoolhouses. To stay in the house we had to buy it with veterans' loans. Paper was coarser, chalk dusted itself on fingers. Everything was shoddier – the students, their studying, their values, their ambitions. Those of us who tried to maintain the old standards suffered of course. *Passé*, people said, smiling politely. It was difficult, for example, to find good Latin teachers.

As for Victoria and Jason, I should blame the war. Not myself, not them. It was the war – though Jason took advantage. This was asked of us: that a generation of fathers become strangers to their children. And this I suppose was what we could not forgive our wives as we lay drowning in mud and shrapnel. (Personally, I found that only anger stilled the nerves when I crouched in the bloodied trenches waiting for death.) We did not forgive our wives for hoarding our last precious seed, scattered in the thoughtless haste of parting while our minds reeled with apocalypse; we did not forgive them, custodians of stolen treasure, for tending it as though we had nothing to do with it. On alien fronts, we missed an entire war. When we returned the custody battles were already over.

And the battle for minds? It was as though we begat aliens. When Jason, when Emily, full of ingenuous righteousness, spoke of Vietnam, of the right to refuse, then the bodies of dead comrades rained down on me and I could never speak. No. We never argued about this. I could not speak at all for fear my jack-hammering blood would explode.

But when I first came home I brought hope like stale rations in my knapsack. I did not immediately concede defeat. Though Victoria shrank from me, I would take her on my knee. I would read Jason stories. I took an interest, I asked questions, I gave fatherly admonitions and exhortations. I did not want them merging into the sluggish flow of other children's lives. I was concerned that the slackness of the times had seeped into their bones. I wanted them to be extraordinary. Perhaps I was too exacting.

I remember I took them to the fair in Springfield one day and Tory was sick on the Ferris wheel. When she put her head on my shoulder, and when Jason clung to my sleeve, I thought with humble wonder: everything is still possible. But then Bessie came home and snapped her fingers of authority and privilege and of course they went to her, conditioned by my long, forced absence.

"Can't you tell when the child is terrified," she asked. "Do you have to make her ill?"

You don't know, I thought. You didn't see her arms around my neck, her head on my shoulder. You know nothing.

At school I saw what was happening to the young. Everywhere, decadence. In the cities, women who once confined themselves for decency were flaunting pregnancies at dinner parties as though biology were a newly discovered triumph. Gentlemen of the old order averted their eyes for shame.

If I had sought out Marta then, she would have looked like one of Fra Lippo Lippi's angels. If I found her now it would be the same: ageless and pure.

I wanted to keep Victoria pure. Perhaps I was too strict.

For Jason I wanted excellence and Harvard. I do not see why a Spartan program should bother a child of the war years. I wanted everything, I gave everything, his future mattered too much for me to unbend. And he has, I suppose, what I wanted him to have – professional and scholarly standing, though I would have preferred law or classics. He chose an obscene field mainly, I would think, to cause me embarrassment. Two books published, which I refuse to read and not because of the blatant dedication: *For my mother Elizabeth.* There are areas where I draw the line. Freud, for instance. Pornography, in my opinion.

What I did not expect was that Jason would graduate into contempt for my pre-war humanism. Home from college one Thanksgiving, I remember he said: "Oh no! Not Wordsworth again!"

I realized it was a tic of my generation. We thought of it as deferring to a shared repository of wisdom. It was a communal act for us. After that I never quoted verse aloud again. (Except perhaps to Bessie on deranged nights when the war eddied into my sleep like smoke and I cried out with horror. She would bring me hot chocolate and my Shakespeare. We would turn on the stereo. Bessie is in many ways a comforting creature.)

Of course I am long past caring for Jason's contempt. I return it. A life going nowhere, a stunted dying tree, no branches.

When they come, all of them – is it tomorrow? the day after? – they will take for granted that Jason will carry me downstairs. I will not let him. Never. I will never forgive him for not writing to me from school, not even when I stooped to begging. When Emily was born I thought it would be different, a fresh chance. (And perhaps after all, if she brings Adam.) Will they really bring Victoria? Will she kill me with her Circe's eye? Is it possible in any sense to feel grateful that they are coming?

Rather than let Jason carry me I will rise to my feet like Samson and let my faulty heart yammer as it will. Adrenalin alone would get me to the foot of the stairs.

Though I would not want to die in front of the child. Not until we have talked.

Emily does not dislike me as Jason does. She has no reason

not to bring the boy. Adam. There is such a sound of hope to it. And Emily's letters have never excluded, always *Dear mother and father....*

Yes, that was how we knew, about three years ago. *Dear mother and father, I have accepted a position in London, address above. I must beg you not to give Tory my address. Her letters to Sydney were so constant and distressing. I expect to be in New York for a concert next month and hope to see....*

"New York!" Bessie said, "Oh, it's been so long." With her eyes like a starling's watching for spring.

And I thought, why not? It is something, a daughter playing on a New York stage, though one could wish for a less nomadic success. Nevertheless. Some people, not understanding the fostering of the exceptional, have claimed that I was a harsh father. Not true. But it is possible that I was exacting with Emily, whom I counted on to atone for other losses.

In any case I wanted to make whatever amends were necessary. At seventy, I wanted to bind wounds.

I did not, I suppose, want to die unloved.

I do not, quite simply, want to die.

I will not go tamely.

If she does not bring the boy it will be over in minutes, like a shell bursting over those steamy villages in Guam.

Will they fly to New York, I wonder?

New York. Her concert. I had forgotten its aftermath. How selective the memory gets, coddling and pandering. Yes, they hold New York against me, of course. They will punish me for that. And yet it is perverse of Emily. She must realize; I cannot believe she does not realize. I cannot absorb shocks so quickly. They should not expect it of me.

In Lincoln Center I was overcome. Even now, recalling it.... Damn. I despise weeping. Tears have always enraged me. If Bessie comes in, I will say the ragweed....

This is what is intolerable about life. (Oh these furies, this wretched tin in my chest. Iago! Iago!) What cannot be borne is this clarity, this torturing knowledge of the turning points, with no possibility of skipping a chapter, going back a page, excising. (One of these spasms, I suppose, will go ripening on and on until I am harvested. Will I be lucid, I wonder, at the last un-rewritable second? I will not go gently! Oh God. This pain is a grappling iron in the ribs!)

The war can be forgiven. Or rather, we can forgive ourselves for the war. It is the moments that could have been otherwise that torment. When Marta extended her milky arms in the gazebo, when Emily lifted her wine glass in Manhattan.... If I had done otherwise then, if I could have those moments over....

(This pain has the jaws of a shark. I will die of rage at my own stupidity.)

This has to be distanced. I have to see the boy, I must live until Adam. This has to be put in perspective, I have to breathe slowly, I have to edit.

In the concert hall the old man thought of doves. It was the flutter of silks perhaps, or the cushioned seats raising and lowering themselves like injured wings. He thought of San Juan Capistrano which he had seen once during the war, a brief respite between dysenteries. He had been amazed, he was still amazed, by rhythms that were heedless of external event: birds massing and gossiping like theatergoers, people flocking to concerts.

As the orchestra assembled on stage in little forays and shufflings and tunings a woman in front of him murmured to her companion:

"However does Julian manage? Hailing taxis and such? It's like a fat mistress, that double bass."

"Anton Kuerti takes his own grand piano with him." Putting things in perspective. "Every concert."

An esoteric language, the old man thought. He was still a beginner, able to make stilted small talk, ignorant of more profound syntax.

Which Stamitz? he heard from somewhere behind his left shoulder. Not Karl, someone responded. Karl did the flute pieces.

Johann then, it was agreed.

His wife knew this language. Her tongue could slide around Köchel ratings as easily as minnows through water. She could correctly assign: early Baroque, late Renaissance. She could distinguish Weimar Bach from Leipzig Bach. The old man could never hope, in his lifetime, to achieve all the necessary colorations, the fine stipplings, that would allow him to pass in her world as a native.

Probably it could be detected that his evening suit was rented. Probably people behind him were speculating: he has come because his wife wanted to; or: he thinks this is expected of out-of-town visitors; or even the truth: he is the father of the guest soloist but has never felt at ease in musical gatherings.

He realized, glancing covertly about, that he should be reading his program notes. A gauge of sorts, separating the devout from the frivolous. Like lowering the kneeling rail when one entered the pew in a cathedral, an indication of serious intention. He bowed his head.

On the page with small photographs the conductor gazed out intensely from between Einstein-like tufts of hair. The old man stared back at him, reading of the conductor's life and achievements and digesting the fragmented newspaper judgments of various critics. One would suppose the critics incapable of complete sentences: "luminous performance," "provocative synthesis," "masterly evocation." Beneath these staccato triumphs was a photograph of a woman with her head tilted so that a waterfall of raffish golden curls snared the eye. She looked like a Burne-Jones angel. In the split second before he read the name, the old man realized that this was his daughter.

The picture interested him greatly since he had not seen her for many years. Odd, he thought, that she was so fair when her mother was dark. Had been. Without moving his head he let his eyes travel sideways to confirm that his wife's hair was indeed now gray as a rain cloud and had for this occasion been professionally molded into soft cumulus curves. His daughter's coloring, then, had come from himself. There was at least that.

Emily Carpenter, he read beneath the picture, studied at Juilliard before taking up a position with the Montreal Philharmonic where she quickly distinguished, etcetera, etcetera.... Sydney, one of the four principals.... London...chamber orchestra...concerts in Europe. This is the first time since, etcetera, etcetera, etcetera, returned to give a concert in her own country.

So, he thought. I learn nothing new. A skeletal life, sprung full-blown from Juilliard like Venus from her birth-shell. *What comes before and after, we know not.* Of course she would deny a prior existence, anything that would have the rank smell of family to it. Anything to extinguish him. He composed his emotions to expect nothing from this reunion. Going through a wardrobe of possible camouflages, fingering fabrics as it were, he chose sardonic detachment. This would be the best he could manage (pure indifference being a cloth too costly for his resources) and would, he hoped, protect him from the giving or taking of blood.

He looked around him at so great a congregation of doves, chirping and fluttering, nesting in balconies above, full of the honorable impulses of community and beauty and tradition, and knew himself a lone bird of prey, excluded, crude, macabre, riddled with envy and contempt, capable of butchery.

But he would wear sardonic detachment.

He experimented. "The Mendelssohn should be interesting as *hors d'oeuvre.*"

His wife smiled.

"Oh Edward." *Con poco vibrato.*

She spoke of dreams fulfilled, not Mendelssohn.

They will exclude me, he thought, casting about to staunch incipient bleeding. Over dinner they will discuss shadings I have never suspected in the second movement, and whether woodwinds gave adequate support.

Not that he should care. He was expert at losing children, he could do it blindfold. An elder daughter marched to mad drummers, communing with strange voices. He had been crawling, when his son was born, on his belly through the world's yeasty private parts. What good could come of this?

His son would be somewhere in the concert hall. With that woman.

There was, in spite of all, a memory of passion from which all of them, wife and children, were excluded. He kept it like a relic in a sacristy of his mind. Its glow sustained him. Probably, here and there, people existed who made do with less.

For the Mendelssohn his daughter did not appear, nor for the Beethoven. He endured the intermission, the bird-like rustle and stir, the molt of broken chatter falling about him: the first violins a trifle out, I thought; admirable adagio, though I question; wouldn't you say the oboe passage; *western* music, well really, Zubin Mehta, Seiji Ozawa, what can one think?

Lights blinking, the flock – the congregation – returning, kneelers lowered, hymn books taken up. As it were. Awaiting the sacrament. His wife reached out and placed her hand over his. From her sleeve an arm ivory and creased as the page of a prayer book exposed itself. As a sheep before its shearers, he thought, as a lamb to the slaughter. He was surprised by tenderness: We made this event. *Ex nihilo*, our bodies coming together.

Gruffly godlike, he whispered: "All those practices, you accompanying, me grumbling about the noise and the cost of lessons." Squeezing her hand.

She raised his fingers to her lips and kissed them, a shocking public act. He had never approved, but now found his eyes as foolishly damp as hers.

There was a hush now, the orchestra fully reassembled, its discourse of tuning, the mating cries of instruments, subsided. And then his daughter entered. He could hear a sort of communal gasp, a glottal stop within the silence, for her beauty. An explosion of applause. She is my daughter, he said to himself, my daughter, my youngest child. As though reiteration would prove: flesh of my flesh.

He felt a confused incestuous rush of desire and guilt. It was not that she looked anything like Marta, his icon, who had been dark, a gypsy memory. Nevertheless something, a translucence, a fragility, was common to them. In this way, as father and lover, he was exalted above other men. He had a finer taste, a Renaissance instinct (in spite of the rented evening suit). Generous, he stroked his wife's black silken sleeve and touched her wrist.

The Sibelius began, the Concerto in D Minor. If she had chosen something in a major key, something wholesome and sunny, he might have been able to reinstate detachment. But from that first keening solo note, that mournful exquisite sound that might have been the voice of Francesca singing love to Paolo in infernal shadows, he was lost. From the cellos, from Paolo's fire-slaked throat, the guttural response: *Passion is eternal.* Across all the circles of Dante's hell, across time, across the old man's memories. And the whole orchestra confirming, a haunting chorus, now mournful, now shrill with exhilaration, celebrating impossible losses and glories and obsessions. Acknowledging the passion for passion – of parents for their remote children, of lovers for unattainable loves.

In the third movement, he slumped back into his seat from the energy demanded of his heart. There was a rondo of such lunatic ecstasy that the arteries in his temples thudded. And that thin seductive call of Francesca, unbearably otherworldly. He did not realize, until he brushed his perspiring brow, that his face was streaked with tears.

So brilliant, so abrupt, was the ending that the audience was winded with surprise. There seemed to be a general sensation of having been dumped down a chute at a fun fair. In the quivering silence Emily lowered her violin and bow and stood fragile, almost with diffidence, as though covering her nakedness with the instrument. For the second time her father thought of Botticelli's Venus. And then the ocean broke around her shell, the surf of bravos and applause. Roses presented, a kiss from the conductor. Exits, returns, applause.

They did not move, the old man and his wife, as chairs folded themselves in two, as people surged. This was partly from depletion of energy. A young woman, sucking herself in to get by them, thought of the word *beatitude* without exactly knowing why. Also, however, there was something of pride. Having become venerable, why should they scurry like ordinary concertgoers?

Edward Carpenter, he thought to himself. School principal *emeritus*. He had a sense of amounting to Latinate distinction.

When the crowd thinned, they walked slowly down the aisle, arm in arm.

The old man demurred: "Suppose they don't let us past?"

"Oh Edward. Of course they will."

Before him, she had had a life where it was natural to go backstage after performances. He felt bewildered, like a child in a new school, among the hubbub of music stands and cases and instruments being dismantled. What came to him was another memory of disorder, of nurses and trolleys, of pacing outside a labor room, of waiting helplessly to be shown his baby daughter through glass. His hands trembled now with the same yearning to hold, to whisper: my child.

"There!" his wife cried, flying on maternal wings.

And he would have flown too, would have folded his arms around that luminous figure as around a rare treasure or a newborn baby, with abandon. Except that his son was there before him. His son's woman was not, at the moment, in evidence.

Jason and Emily were holding each other at arm's length, as two people do who have just embraced but can scarcely believe they have met again. They were laughing and crying. Into the charmed circle flew his wife and was absorbed.

The old man waited, the momentum of his love balked. He could not, in front of Jason, *display* himself. After his son left, the reined-in desire would leap again.

Emily's eyes swept the room.

"Father!" She came to him and took both hands and kissed his cheek.

"Emily," he said shakily. And because Jason looked: "Your mother and I are very proud of you."

He caught Jason's grimace, heard him thinking: Stiff, as always.

"Father," Jason said, acknowledging a regrettable given. They shook hands like polite acquaintances. "How are you keeping?"

Just in time he checked himself from responding: *On Fortune's cap we are not the very button*. But evidently too late, and to little avail.

"No quotations, father? No *sweets for the sweet* or *music, when soft voices die*?" Having drawn blood, he added lightly: "Just teasing."

"Jason," his mother warned. She touched his wrist in gentle reproach and he, instinctively, leaned over and kissed her on the forehead.

The old man felt a dangerous agitation in his hands. How all occasions do inform against me. I have not, he wanted to point out, aggrieved, recited anything aloud for ten years. Not since you were in college. Not since you so wittily pointed out.

He said: "Your woman is not with you?" It came out mildly, evening the score.

"Waiting in the lounge, father. She thought this should be a family moment. She has delicacy." With only the faintest emphasis. He smiled. "Did you wish to see her?"

"Jason." Emily made a gesture which might have been that of a weary arbitrator in a protracted union dispute. "You and Ruth are joining us for dinner?"

"Delicacy forbids. We decided you three should have this evening to yourselves." Graciously condescending to permit. "Pick you up in the morning as arranged, Emily." Prior collusion, like territorial rights, must of course be established. "Bye, mother." He displayed his ascendant manhood, lifting her slightly in his embrace. "Take care."

"Father." The hand proffered again.

Like duelists', their manners were impeccable.

In the restaurant alcove there was a single rose and candle-light. His wife and daughter were talking in little rushes of excitement, rummaging through a box of memories like children through old clothing trunks at Halloween. Edward watched them and felt the tide of poison recede.

His daughter, his wife, one fair, one formerly dark, both vibrant. Always, for him, they had had that charged stillness that reminds of herons or gazelles. And Marta also. Such women, he thought, in my life. It set him apart. But then he remembered his other daughter, disfigured with madness, and found it necessary to drain his wine glass.

He filled it again – a dry red – and raised it so that [illegible] candle flame glowed through, a burning jewel in his h[illegible]

Through the upper clear curve of glass he continued to watch his daughter, appraising, with one eye closed. She was indeed extraordinarily beautiful, with hair like flakes of gold. (Thirty, was it now? Thirty-one. Yet who would possibly guess?) And held an auditorium of people in her hand like so much confetti.

In a moment, in just another moment as the wine washed away Jason, he would be able to say he loved and adored her. He would be able to weep openly, to propose a toast, to take her – even in this public place – in his arms. His child, untainted and pure, the hope of his old age.

"Emily," he ventured, and she turned, her glass poised in mid-air.

He could not continue.

"Oh daddy!"

His tears had some irrevocable impact. A decision was reached. He could see it in the impress of her lips, the fluttering lashes. She put down her glass and reached across the table to take a hand of each parent. In a moment he would be indifferent to waiters. In a moment he would rise and clasp her to himself. He saw it as in a Burne-Jones tableau: the gnarled old king and his virgin daughter lambent as candlelight on snow; Pericles and Marina.

"I have to tell you both about Adam," she said.

He withdrew his hand from hers, but gently, not wanting to mar with his spasm of jealousy. To lose her again so soon. Yet it would be a splendid thing, giving her in marriage. He warmed to his vision.

She turned her glass with the released hand, twirling the stem like a top. She raised it and sipped, held it suspended like a shield or charm. Afterwards, this was the moment he always returned to: her raised wine glass, still intact. The last moment of innocence, Eve's hand extended toward the apple.

[illegible]le is five now," she said. "Of course it's unforgivable, not [illegible] you all these years. But you know how things were. I [illegible] Montreal and the affair itself was...complicated. I [illegible] have talked about it. A married man, naturally. [illegible]ignificant now. By the time Adam was due I was in [illegible]nd it seemed so remote. It was easy to believe it didn't concern you. Dave wanted to, actually, but I wouldn't let...for one thing, I didn't want to have to explain *him*. You did always make that sort of thing difficult, daddy. Actually" – the stillness of a lull in battle, the wine glass still raised like a truce flag, the old man's hands not visible below the table – "you and Dave would enjoy each other. Adam adored him. Still, that's over now, and since we're in England.... Next time, I'll bring him. He's" – she took a deep shuddering breath – "he's my life. He is quite simply a beautiful and amazing child, your grandson."

A thin high note of the kind that shatters crystal had begun to sound inside the old man's skull, had risen to a disorienting crescendo so that as he rose to his feet he had difficulty keeping his balance. He was aware of the backward crash of the chair but otherwise there was no time to gauge or plan, no chance to rehearse the sweep of his arm.

A word flew from his mouth like a stone. Slut, perhaps. Or tramp. He did not so much formulate it as see the white laceration it made on her cheek.

The wine glass had been struck free of her hand and soared like a falcon released, its droppings of wine splashing them. It dipped, quivered, plummeted to the tablecloth. Splinters everywhere. He saw blood on Emily's hands, the ashen face of his wife.

He could not stop himself. It seemed to him he was coughing blood, not vitriol.

"Dear God, dear God," his wife moaned, a hand at her throat. As though in sleep, not quite believing, she moved to him, a butterfly against a tank.

"Edward, dearest, please don't. Your heart, Edward. Oh please don't."

Other chairs were being pushed back, people rising, waiters gathering like ushers at a funeral, obsequious yet forceful. A public performance. How Jason would sneer.

The old man put his hand to the tumult at his temple and felt the artery cavorting like a gymnast. In another second, strong hands would be laid on him.

He leaned close to Emily and whispered: "I will not ha[illegible] bastard in my house. I never wish to see him. Never."

And then his screaming blood was in his eyes and ears and mouth, the strong hands descended, darkness fell.

"She visited," his wife told him.

He was in a white bedroom, tied to tubes and a video screen.

"She sat with you through the first night. We all did. Jason too."

And said: *How are the mighty fallen,* no doubt.

"But the doctor said there was no danger and she had concerts in England. She had to go."

No danger, he thought, not considering it a favor. He let her stroke his forehead, warming himself against this small flame. Beneath the sheet, his body felt to him cold and heavy as ice.

"It's beating normally now," she said, watching a palsied line jerk across the screen. "They've put a pacemaker in."

He lay silent with the appalling weariness of seventy years, watching his wife, thinking: she is like tissue over a fine steel frame. Perhaps it has exhausted her, all these years as go-between.

Yet she seemed immortal, buttressed as always with quiet self-possession, dispensing small comforts.

Suddenly before his eyes she crumpled. Dissolved. Laid her gray head beside his on the pillow. Noiselessly she sobbed; he could feel the heaving like an earth tremor in his bed. After this subsided, after her chafing of his newly sluggish hands, she consoled: "She understands, you know. I told her it was just the shock. We're not used to so much event, living out in the country. And the concert was so...it made us more vulnerable." Pleading with him to confirm. "I told her you didn't mean it."

If I could just nod, he thought. If I could simply say: ...rgive me."

... grandson," she said. "Think of it."

... put her fingertips to his lips, a sign of blessing.

...ould just smile. If I could kiss her fingers. If I could ...*n.*

...oth waited for his voice as though for an unpredicta-...y, habitually late.

Am I, he asked himself, evil or merely cursed?

There were two moments etched into sleep and waking: Marta's arms (into which he did not walk) extended in the moonlight a lifetime ago; Emily's glass raised in the candlelight.

There is a tide in the affairs of men. But he had never, alas, taken anything at the flood. Ahead of him stretched miles and miles of mud flats and in the remote distance, toward which he toiled dragging shackles, the inaccessible plea: "I want to see Adam. I want my grandson."

He turned his face to the wall. Words were not pliant to his bidding. They went their own way as his children had done.

Sorrowfully his wife leaned over him and kissed his cheek. Some dampness at her eyes, the brine of an ebb tide, wet him. And still the words which would have saved him did not come.

XIV Elizabeth

Elizabeth is planting peonies. Extravagance is promised: double blossoms, a glut of petals, more translucence to the inch. Summer after summer after summer. She has a definite preference for perennials, anything that speaks of winter as brief intermission.

Thursday, she thinks. They are on their way, somewhere over the Atlantic, entrusted to air. The elements, their magic properties, astonish. She uses a trowel and her bare hands, scooping out handfuls of soil. Sometimes she pauses to watch an earthworm undulate back into darkness – violated, she is aware, by the light she has unleashed. The gracefulness of its trauma takes her breath away. To move like that. Instinctively she transposes, composes: song of the earthworm. After the planting, she will commit it to notes.

She watches the last of it pull itself into safety. Like a lolling pink tongue sucked back into a mouthful of soil. She covers it with an extra handful of June's warm earth, making amends, and in doing so lays bare its brother. How the light sears them. A ballet of shock, the exposed skin comforting itself in love knots.

Intrusions, adjustments, reparations, she thinks. Like gerbils on wheels, we go in circles. We move, we damage, we bind up and tend.

Behind her, troops of potted peonies await orders. Reinforcements. Though regiments already flourish in many directions. There cannot be too much white or pink, Elizabeth believes. Eloquent clusters, they sing of the light made flesh, dwelling miraculously among us.

Elizabeth baptizes each plant, dangling the garden hose over it. She releases it from constriction with discreet prods and tappings, holds the potted earth intact around it, puts it to its mother's breast. The tuberous roots slurp at nourishment.

A gentle place, Elizabeth thinks, feeling along the rootways. She touches bulbs busy with the brewing of next spring. It won't be so bad, down there, when the time comes. Consorting with earthworms and birth.

She needs to see death that way. She acknowledges this freely to herself. She prefers perennials to annuals, evergreens to deciduous trees. She would like to minimize the finality of death.

Abstraction settles on her. On the way to connecting another peony with the earth, her soil-caked hands lose their way, forget, fold themselves in her lap. The potted plants huddle and wait.

Elizabeth is remembering a death and a brush with death.

The death was a long time ago. Though when it is importunate, as now, asserting itself, it seems to have happened yesterday. Somewhere it nourishes vines more lunatic than honeysuckle. She has seen pictures: stems thicker than an arm, leaves vast as flags, a punctuation of blood-red flowers. Somewhere a jungle heard her name – *Liz, Liz* – and grew over the sound.

A winter falls into Elizabeth, the cold gets to her, she falters, she senses the drifts closing over. Through the cracks of unguarded moments, ice fingers her.

She plunges her hands into earth, she claws at warmth, she stops up drafty places. Another peony, dizzy with abrupt transplant, is pitched into juvenescence. And another. And another. A fever of fruitfulness.

Nothing is gained, Elizabeth tells herself, by acknowledging the inexorable nature of the opposition. No prizes for being overwhelmed.

Scoop, transplant, tamp the soil. Expand the ranks of the flourishing. She bends low, intent, lifts one more handful of mud, and another earthworm confronts her moistly. The abiding question. Never look Circe in the eye, she tells it, and buries it in the peony's cradle.

Anything calling for action, for transposition into beauty, this is her credo. Stay busy with birth and mending. The mere brush with death she could cope with. There was plenty to be done that time, after the concert in New York, when Edward's heart threw a tantrum. Enough, enough, it screamed, threatening to shut down until further notice. A jungle of tubing flowered over it.

Elizabeth felt the coldness, she came close to losing hope, but she held her breath and kept watch. She has a gift for life. Her hands massaged, caressed, coaxed him back. Not yet, she had willed. Not like this. Not before this family has achieved wholeness.

Mending.

There was more to be done.

They were centering now, coming in from the corners of the earth. She was reining them in, from London, from Sydney, from New York.

She pulled Adam and Emily from air. Dave waited, expectant; she was playing him into the piece. Catalysis, catalysis. Into her thoughts fell Jason. The peonies sang. Tory, fragrant with homecoming, flowered between her fingers.

In the garden Elizabeth dreams of, everything flourishes. The young are in one another's arms.

XV Converging

(i)

"Newfoundland is on our starboard side now, but too far to see. The steward told me." Adam collected mentors the way other boys did scraped knees. "Unless there's a storm. Then we might have to enter Canadian air space."

"That's where you began."

He was politely uninterested, being loyal to Dave, but felt obliged to ask: "Am I Canadian too?"

He felt a kinship with mongrel dogs – the fluffy lovable kind – nationalities adhering to him like chunks of various breeding lines.

It struck his mother as a singularly amusing question.

"No. That's something they haven't managed to catalogue. As yet. You're thoroughly documented for the U.S. and Australia. And there are our visas for the U.K. But they have no way of monitoring conception." She winked at him, sharing a sophisticated joke. "There's no record whatsoever of your passage through Canada. You got away with it."

If Dave had been there, he would have said: "No flies on *you*, mate."

He wished he could turn to her and say: "For my next birthday, I want Dave back."

But it was something, like death, that could not be mentioned. Once when he had done so a tic had absorbed the entire right side of her face, like a frightened bird beating its wings against the inner wall of her cheek.

More often she did what he thought of as "walking away from herself." He would know from her eyes that she had gone from behind them. When he was ready to revert to sensible things, she seemed to intimate, they would resume conversation.

He watched her absorption in the cloud ballet beyond her window. She was thinking, perhaps, of Canada and of the man in Montreal who was technically his father. This information, for him, existed on the same level as his awareness that he was technically a citizen of the United States though he had yet to set foot on American soil.

He heard her catch her breath in instinctive appreciation of the graceful somersaults of cirrus puffs. He watched the gentleman across the aisle watching her. He thought of Dave and of the rare turquoise butterfly that was never still. He watched the gentleman's wife watching the gentleman watching his mother. In his dreams, sometimes, he and Dave made butterfly nets.

⯁⯁⯁

Emily contemplated the inside of clouds, reassured by their disorderly secrets. Movement soothed her. She would have delighted in a storm for what it would offer in dramatic gesture as well as for any delay or detour it might promise in reaching New York. Only in transit did she feel at ease. If she had not had the good fortune to be a concert musician she would, she supposed, have had to sell pharmaceuticals or office equipment – a company car, a wide territory, a life on the road.

Silkily the plane cleaved through a gray-white turbulence that had once drifted along the St. Lawrence; that had perhaps, two or three days ago, brought rain to Montreal. On Place Jacques Cartier the chairs and tables would have been pulled back into the shelter of awnings, the flower sellers would have tucked buckets of roses and ferns under trestle counters, rivulets would have coursed in the grooves between cobblestones, and quite possibly Sergei would have presented one sweetheart rose to a young woman with rain-wet hair and a future. A little later he might have begotten another child while the weather fogged the young woman's apartment windows.

For this she reproached him not at all, and herself, for the mistakes of youth, only a little. How could she regret Adam? She thought of Sergei, now that he was safely sealed into the past, as an interlude, yes, an educational interlude, a buffer zone, in her life. Also, he had taught her jealousy and for that too she was grateful – grateful in the way of a mother who has repeatedly warned a child about playing by the hot stove; the child burns one hand in a fleeting brush with the element; a lesson is learned, a greater danger forestalled.

After New York and Juilliard, where she had tried men much as she had tried artichokes, pot, anti-war demonstrations, and subscriptions to *Gourmet* and *Ramparts*, Montreal had seemed, in 1970, like a voyage to the Old World.

Yet in fact the city had been a ferment of hysteria and martial law. At the time all that had seemed like so much background noise.

In the pages of newspapers, monitoring the rise of her own star, she had sought music reviews before news bulletins. If she had thought much about the words scrawled in spray paint across walls – *Vive le Québec libre* – it had been to assent inwardly to the blissful freedom of a world remote from family and father, a Quebec where she could spend illicit midnights with Sergei and be deluged with his flowers backstage – a publicly private affair.

She had believed that the passion would last forever – such was the gift, the illusory magic of Sergei, purveyor of love as art form. She had crossed a border. In New York in the sixties, love was a politically unacceptable anachronism.

In New York her succession of couplings had been so arid that she had begun to fear she was sexually or emotionally impaired. Not that there were technical problems. Rather she discovered that orgasm itself could be almost joyless – like laughter in a television sitcom machine. Or perhaps, as Rob put it, she was politically and sexually infantile, hankering after affection and the *forms* of romance. For Rob, sex was a balance sheet that must come out even on each side, each time, even when she assured him she would have been quite happy to run a slight debit.

For more spiritual intercourse she had turned to Jim who

read to her in bed – Norman O. Brown before and Marcuse after. This was uplifting but failed to spark an abiding passion.

There had been various other men whose energies had seemed to promise much. They had declaimed on campuses and co-opted her for poster making and berated her for such an irrelevancy as the violin when the world was crumbling. They made love as though it were a military act and they taught her lingering guilt. She made more and more frequent contributions to *Save the Children* to atone for the price of concert tickets.

These men were also, incongruously, addicted to permanence.

"You know you want me back," Rob would storm into the phone. "You know this is infantile. You've made your point now. My shrink told me it's your way of throwing a tantrum. Look, Rob, no hands!"

And Jim would drop by with a new book.

"This independence thing," he would say. "Don't you think you're carrying it too far? We should discuss it. Why don't I stay over and we can work through this book?"

Baby, the various angry young militants said, quoting Stokely Carmichael (or was it Rap Brown?), the only position for women in this movement is prone. Violins are elitist. Lay it aside and lie back, or leave.

I'll leave, she would offer politely.

Outraged, they accused: castrating bitch!

Hey, wait a minute! they pleaded, confused. Can't we reconsider?

By 1970 New York was mined with lovers who felt discarded. Between the tall buildings they stalked her. Each day the city seemed to shrink, to resemble the small town in western Massachusetts from which she had fled, to smell stale with use. When the Montreal offer came, it was like the gift of a respirator to a victim of asthma.

"Metals I do not consider urgent," Sergei said. "Real estate, yes, because of inflation and for safety. But music is my best investment." He had made his money in shoes but now owned whole blocks of Montreal and one of its newspapers and was one of the orchestra's most generous benefactors. "For my grandfather," he said, "who never saw this land of promise but who played the violin to me in the evenings when I was a child. That was before our world fell apart."

Emily, drinking his champagne at a festive opening of the season, smiled politely. She considered how well age suited some men, imagining him at a long table in some baroque room presided over by Metternich or Tolstoy or a patriarch of the Académie Française. His only slightly graying hair would be falling across his forehead in just this way while cultured women in salons all over Europe were pining for him.

"You must come and play for us at our little chamber concerts," he said. "Must she not, Anna?"

His wife, who might once have been a dancer or a countess, a gaunt handsome woman in black and pearls, said dryly: "We must certainly keep an eye on her."

And her lively dark eyes had conveyed to Emily the most extraordinary semaphore: pride, amused disdain, indulgence. An air even of collusion: this is the way he is; we must make shift with it.

And of pity: poor child.

A little later a young man of about her own age, beautiful in the style of a Viennese aesthete or a friend of Oscar Wilde, offered Emily *canapés*.

"Ah well," he said. "It has been duly noted. You're next. We must resign ourselves, I suppose."

"Pardon?"

"I'm Sasha."

"Emily Carpenter. How do you do?"

"His *son*."

She smiled, bewildered.

"I hope," he said, "when you've finished being blinded by him, that you'll stay long enough to get to know me. Could I take you out for drinks after this charade, or am I already too late?"

"Actually," she said, feeling crowded, the ghosts of New York lovers jostling her, "I need to unpack. I just got an apartment yesterday. I've been camping with a friend in graduate residence at McGill up till now."

The next morning there were two deliveries of flowers. From Sergei and from Sasha. Arms full of blossoms and fragrance, she debated whether to answer the phone or the door first.

"Could you hold for one minute?" she said into the receiver. "I have to answer the doorbell."

"You look enchanting by morning light." Sergei indicated his car in the street. "We have reservations for lunch, but I thought a drive up Mount Royal first?"

"I'm unpacking crates," she said, breathless. "I'm... you see...." Gesturing at her jeans and sweatshirt.

"I'll wait while you change."

In the hallway he said: "Your phone."

"Oh, I forgot. Excuse me."

She picked up the receiver.

"Emily? This is Sasha. May I come over and help you unpack?"

"Uh... actually, I'm just going out. Maybe later. It's awfully sweet of you."

"Don't come crying," Sasha said, "when it's all over. I don't touch his rejects."

"That's quite... uncalled for, I think. The flowers..."

"I can tell from your breathing."

"The flowers are gorgeous. May I thank you?"

"It's nothing. You could change your mind."

"Would this afternoon...?"

"Forget it."

She heard the plastic click of renunciation.

"It's just a stage," Sergei said. "He'll get over it. Do you have something blue?"

He took her face between his hands and ran his index finger gently across her eyelids. As a bishop might have anointed the eyes of a young acolyte. "With such eyes it should be blue. And for such a body, soft as thistledown."

She strove to see it as elaborate playacting, as almost comically out of date, yet felt absurd tidal movements in the blood. When she walked to the bedroom to find something blue and soft in her suitcases, it was as though a sac of flesh had ballooned suddenly between her thighs. She could scarcely stand for the sweet aching and the shift of gravity. I am dissolving, she thought. This is it. I am finally experiencing passion.

What was tantalizing about Sergei was that he let her seep and ferment with desire for weeks before he did more than kiss her fingertips or stroke her hair.

On Mount Royal they climbed the last slope beyond the parking lot to the gigantic cross. Below them in the crisp air the city stirred like a languid woman in October gold.

"You will never forget Montréal." He pronounced it in the French way. "I will see to it."

He took both her hands and kissed her lightly on the forehead and led her back to the car. On the car radio, an announcer was saying that James Richard Cross, British Trade Commissioner to the Province of Quebec, had been kidnapped from his home early that morning. Ransom demands of the *Front de Libération du Québec* had just been found in a letter.

"Messy business," Sergei said. "I hope to God Sasha has enough sense...."

"Sasha is a sympathizer?"

"It's his university crowd. Fashionable stuff at the moment and he's fluently bilingual. Also fancies the role of victim."

The FLQ, said the announcer, gave the authorities forty-eight hours to meet their demands.

Sergei turned off the radio and took her to L'Epicure.

Each day Sergei would sit in the gloom of the empty auditorium and Emily would note the suppressed smiles, the telegraphy of eyes. She would not have minded had she not feared that the members of the orchestra smirked because they detected her ravenous unconsummated hunger. Striving to look tranquil and satiated, she was aware that her hands sometimes trembled, that her eyes and skin had the luminous look of starvation.

Every day Sasha called her, vicious and pleading. I dream

about you, he would say. Don't expect me to care what you do. She promised to have lunch with him. Some time soon. She yearned to ask: What are your father's intentions?

Daily, after rehearsal, Sergei would take her somewhere for drinks and any bartender would have thought: two lovers. They would drive to her apartment, he would open her door, give a courtly bow, kiss her hand, and leave. After ten days of thinking *Surely tonight*, of shifting from wry regret to disbelief to frenzy, she ventured:

"Will you come in for dinner? I have a cold chicken and I make a wonderful spinach salad. Everyone says so."

"*Ma petite* Emily," he sighed. "How delightful that would be."

But dinner, he explained, was a grand occasion *chez* Anna. The whole family, the silverware, the best china, candlelight. As in the Old World. He could never disappoint.

"Besides," he chided, "you must practise. You are disappointing me, relying too much on natural ability. How many hours a day are you doing, aside from orchestra rehearsal?"

"Three. All morning."

His eyes reproached. "This is not enough. If you are going to be famous, and I have decided that you will be, you must be perfect. You must start earlier in the morning. And three hours more tonight. You will promise?"

In New York a month ago, someone (Liam? Jeff?) had said: "Three hours a day! What monumental self-indulgence! Meanwhile villages are being bombed and children are dying."

"Three more hours," she promised meekly.

He kissed her hand in farewell. "Tomorrow I will notice a difference in the playing." And he kissed her forehead.

Perhaps this is what he does, she thought sadly, watching the receding car from her window. Perhaps when Sasha said "duly noted" he meant that I had been singled out for hard labor and celibacy, for twelve hours of practice a day and a tilt at the golden ring.

Music is my best investment.

He was, after all, simply an impresario, avuncular and

intransigent. Practise, practise, practise. *I have decided you will be famous.*

Abandoned, she was tempted to curl up in bed and weep. Never before, as she rosined her bow, had she thought of her violin as a rival, more desirable than she.

She practised with an intensity designed to numb her want – and to please him, to dazzle him, to have him say "much improved," to seduce him with music. Just to have him touch her eyelids, kiss her forehead again. When she dragged herself to bed she went to sleep with a pillow hugged between her legs and dreamed Sergei was undressing her.

For breakfast she had coffee and a Bartok score. He wanted her to work on it "for one of our little chamber concerts." Under the sardonic eye of the empress Anna she would have to perform gymnastics with fingers and bow. Like a court jester. And will they all know? Is it always like this – a family joke?

Don't come crying....

She worked at the Bartok with savage concentration. When she paused after two hours she felt better. Like a long-distance runner who extends herself beyond pain, tapping the second wind. I am getting it, I will show them, even Anna will lower her eyes and applaud.

Languidly she stretched, flexing her cramped fingers. She would shower and do three more hours before lunch. Virtue filled her like cinnamon-scented black coffee, making the world vibrant, everything sensuous and full of promise. She opened the window to a brisk rush of October air, lay on the rug and lifted her arms and legs ten times, touching fingers to toes. If I'm going to be famous, I have to be perfect – and then Sergei one night would simply say "May I come in?," parting her yearning thighs. Under the shower she sang and shampooed her hair, toweled herself lightly, put on a soft bathrobe, still singing.

In her mind's eye she observed herself: taking from a pine sideboard a blue and white china plate and a pearl-handled knife, selecting an orange from the bowl, sitting by the window, a lucent spiral of rind falling like a bracelet from the fruit. *Young Woman Peeling Orange in Sunlight* – a Dutch interior. *Young Woman Waiting for a Phone Call.*

When the doorbell rang she was not surprised, feeling only a *frisson* of satisfaction for her wet curls and bathrobe. Now he will reward me. The bell rang again and again, shrilly, in a frenzy of dammed-up desire. Bathrobe flying, she released the lock.

It was Sasha who catapulted in. He slammed the door behind him and locked it, stood leaning against it, his face buried in his hands.

"Sasha, my god, what is it? What's happened to him?"

"Who knows? Jail, concentration camp, the world's gone mad. No warrants, no charges, nothing!"

"My god, Sasha, explain, *explain*!" Cat-like, claws out, she shook him as though he were a sparrow. "Where is Sergei?"

"My *father*!" He stared at her through his fingers and gave a shout of derisive laughter. "Oh, I assure you, no harm can come to my father." He began pacing up and down her living room, wringing his hands. "No, no. He is probably conferring with the government, slipping money for law and order."

"What is it then? What's happened?"

"Hundreds of people. Practically anyone who looks poor and speaks French."

"Sasha, please. I don't know what you're talking about."

"Oh, Emily, Emily!" he was distraught, waving his arms as though trying to tear away a nightmare that clung like a cobweb. He seized her and held her against himself so that she could scarcely breathe, but it had nothing to do with desire. In the vibrato of his limbs, in the desperate clench of his hands, she sensed that he held her as a man drowning might grasp at a lifeguard; as a child who has seen unspeakable horrors in the night might cling to his mother.

"Sasha, *tell* me! What is it?"

"People herded up like cattle!" He could not keep still. It occurred to her that he was hallucinating. (A party? Drugs?) He kept rubbing his forehead and temples. "One grows up with such myths. Especially *here*. The dreams of two cultures: *liberté, égalité, fraternité*; government of the people by the people for the people. Beautiful, beautiful. And one day you wake up and see the real face of power – a stink hole crawling with maggots."

"Please *explain*, Sasha. I haven't seen the news, I've been practising all morning."

"They've invoked the War Measures Act. They don't need warrants or reasons. They can break in anywhere, arrest anyone they want. They got Gilles and Sylvie at five o'clock this morning, the animals."

He leapt up and began pacing again. "*French* policemen too. How is it possible? With liberty and justice for all." He pounded on the wall with his fists. "Can you imagine? Can you imagine? The babies left crying in their cribs?"

"Babies?"

"If the parents are dangerous, we can't be worried about details like their babies, can we? Sylvie had two minutes to tell a neighbor. The neighbor called me."

"All this is because of Cross?"

"And Laporte."

"Laporte?"

"Don't you live in the real world, Emily? Laporte was kidnapped six days ago."

As in New York, as with Sergei last night, she grieved for her congenital triviality.

"It has to be someone like Gilles, of course. Mediocrity can get by, but anyone brilliant and compassionate...to be an intellectual is proof of guilt." He was talking more calmly now, her ignorance sobering him. "And poor. That's a dreadful crime."

"What have they done, this Gilles and Sylvie?"

"Oh well," his voice was heavy with bitterness. "Sylvie helped organize a day-care center. *That's* certainly subversive. And Gilles is known to hold separatist views. Due process doesn't apply."

She let him pace, fascinated by his rage as by something inaccessible to her.

"They were dragged out of bed this morning. No knocking. Just police in the bedroom. No calls to a lawyer allowed. No reasons given. Just come with us. As a special concession you can tell a neighbor to look in on the children."

"That's horrible. I can't believe it."

"When I went there the two-year-old was crying and vomiting with fright. I took him to a clinic then home to my mother. My father has to have some use. The other one, the baby, is with the neighbor."

"Are you in danger?"

"Ha! What do you think, Emily? I live in Westmount. My father donates to Bourassa's campaigns."

He picked up the orange she had peeled and began to eat it. The fire of his outrage had slackened, he looked haggard, he slumped at her table.

"I just needed to tell someone. I wanted to see if there were still human beings who would be shocked. I'm sorry, Emily. I've interfered with your practice."

If criticism was implied, it could not be detected in his tone of voice.

"I'll go now," he said.

And left.

That afternoon, a Friday, Sergei was not at rehearsal.

It is the child, she thought. Their lives have become complicated, implicated. She could not decide which was the more indulgent: to listen to the radio all evening or to practise with single-minded zeal. Trying both, trying to quash the shameful fantasies of her body, she toyed ineffectually with Bartok, ricocheted from news bulletins to hovering by the telephone. (Should I call? under pretext of asking for Sasha, asking how is the child?)

She thought how fortunate she had been when he simply sat in the empty auditorium watching her. An embarrassment of riches. Through greed she had upset some delicate ecology of the emotions and lost him.

The phone rang and she flew to it, but it was Jim from New York.

"How on earth did you get my phone number?"

"From the CIA," he joked.

"Seriously."

"Seriously, what could be simpler? I called the secretary of the Montreal Symphony. And I'm sure the CIA did the same."

"It's terrible here. Like an apocalypse. Are we on the news there?"

"Of course. Fascism unmasked: the true face of the propertied classes revealed. Who is surprised?"

"I am surprised."

"You would be. I called to see if you were caught in the tangle in any way, though I felt reasonably confident you'd be engaged with your violin."

"That's right," she said wearily. "I think I'll go now, Jim. I'm keeping Bartok waiting."

"Have you any idea what's happening in Vietnam right now? You need someone to keep you in touch with reality, Emily."

As she lowered the receiver, she could hear him crying: "Don't you care about justice? Don't you care what you're doing to me?"

On the route of Sasha's distress, she paced her apartment. She turned on the radio. "... safe conduct out of Canada," Bourassa was promising, "in exchange for the safe return of Mr. Cross and Mr. Laporte. But there will be no negotiation...." She turned it off. Where was there safety from guilt? And from self-disgust? And from yearning? If rice paddies burned while she fiddled, if a child whimpered in Westmount for its mother while she longed only and obsessively for Sergei, what hope lay in music, however exalted? She felt unclean, she showered again, and douched.

As sin-wracked medieval penitents found peace only in hair shirts and excess, she practised for five hours without sitting, without dinner, without pause. She practised until one a.m. when someone from another apartment thumped on her door and demanded to know when she was going to let mere mortals sleep.

When she looked across the table at him she kept saying to herself *Sergei, Sergei*, afraid he would disappear. It was already dark when he came, late on Saturday. After dinner *chez* Anna.

After, for Emily, a day of fitful sleep and hallucination and manic bursts of practising.

She reached out to touch him and he took her hand in both of his. He had not spoken since saying at the door: "Emily."

Powerless to feel irritated, she thought: he assumes that my time, my apartment, are at his disposal. My rhythms must match his whims.

And it was so.

Surely her desire must be apparent as an aureole, a visible halo of want. If he leaned an inch closer he would be swallowed up in the magnetic field of her body. When he took her hand she felt a physical displacement, a seeping of herself on to her chair. Soon she would simply flow around him so that he, an undefended island, would be bathed in her warm compelling sea.

Sergei sat without moving, without speaking, seemingly unaware of her presence in spite of the hand clasped in his.

She said softly: "Does the child in your house upset you?"

And he stirred like someone trying to shake off the effects of a sleeping pill.

"I have provided generously. There's a man, one of my printers at the newspaper, a good family, French. Until all this is over."

"Sasha?" she ventured.

"It's not a fault, idealism in the young." He raked his fingers through his hair, troubled by uncertainty, a novel emotion. "Inevitably there are excesses with the police. It was badly done." He toyed with her fingers as though with worry beads. "Sasha did the right thing. For his sake I got word through to the parents. I assured them the children would be cared for."

How simple power is, she thought. Compassionate power.

She saw tears in his eyes and felt insanely jealous of Sasha.

"But so naive," he sighed, shaking his head. "So hopelessly romantic."

Again he retreated to silent abstraction. With anguish she thought: he will leave abruptly, as Sasha did. I can never intrude on that family. They are obsessed, they think constantly of each other.

She willed herself to absolute stillness. If he would just sit there all night, holding her hand, it would be enough.

He stood suddenly and her heart keeled over like a torpedoed ship. Pacing, on a route now well worn, he talked partly to her, partly to himself. As if it is new to me, social injustice.... Why should he think...? We arrived here penniless, doesn't he consider...? Is it not as universal as air? Is anything possible without power? Why does he think I have surrounded him with wealth and safety?

She was not required to comment. She was afraid to offer tea or solace for fear of what she might precipitate. He turned on the radio and she hated the third presence in the room. Mercifully there was mostly music while Sergei paced or stared moodily from her window. But then the voice of an announcer would intrude like a handful of gravel. She longed, but did not dare, to turn it off. Recorded in London on the Vanguard label, Sir Thomas Beecham conducting.... More music. Then the voice again, a voyeur obscenely sharing her vigil. Chicago under Sir Georg Solti.... And more music. We interrupt for a bulletin....

Sergei stopped pacing, waited like a bow pulled taut.

> Following directions found in a note left at Théâtre Port-Royal, police have found the body of Pierre Laporte. The text of the note reads as follows:
>
> "Faced with the arrogance of the federal government and its valet Bourassa, faced with obvious bad faith, the FLQ has decided to act. Pierre Laporte, Minister of Unemployment and Assimilation, was executed at 6:18 tonight by the Dieppe Cell (Royal 22nd). You will find the body in the trunk of the green Chevrolet 9J-2420 at the St. Hubert Base. *Nous vaincrons.* FLQ"

"*Mon Dieu*!" Sergei cried. "And that is the nobility of the revolutionaries! That is the new order of justice. Animals, mere animals!"

"Horrible." Emily could barely whisper. "Horrible."

Now he will go, she thought with inner panic. Now that the world is turning savage he will leave me and go to Sasha, to restrain him, to reason with him, to comfort him. She began to cry helplessly, propping her face in her hand, her elbow resting on the table, her hair falling in a curtain so that he would not notice.

"Emily, are you crying?" He took her in his arms. "Civilization has survived worse. One has to believe."

He began kissing her forehead, her eyelids, her lips, he buried his face in her hair and with his fingertips explored her face, the curve of her throat, her breasts.

"Oh Sergei, Sergei." She was practically sobbing with relief, tearing at her clothes, when he lifted her up as lightly as though she were the child abandoned at dawn, and carried her into her own bedroom.

In Emily's mind the next two and a half years passed like a blink of her eyelid. For such a passionate time, her days were strangely celibate. She might have been a novice in some order dedicated to excellence: the solitary arduous mornings of practice, the afternoon rehearsals, the evenings again with only violin and hard work for company.

There were countless lunches, but never dinners, with Sergei. He would not disappoint Anna, he considered Emily's practising inviolable. Around eleven each night he would arrive – from whatever corporate affairs or social engagements involved him – bearing usually a rose or a bunch of narcissus or daffodils. They would sip wine and talk and listen to music and make love. Somewhere between two and three in the morning he would go home to Anna.

At first Emily would beg: "Don't leave me." But she came to accept the pattern of their love. She felt married.

At the not-so-little chamber concerts, she dazzled. Always Anna commented on her progress, her piercing eyes approving and mocking, her wide mobile mouth, it seemed to Emily, intimating words other than those spoken. Once she said cryptically: "You are almost ready to graduate."

Emily was bewildered. "From the concerts?"

But Anna simply smiled as though all knowledge had already passed between them. Sasha, like an attendant lord, led her to a windowseat.

"You look like alabaster," he said, "with the moon locked inside. You have the world at your feet. Not to mention the reviewers."

Reviews, indeed, had spilled as from a jewel box, lavish, exotic, glittering with superlatives.

She said self-deprecatingly: "It doesn't hurt, I'm sure, to be the protégé of a newspaper magnate."

"But the other papers too," he said. "They're all under your spell. As I am."

"Sasha." She touched his hand fondly. As a sister. A rival sibling for Sergei's love. He drew it away irritably.

"I don't want your pity. Besides" – there was an edge of urgency in his voice – "I'm worried about you. It's that blooming look – you're expecting more than you can possibly have. I know you'll think this is spite, but it can't last, you know. It simply won't be allowed. You won't do anything silly, will you?"

"Silly?"

"He goes through these stages. I can see it coming on. I hope you'll be sensible."

It was later that week that she woke one morning to find Sergei still in bed with her.

"*Merde*!" he laughed. "I fell asleep!" And they made love as the morning sun gilded them.

They agreed it was enchanting, and she brought coffee and French toast. She cautioned herself not to become addicted.

A few nights later it happened again. This could, they told each other, become a habit.

Shortly after he had left on the morning of the fourth occurrence – so that her practice would not be interfered with – Emily received a hand-delivered note from Anna inviting her to be present within the hour at morning tea in Westmount. It did not seem to be the kind of invitation that could be declined.

"Child," Anna said. "I want you to understand that I find you utterly charming and therefore I hope, quite sincerely, that you will not be hurt. Since you are also intelligent, I am confident that things will work out well. You must understand that a certain point has been reached. It is quite over now."

"I can't give him up, you know. I love him."

Anna shrugged. "We all love him, child. Now, I have three possibilities for you, each excellent. You are aware that your musicality has reached a pitch that will not go unremarked in the world. Very quickly you will become famous and will forget all about us. You have offers from the orchestras of Dallas, Minneapolis, and Sydney, Australia. The auditions, of course, took place at our little concerts. Now, which one do you choose?"

With infinite care, Emily set down her china teacup in its saucer and said coldly: "I believe I will go now."

"When you are ready to send your telegram of acceptance, Sasha will come and help with the necessary arrangements."

Emily left for rehearsal. That night Sergei did not come and at lunch the next day, he was abstracted. A flicker, like the shadow of a small swiftly flying bird, passed over Emily's confidence.

"Sergei, is something the matter?"

"My love, it is too distressing. I cannot come again tonight. Another of our little concerts, a fledgling performer, rather tedious I'm afraid. Which is why I spare you from coming. You need rest and practice."

For a week, though the lunches and nocturnal visits grew erratic, she felt no anxiety. It was a major decision and she knew who would win. When, during the second week, she saw him scarcely at all, she had difficulty eating and her sleep and playing were affected. Nothing, he assured her, was wrong. In the third week, during which he neither came nor telephoned, she became ill and missed two rehearsals. By the fourth week, she was frantic.

She telephoned Anna and raved in a manner she would never have believed possible: "Where is he? What lies have you told him? You are monstrous and evil! You are a witch!"

She could hear Anna's sigh. "I do wish you would not be so hurt. I did explain."

She phoned his newspaper, the florist, his apartment buildings, his broker, the waiters at restaurants they had frequented. If she could just *speak* to him. He was never available. He had always just left.

In the sixth week, Sasha called.

"Do you wish to see my father?"

"Oh Sasha," she sobbed. "Please."

"I'll come and get you."

In Sasha's car they drove to a section of Old Montreal, a section of cobbles and restaurants with tiny courtyards.

"We'll go round the back way. You must promise you will be discreet."

Numbly she followed and through a crevice in an ivy-covered stone wall saw the courtyard, the intimate tête-à-tête, Sergei leaning across a table toward a willowy young woman in white. She saw Sergei's eyes, smoky with obsession.

"Mother found her at the Sorbonne," Sasha said. "A cellist, winner of various prizes in Paris and of a European-wide contest. A few weeks ago she played at one of our little chamber concerts. Enormous promise, everyone thinks. Father wants her for the orchestra. Have you seen enough?"

Emily half turned to him, brushing her hand across her eyes as though for some pain or dizziness, and fainted. When she came to, she was in a doctor's office. She was, he told her, pregnant.

Afterwards she could never be sure if she had changed from the pill to less certain methods because she had read an article warning of dire side effects or because Sergei had stayed for breakfast and she had begun to crave more than a shadow life.

Driving her home, Sasha demanded: "Well, what did the doctor say?"

"Exhaustion and shock, that's all. He said I need rest. I want to get away."

"Dallas or Minneapolis?"

"Sydney."

At her door Sasha said: "When you're ready, I'll help with the packing and everything. I'll take you to the airport."

Tentatively he touched her arm. "I do adore you, Emily. I will probably always be faithful to you."

For days she slept and cried. She did not want to eat but feared for the baby and forced herself. She was often sick. Sometimes she thought she might never have emerged from her apartment, never have opened her violin case again, never have left for Australia, if Victoria had not arrived as mysteriously and alarmingly as the priestess Pythia from a cave at Delphi, mouthing oracular predictions.

"Who is it?" Emily demanded of the silence in the receiver. She had never deluded herself that Sergei would call, having seen his eyes on *la celliste ravissante.* "Is it Anna? Are you waiting for a formal surrender?"

Silence. Heavy breathing.

She felt a spasm of unease because Anna would never....

"Emily, there's a man watching me. I can't leave the phone booth."

"What? Who is this?"

"It's Tory, Emily. Help me!"

"Tory?" Roaming confusedly through Montreal acquaintances, her memory took several seconds to alight on her sister. "My god, *Tory*! Where are you?"

"At the airport. There's a man watching me."

"*Which* airport?"

"Here. In Montreal. Dorval, is it? He followed me from Boston. Should I speak to him? Perhaps he likes me. But it might be for rape. I'm scared."

"Tory, darling Tory. I won't let anyone harm you. Stay right where you are and I'll come and get you. Now tell me, exactly where in the airport?"

"Eastern Airlines. I'm at the Eastern Airlines terminal."

"It will take me half an hour at least, Tory. You mustn't worry. I'll get there as fast as I can." Emily pressed her thumping heart, striving to impart calm. "But I promise nothing will happen to you. That's a *promise*, okay? Just stay right where you are."

She called Sasha, and while she waited for him to come, called Jason.

"Thank God," Jason said. "She's been missing since early this morning. She seemed perfectly calm last night and when they went to her room this morning she was gone."

"Why didn't anyone call me?"

"How could we expect it would involve you? It's incredible that she could have got into Boston and got a plane by herself.

But we knew she had money. Took it from father's desk.

"Father's desk?"

"She's been at home for a month. You don't exactly keep in touch, do you? We thought she was doing extremely well; something happened with father no doubt. I didn't like the arrangement in the first place, it never works out, but he keeps trying to atone, you know. And mother hopes for so much. A disaster."

"What should I do?"

"I'll come up tomorrow and bring her back. Oh god. Poor Tory. But you won't find her difficult. She's pathetically docile, writes letters to us constantly, and poetry incessantly. That's where her rage goes. Haven't you had any?"

"No. She wouldn't have my address." Then, puzzled: "But she must...."

"May have just got it from home. Must have been what gave her the idea. Could she stay for a while?"

Emily reeled with panic and nausea.

"Jason, no! I mean, I'd like to. But I leave for Australia in a few days."

"Australia?!"

"Sydney Symphony. I've been offered a position."

"Good grief! Is something the matter?"

"What kind of question is that? It's an offer I can't refuse. About Tory. How's mother taking this?"

"Distraught. Father's fit to be tied. The guiltier he feels, the worse he behaves, as usual."

"Oh god."

"Stupid mistake to have Tory back home. Mustn't happen again."

"No. And yet institutions... when she's doing well. What a mess."

They were silent, both miserable with guilt, knowing they were not equal to.... Some time in my life, Emily promised herself, when I am not pregnant and falling apart at the seams, I will have Tory live with me. I will make her happy. Some time.

"Here's my car," she said. "I'll see you tomorrow then."

Incongruously, as she got into Sasha's car, she remembered

Tory lifting her into a wheelbarrow and trundling her around the garden. Shrieks of pleasure. More, Tory, more, she was calling. Don't stop!

Emily rushed toward Tory at the speed of thought, hurtling through air. Don't stop, she wanted to beg the pilot. This was her preferred relationship to the past: skimming over it in the arms of a Boeing 747.

Montreal was a long way off, eight years to starboard.

But New York and Tory came closer by the minute.

(*ii*)

"I think it's Thursday," Victoria said to herself, aloud. She wrote it at the top of her page, and then she wrote *New York. Dear Emily*, she continued.

> *It is beautiful here in Jason's apartment. There are soft things and white things and the sofa feels like lying on rough grasses down by the creek near old Mr. Hamilton's house. You remember, the school cleaner? Ruth's kitchen smells of cinnamon. I love it here and I hope I won't have to leave. At the place where I was staying everything smells of nurses. Jason has a Ruth, did you know? But they do not sleep in the same bed which is very wise in case father finds out.*
>
> *I am so excited you are coming. Jason said he will bring you home tonight. From the airport. I remember the airport. When you came to the airport you were with a young man but I promised I would not tell father and I have never told. I keep my promises though you did not keep yours, Emily. You did not write to me. You promised to write and you did not did not.*
>
> *Jason says Australia and England and all over Europe. Did you come to Elsinore in Denmark?*

There's something rotten in the state of Denmark and in the rest of the world too. Remember how father made us memorize Shakespeare? These tedious old fools. Or was it just me and Jason? Did he make you too? Still harping on his daughter. I am but mad north-north-west; when the wind is southerly I know a hawk from a handsaw.

I'll tell you a secret Emily. I wanted to go all over the world, I wanted to have young men. You have got too much and have to share. In our family, haven't you noticed, I got all the loneliness? Do you think this is fair?

One is one is one is one.
What's this on the butcher's bench
slit open
for all the doctors to stare at?
They feed her honeysuckle
which is poisonous,
and take measurements
analyzing
analyzing

You owe me letters. Letters and letters. You owe me 416 letters, one a week for eight years, since you sent me away from Montreal with promises. You say to yourselves: Tory will forget, she knows nothing.

When I saw your pretty young man at the airport I said it would result in a son. Remember I said that?

When I said son, seeing him through the veins
of blood,
your skin blanched like almonds
in fire.
But the young man touched you
and said
tell me more.

Jason said yes, there is a son. When he comes I will see if he has the young man's eyes.

Emily, I will forgive the letters, only speak to father for me. We are going to see father, did you know? Someone has to tell him I am sorry so he will not be angry with me. I'm sorry for vomiting, I'm sorry about the young man. I promise I will stay away from the honeysuckle. If he is angry, will mother protect us, that is the question? Will she remember us?

It's easier when I write to say these things. My words when I speak are not good swimmers, they scatter in different currents, sometimes they drown. I have a special request: everyone should share and not be greedy, isn't that right? Now that you have your son, can I have your young man? Just for a little while. He was so lovely, golden and sweet as fresh-churned butter. On Russell Davison's farm he had two cows and they made butter and we shared. Do you remember? No one lets me have anything of my own now, though Jason is very kind to me. When you were little I used to push you and Jason on the swings. I gave you all my books and my old dolls. They took away my young man and I never found him again but if I can have yours it will be all right.

How should I your true love know
From another one?
By his cockle hat and staff
and his sandal shoon.

He is dead and gone, lady,
He is dead and gone:
They strangled him with honeysuckle
And left you all alone.

I know a place in Central Park where you can watch children sail boats. Tomorrow I will show you. This afternoon Jason's Ruth is going to take me downtown to the shops and a restaurant, and on Saturday afternoon we are all driving up to Ashville for a party on Sunday.

Will you promise to speak to father for me?

Love, Tory.

(*iii*)

Over the intercom Jason's secretary said: "Stephen Waller is here. Shall I send him in?"

"Give me five mintues to make a call first. I'll buzz when I'm ready."

He began dialing Jessica's number then hesitated, indecisive, and replaced the receiver. But yes, it really was time. Lately, making love to her, even being with her, was like losing hold of the reins of a team of galloping horses.

Jason did not care ever to surrender power.

And yes, it was time. Before Ruth was hurt, before Jessica was too badly hurt, before he himself became irreversibly vulnerable. Already he had been distancing himself from the white-water turbulence of her presence.

Mentally he rehearsed: Two weeks, I know, I feel guilty as hell...incredibly busy...too hectic even to *think* about you, which is criminal (nicely ambiguous)...and now the craziest thing...my sister flying in from London this evening...family reunion...another whole week, I'm afraid.

Easing out, not without regret. In any case, she had known from the start.

"Nothing can come of this." Always he made that clear right at the beginning. "I have an ongoing commitment."

One of his saving graces, he felt, was his honesty, including his unblinking acceptance of his own deficiencies. I'm a bastard to live with, he would say to himself. He had also said this to Nina, and to Ruth, and to a number of other women. Laying his cards on the table. No rose-tinted illusions. Though to himself he would add: but considering everything....

There was also his gentleness, the fact that he took no pleasure in causing pain. If he had to hurt, if there were women who willed themselves to forget the agreed-upon terms, then he did so with as light a touch as possible.

Decisively he dialed Jessica's number. Now that it was over, a vision of her lithe brown dancer's body filled him with exquisite sorrow. When, on the fifth ring, she had still not answered, he imagined her doing *pliés* before the bedroom mirror, or standing naked in the bathroom, still wet from the shower, high-kicking one sun-gold leg after the other, her dainty foot pointed like a swallow at the ceiling, the petal-soft honey-warm crevice between her legs opening and closing like a rare orchid.

He drew strength from the knowledge that, having reached a decision, he was immune. Regardless of the misbehavior of his blood and the sentimentality of his sexual organ (which he stroked gently as though calming a foolish and exuberant puppy) he would not, in fact, consent to any tearful pleas for "just one more time."

She was letting the phone ring an unconscionably long time, but he knew she would be at home at this hour of the morning. It was entirely probable that she was willing herself not to answer in order to punish him for the last two weeks. Of course sleeping pills were always a possibility, a syndrome with which he was not unfamiliar either as a therapist or as a lover extricating himself from relationships that had run their course. But in Jessica's case he thought the refusal to answer was more likely. Part of her attraction was the stubborness that went along with her coltish grace.

"Well," she had said lightly right at the beginning – at the Schonberg's party where they had met. "That would be perfectly all right because I have one too. An ongoing commitment."

He had been leaning, whiskey-mellow, on the piano and had whispered that he desired her inordinately but he was afraid nothing could come of it, etcetera.

"It is," he said reproachfully, "quite uncalled for in your case. A commitment. He's here at the party?"

"As a matter of fact, he's in Europe for a few months. Company assignment. But I couldn't possibly pass up the show I'm doing at the moment so I stayed behind. And your wife?"

"Ruth's at a board meeting. What does your husband do?"

"Not husband, in point of fact."

"Ah. In my case also, actually, not wife. We intend a more lasting commitment."

"Indeed?" She raised a sardonic eyebrow. "It's working well, I see."

Chagrined he explicated: "An open and honest one."

"Oh of course. Ned and I, on the other hand, are just playing it by ear. No specific vows of permanence."

"And what does Ned do?"

"Corporation lawyer. Aren't you? Do the Schonbergs know any other kind of people, allowing for minor divergences into international law, industrial law, and taxation law?"

"As a matter of fact, I'm a clinical therapist. And a psychology professor on the side. I teach a couple of courses."

"How did you get in the Schonberg's front door? You're not her shrink, are you?"

"No. She took one of my courses."

"*Contemporary Neuroses* or *How to Get More Out of Your Sex Life?*"

"Cruel," he said. "To both of us."

"Therapists bring out the worst in me."

"You've had a bad experience with one?"

"I wouldn't touch one."

"What a blow," he said archly. "And here I was hoping."

"But we already agreed that this could go nowhere."

"Your hostility is definitely showing. What do you have against therapists?"

"They manipulate. They're power freaks. Also I have several friends who've been turned into dependency junkies. Have to call their therapists every second day for a fix."

"In my defense, let me say only that there have been people who came to me incapacitated with misery, who went away functioning and happy."

"But most of all, I hate their arrogance. That sickening sense of themselves as God."

In retrospect, he thought, it was not surprising that she had induced a mild frenzy of possessive desire.

On what must have been the twentieth ring, the phone was answered. Breathlessly.

"Sorry. (Gasp). Heard it ring as I unlocked. (Gasp). Just ran up the stairs."

It was not Jessica's voice.

"Excuse me. I must have the wrong number."

"Did you want Jessica?"

"Ah...yes. Who are you?"

"New tenant. Lise. Jessica moved out a week ago."

"Moved out? That's impossible. Why?"

"Don't ask me. I just answered her ad on the bulletin board at the theater. Because of the guy, I suppose. Some guy came back into her life, she said."

"Oh. Ned from Europe."

"Ned? No, that wasn't his name. I met him when I was moving in. But I remember now: she said if Ned called, tell him she'd write."

"I see. Any other messages?"

"Not that I recall. Oh yes. Just that I wasn't to give anyone her phone number. She said anyone who mattered knew where to find her at rehearsal. But she still has to come back to pick up a couple of things if you want to leave a message.... Hello?...Hello?"

He was stunned. Outraged. Two weeks of disciplined self-denial designed to convey a subtle message, to accustom her gently....

Tramp, he thought.

Good riddance.

As he pressed the intercom button he noticed that his hand was trembling. Was it possible, after such tempestuous nights, such profound discussions over wine, that he could mean so little to her? Not even a pretence at farewell? It was monstrous.

"Send Stephen Waller in, Julie."

No. It was not possible. It was not possible to fake the kind of passion that had been between them for months. Without question she was in love with him. This was a devious revenge for his not calling for two weeks. Collusion with some girl friend, designed to shake him. Well, they would see who was the smarter game player. He would simply ignore the whole thing. Spare himself the trouble of easing out.

"Of course," Stephen Waller was saying, feeling the coarse weave of a vest made high in the Andes as though doing a quick check on his I.D., "I don't accept the validity of anything you say. Your task is to iron out the exceptional, the worst kind of moral reductionism really. Bring everything down to the level of the well-adjusted. That is to say, the banal."

Such an intense memory of Jessica swamped Jason that the room seemed full of musk and jasmine, her tropical odors, overpowering. He could scarcely breathe and rose abruptly from his desk, crossing to the window. Disoriented at finding it already open, he turned on the fan.

"What are you doing?" Stephen asked sharply. "You've activated something, haven't you? Is the room bugged? I would have thought at least some places were sacred." He laughed. "Is it possible I still have illusions?"

The smell of Jessica hung between them like incense. Jason leaned on his desk, his head in his hands. "It's a question of deciding what one wants," he mused aloud. "Are the possible consequences worth it?"

"Well," Stephen responded out of a different world, "I know all about possible consequences, don't I? My problem is, do I have any right whatsoever to bother about personal consequences considering what *they*, what the consequences for *them* . . . ."

Jessica was dispersing, blowing out the window. Now that he thought about it, the fact of her not saying goodbye was proof. If she were genuinely indifferent, of course she would have called, explained, invented excuses, planned a farewell dinner. He could breathe again.

"How can even syntax – you see the scope of the problem?" Stephen went on. "How can anything hang together? I find I can't . . . even connect words. . . . If you'd seen her, you'd understand. I think I'm going to be sick, you'll have to excuse me."

Jason focussed, surfacing from Jessica, on Stephen's heaving body.

"It's . . . logic snapped, you see," Stephen said. "Sentences don't finish. All connections." There was a noise from his throat as of gears grinding. "The gap between action and consequence. Nothing since. . . . Off its traces, you might say. I have trouble with words, they float away from their meanings."

He sank to his knees and put his cupped hands to his

mouth, his body undulating as though in obeisance to some barbaric deity.

"Every morning I am surprised, moved to tears. For five minutes I feel hope: the sun has risen as predicted, the center holds. But I have no confidence that day will continue to follow night."

With awful quietness a gray river of vomit flowed into his cupped hands.

"Oh god," Jason said softly. He came from behind his desk, and led Stephen to the small bathroom at one side of the office. Stephen continued to vomit into the toilet. Very gently, when the physical trauma had expended itself, Jason sponged the young man's face and arms with a washcloth.

"I'm sorry," Stephen said, ashen. "I'm sorry. All I want is for you to make it possible for me to go on living because my death can't help them."

"Can you describe what it is that...? I think it will be better once you can do that."

"I don't think I can. I'll try. No, I don't think I can. It's so... so..." He drew complex figures in the air, like an ancient astromancer. "It's not amenable to belief. You see, I can't fill the role, my reasons for going were so frivolous. Oh a certain amount of idealism, I guess, but mostly just for the adventure. A chance to use my Spanish. Fascination with another culture. Even ambition. It doesn't hurt on the résumé of an agricultural scientist, improving third-world technology. All college reasons, selfish reasons.

"Of course you want to know about college. Was I political? Manic-depressive? Suicidal?" Stephen laughed mirthlessly. "I can assure you that has been gone over very thoroughly. They couldn't find a thing. Disgustingly ordinary apolitical jock." His eyes darted around the room. "Are we bugged?"

Jason shook his head. "You contacted me, remember?"

"Yes, yes. Someone recommended. Said you were human. But that could all be part of the.... I've lost six jobs, though they don't have to be behind that. I can do that all on my own. Father keeps getting new ones for me, poor devil. He has excellent connections. Big brass at IBM and doesn't even see the irony. Poor bastard has got ulcers over me, and one heart seizure. I'd like to improve, you know, for his sake. Oh god, I started to tell him about it once. You understand, he wanted the takeover, he was against Allende from the start."

Stephen raised his arms in front of his face, warding off blows.

"Yes?" Jason prompted.

"It didn't happen yesterday, did it? No, I don't think it did. Another problem I have is with time. Does it pass?"

"You came here on time."

"Father brought me. Yes, but when did I come back? How long was I there? How did they get me out?"

"Can you tell me?"

"Thirty pounds ago. They had to buy me new clothes. Am I thin?"

"Well, yes. You're of slight build."

"No. That happened. I used to play football in college. Thirty pounds ago, maybe longer than that. Let's see. I graduated in sixty-nine, I left in the fall, yes. I was there for the election, for Allende, that was late seventy. We were building the dam in the village. The summers are so dry, they weren't conserving the winter rain or the melting snows. That same fall Father Gabriel and the sisters began the classes. Sister Concepción was very young, she taught the children, and Sister Serena took the women and Father Gabriel taught the farmers. I sat in sometimes with the men. They'd finished the alphabet and their names, they were starting on the Gospel of Matthew. And then you know Allende fell and the army came to the village and after that...after that the boa constrictors seemed innocent as garden lizards.

"But there aren't any reasons. There can't be explanations. I know that colonel, I knew the chief of police, I had drunk wine with them. I remember the police chief's little girl, how he carried her on his back. So you see why.... You could smile at me and call your secretary in and ask her politely to cut off my ears. You could make me eat them. Why not? These things happen." Stephen traced hieroglyphs in the air. "Where is logic?"

He leaned forward. "Words are deadly as poisoned boomerangs."

Accusingly he demanded, "And if Father Gabriel, why not me? Can you tell me that? Why not me? Because I'm American? Now *there's* a nice nugget of logic. Whenever two and two still make four, I have hope. Or maybe father's connections, there's another gleam of causality. Shall I tell you what I saw?"

"It will help if you can."

"I only saw Sister Concepción, but the villagers told me about Father Gabriel. Neatly bundled in a grain sack, they said, at the church door. Like a jigsaw puzzle, so many pieces: arms, legs, hands, feet, his penis stuffed into his mouth. I didn't see that.

"But Concepción, they left her at my door. I don't know why. A warning, I suppose." He put his hands over his eyes and began retching again, his breathing ragged as a broken air conditioner. "She was not dismembered. No. It was the burns, the mutilation.... I'm sorry, I can't go on."

Watching the convulsions of Stephen's neck, Jason was reminded of a cat he had once seen trying to regurgitate a small snake. He put his hand over his own mouth and felt a giving way in his intestines, as of subsidence along a fault line in his body.

"Don't try...to recall any more...just now."

Stephen nodded. A thin stream of bile trickled down his chin and he bent over and felt his way to the bathroom. Jason remained motionless at his desk. Fifteen minutes elapsed.

"The problem" – Stephen emerged talking as though an ongoing discussion had never ceased – "is how to *atone*. And how to go on. Do you see? Even in the simplest position, even as a lab technician...I ask myself, what is science? The support structure is gone. We exist off the rails. What did they do? They taught peasants to read. Do you see? It is not...it is not...." The veins in his temples throbbed visibly as though a marathon effort were being made. "It is not *commensurate*."

"No." Jason's voice could barely be heard. "It is not commensurate."

They both sat in a trance, neither moving.

At last Stephen said: "When I got back, no one believed. But how can I blame? Who can believe? They ordered psychiatric tests. They said the prison in Santiago, malnutrition, and so on. At first that enraged me, but then I wanted it to be true. Do you see? If the explanation is that I was mad, then there's hope. I could be sane again."

"When you come to me, what is it you want?"

"My father wants. You're the fourth or fifth. It's costing him a fortune."

"But you. What do you want?"

"I want to forget."

"To forget?"

"Yes. No. I don't know. I don't think I should forget but I want the nightmares to stop, I want to stop *seeing* her. I would like to atone, to bear witness, but it is beyond me, a task for saints like Father Gabriel and her. I tremble, I vomit, I startle at shadows, I forget where I am, what year it is. It is worst when I see a priest or a nun. I believe I am followed and bugged and that people are trying to kill me. I also know I am paranoid but after...all that...and the prison in Santiago, it is difficult to know where to distinguish. Most of the time I'm functional, but without direction. Your hands are shaking, doctor."

Jason made some vague gesture. It seemed to him that an unspeakable vision of Sister Concepción had entered him like a virus.

"Doctor." Stephen leaned forward, his arms on the other side of the desk. "Do you believe me?"

Jason saw that the plea to acknowledge and the plea to deny were equally intense. He could not answer.

After a long silence Stephen asked: "If it happened – we both fear it happened – can you help me?"

Jason's hands parted, fragile as dove's wings, and came together. Almost, one might have thought, in prayer.

"It has always been this way, hasn't it? Mere flickerings against the night." Stephen had to strain forward to hear him. "We can light candles, that is all. As your...as Father Gabriel and Sister Concepción did."

After Stephen left, Jason instructed his secretary: "Cancel the afternoon appointments and hold all my calls."

For a long time he sat with his head in his hands. He found that he had written on his blotter: *What a piece of work is man! How noble in reason, how infinite in faculty. And yet, to me, what is this quintessence of dust?*

Oh father, he sighed, how you would bark with derision, reading over my shoulder.

When his secretary buzzed to see if he wanted lunch brought in, he realized hours had passed. He heard his office clock chime two. Then three. Three had some special significance. Jessica's rehearsal time.

It was, suddenly, essential that he see Jessica, that he warm himself against her, stave off the hobgoblins.

He was in the street. He gave the taxi driver the address.

In the dressing room mirror he caught her unguarded shock. And then the flippant mask fell into place like a visor. She was wearing leotards and leg warmers that rolled over into cuffs high on her thighs and gave her the rakish look of a barefoot buccaneer. She swiveled her chair around to face him, her chestnut hair falling around her shoulders.

"I would've called eventually, Jason. But hell...." She shrugged disarmingly. "You would've gotten so moral. And how can I explain why these things happen? I'm just a flighty dancer. You're better off without me."

He felt as though, flying, he had hit an air pocket and just dropped fifty feet. He had been going to accuse: you staged this whole thing. I saw your face in the mirror. You're manipulating me.

Disoriented he said: "Will you talk to me? Something very...disturbing happened this morning."

It was as though the gray membrane of a cocoon fell away from a luminous essence.

"Oh Jason, what is it? What's wrong?" She took his hands in hers and her voice, he thought, was how the voice of Sister Concepción might have sounded comforting some Indian peasant woman in labor.

"Jason, you're feverish! What is it?" She drew him towards herself and he sat on the floor beside her chair and put his head in her lap.

"You know how you hate the therapist-as-God syndrome?"

"Mmm."

"There's a case to be made though. There are people begging for cohesion. If I myself gave in to this tidal wave of chaos that threatens to swamp us all...where would those people go? If I don't stay glued together, who will help the Stephens? Who will help Tory?"

She stroked his hair. "What happened?"

As he told her about Stephen, she slid down beside him on the floor and put her face against his. They kissed, starved for each other.

"You're crying," he said wonderingly. "You *do* want me." (He almost said "love me.") And less certainly: "Don't you?"

"Oh yes. Damn you. But don't let it bother you."

"Then this other man...? I *knew* it was an act...."

"No. He exists. I've moved in, all right. It's a mutually suitable temporary arrangement. I may not be terribly smart, Jason, but I know all about self-protection and survival. I don't wait around for the knock-out and final count."

"Jessica, I need you."

"Need." She turned the word over in her mind. It might have been an eggplant or summer squash she was examining suspiciously in a market. "I don't know about you and need, Jason. You use people up. Perhaps it's justifiable, as you say. For the Stephens and the Torys. It's just that I'm not the saintly type, I can't afford to be used up, I need me for dancing."

"Please, dance for *me*. I need to make love to you, I need to be held."

He pressed her against himself and kissed her until he felt the ramrod of her will weaken. "Come with me."

"I can't *now*, Jason. I've got rehearsal."

"Once won't hurt. Say you're sick. Please."

"But where? We can't go to my apartment any more."

"Mine. Ruth's taken Tory shopping for the afternoon. They won't be home till after six. Please. If you don't come, I'll...I don't know how I'll hold together tonight."

"That's hard to believe, but I'll come."

She had never seen the inside of his co-op before.

"It's so clinical!" she exclaimed, and her judgment hit him like a lash. "All white and off-white and beige, straight out of a magazine. So passionless. Oh, except for this!" It was Nina's wooden carving she had noticed and she stroked it with her hands.

Not listening now he put on the Bach flute sonatas. To those haunting notes, he laid her on the off-white textured rug and unbuttoned her shirt and peeled off the leotard.

"Dance for me."

As seaweed sways in the ocean she moved. Languid, effortless, weightless. He thought of crocuses pushing through late snow, of lilacs beginning to bloom, of Sister Concepción moving among angels. He took off his clothes and danced with her, first only their fingers touching, then hands, then their bodies merging.

Behind his closed eyes he saw the glassy concave tunnel of the wave that he always feared would drown him. The current had him, he was borne headlong, he was rushing up up up to the breaking point. Someone, perhaps both of them, cried out as the crest exploded over their bodies.

Much later, when they had drifted into lassitude, they still clung wetly together.

Jason looked at his watch.

"Oh my god!" He leaped to his feet, began a frantic reassembling of clothing, paused. "I'll have to shower, they'll be home in fifteen minutes. Get yourself a taxi, quick! Oh god, smell this place! Ruth will know the second she walks in the door." Clutching his clothes in one arm, he began darting around the room opening windows. "What do you do, bathe in musk, for god's sake?"

White-faced, Jessica sat with the back of one hand pressed against her lips. Then she picked up her clothes and went into the bathroom. I will not cry, she promised herself.

There was a box of Kleenex above the toilet and she hastily swabbed her sticky thighs. The wastepaper basket was empty, clean and deodorized as a hospital bathroom. Could Jason ever countenance detritus? she wondered. Would he permit vicious little signs of decay like soiled tissues, flattened toothpaste tubes, stubble-clotted Trac II razorblades? Perhaps he emptied the baskets every hour.

She was dressed. He was in the cramped room with her.

"Dear god," he said. "Are you mad? What are you doing? Are you trying to gloat over Ruth? Are you into cheap triumphs?"

He picked up the balled wad of tissues and lubricant and sperm, holding it at arm's length between thumb and forefinger.

"I'll find a taxi somewhere down the street," she said.

He was already showering as she clicked the front door behind her and when a taxi pulled up she could barely see. She got in and gave her address.

"Hell, kid!" The driver was concerned. "You're in lousy shape."

"Don't mind me. I'm just stupid." She dabbed at her swollen eyes and at the smudged rivers of mascara. "And to think I've always believed I'm not a masochist."

"He's not worth it," the driver said. "I tell my four daughters all the time. Men just aren't worth it, you know."

"I know."

At her door, he was fatherly. "Let me buy you a cup of coffee. Gonna worry all night otherwise. Can't stand to see a pretty kid cry like that."

"Bless you," she said. "Why not?"

XVI Edward

I have set something irreversible in motion.

In my mind there arises an image of a juggernaut seen in some documentary of India – a massively carved temple cart with ponderous wooden wheels like cask lids. Under its canopy, bronze and sandalwood deities huddle in suspense while jasmine-chains and streamers of gaudy cloth whirl before their eyes, promising drama. Below the wagon, red sand slopes down to the ocean, and a frail little man, a priest, gives a push with his hand. Slowly, as though stirring from sleep, the gigantic wheels rock, lurch, lumber into wakefulness, greedy now, gobbling up sand, thirsty for seawater, rabid for baptism, hurling their titanic superstructure and divine cargo into spectacular collision with the plumed and inexorably advancing waves.

I also think of Caesar crossing the Rubicon and of Napoleon making his fateful decision to advance on the Russian winter and of Marlowe's *Faustus. Her lips suck forth my soul: see where it flies!*

Why should these all be images of destruction and damnation? Why not of hope?

In any case, nothing may come of it.

When Marta came through the moonlight that night, I could not speak. I forgot about Victoria, a pensive child in a white shift at an upstairs window. The night was full of Marta who seemed lighter than air, her gauzy dress an incandescence, her mane of black curls a fragrant snare. I wanted to tangle my fingers, to bury my face in that thicket. A disturbance of fragrance, of something compellingly tropical, filled the gazebo.

In Guam, sometimes, a shift of nightwinds would brush her

against my senses and I would feel weak with longing and terror and confusion and a sense of grossly improper association. As though I had violated her with mud and death. And yet her presence was always fraught with impending cataclysm.

In the gazebo I could not move. The weight in my genitals anchored me, as surely as a ball and chain would have done, to the wooden bench. I feared, in fact, that I might faint and humiliate myself, such a painful throbbing downward-dragging agitation clawed at my flesh.

"Oh Edward, you and I," she sighed, twining herself around the central upright like a bright ribbon around a maypole, "we had such foolish expectations of the proper marriage. The romanticism of the disadvantaged. And we're so hopelessly prim."

I did not understand, but part of her hold over me was her unpredictability. I believed that a meaning would unfold itself.

Silence flowed between us, a palpable sensuous bond. She was contemplating, it seemed to me, the chaos of the inevitable, the fate that bound us. I decided I would do nothing, I would rely on her timing, initiative not being within my power. I simply waited, a cork on the floodtide of our destiny.

"They're different from us, Edward. They could slough us off like old skin. Should we simply capitulate and make it easy for them?"

We are going to flee tonight, I thought. We will leave them with a face-saving scandal, public sympathy all on their side. And we like smugglers, absconding with ill-gotten but fabulous gains.

"Almost everyone's gone. Joe thinks I've walked home. To pay the babysitter, I said. They'll be alone in there soon."

I thought of her with her little girl and a vision came to me, beatific, of our love children, a shower of bright beings. And hard on its tail, like a storm cloud: the children! Must we lose the children? My delicate Tory, Marta's infant Sonia. I looked up at the window, but Tory had gone from the landing.

"I'm so generous, so noble," Marta laughed. "Born to the tragic role."

Her laughter was like that of a clown, a hard-won sobbing sound. It's because of the children, I thought, and my mind leaped to Tory shivering on the stairs in her bare feet. Or perhaps alone and frightened in her bedroom. Antony, I thought, lost a kingdom for Cleopatra. But how can one contemplate the loss of a child?

Marta's voice broke. "Oh Edward, what shall we do?" She turned to me, extending her milky arms.

Stricken, I lurched toward her. There could be no turning back now. Once I touched her we would ignite, the conflagration would be unquenchable.

And then, like conscience herself, like the spirit of innocence, I saw Victoria. Or rather, I saw a flutter of white in the garden.

Blindly I stumbled past Marta's outstretched arms and floundered into the night. I reeled about the garden like a drunken ship with shredded sails and splintered hull. When I collided with Bessie I felt like a pirate brought to retribution.

I will plead guilty, I thought. I will beg for forgiveness. I will throw myself on her mercy.

"Victoria," she said frantically. "I can't find Victoria! She's not in the house."

It was like a reprieve. Scope for atonement.

When we found her, damp and shivering in the honeysuckle, we outdid each other with concern, with self-reproach. It was my embrace that Tory reached for, I remember that, mine. In my arms she was light and precious as silk. She whimpered against my heart and I kissed her hair and carried her into the house. There was not a sound, the last car had left, the last guest gone. Marta, I suppose, had crept away. We carried Tory up the stairs and then knelt, one at each side of her bed, holding her white little hands until sleep quieted the rushes of breathing. Then I took my wife into my arms, my wife Elizabeth, my beautiful pale elegant aristocrat.

"Bessie," I murmured, as though anchoring myself to all I had struggled for, all that was sane.

"Edward," she whispered. And then she told me: "I'm going to have another baby."

And I thought: entrapment! She knew all along; she has made all alternatives impossible.

I resented, then, the theft of choice. No hope of weighing costs, of second thoughts. Wedlock, childlock, all those shackles.

When Jason first drew air into his lungs I was surrounded by the death cries of men in agony. It seemed an accompaniment not altogether unfitting.

I feel I have moved the rock that was stemming an avalanche. There will be seismic repercussions.

And yet it could come to nothing.

This is what I have done: When Bessie was out this morning I called the school board and asked to speak to Miss Perkins, an efficient soul permitted by a special dispensation to stay on past retirement age. A leftover from my administration, married to the job, a willing slave, out to pasture now in the records division.

"Oh, Mr. Carpenter!" she gushed, eager to help.

Before the war, I told her, there was a Joseph Wilson, my deputy principal. He was killed in action. His wife's name.... But I could not say it. He had a wife, I said. I believe she still lives in New York, though of course she may have remarried. Can you trace her at such short notice?

Miss Perkins does that sort of thing. She will phone registry offices and postal departments around the country if necessary, she will tap electronic memories, an adaptation on her part that astonishes me.

If you could send an official school board invitation for Sunday, I said. By telephone or telegram. Without mentioning I suggested it.

"It's *Friday*, Mr. Carpenter," she said doubtfully, "but I'll do my best."

Only two days' notice. But Marta was always a creature of impulse.

Miss Perkins, I said, this is my little secret for the celebrations. If my wife answers, you understand....

"Oh absolutely, Mr. Carpenter. The soul of discretion."

By mid-afternoon she called back. Luckily Bessie had gone off to the post office or somewhere. A Mrs. Marta Wilson, Miss Perkins said – and I stopped breathing for several seconds – had been located in New York City. She had never remarried, her identity had been confirmed by a telephone call. A formal telegram of invitation had been sent.

It must be rather like this – a vibrant palpitation of nerves, of wings stretched – when the butterfly senses the dissolving of cocoon walls, smells the life discarded and the coming birth.

I am young with excitement.

XVII Elizabeth

Elizabeth forgets to hang up. She cradles the receiver between her breasts and fondles it absent-mindedly as though it were a kitten.

They are here!

They are all in New York. She has spoken to them on the telephone. A neatly arranged score: it is all going to happen now exactly as she has written it. A final scherzo of celebration.

It is Friday. By tomorrow evening they will be in the house.

Elizabeth stands at the French windows, lifting her arms to the sun. She decides she will say nothing to Edward. He will only blunder into irritation, say things he regrets, back himself into a corner, forbid Adam to enter the house.

Elizabeth has double-checked her list. Weeks ago she sent out the local invitations and the ones to Boston. The acceptances are in neat piles on the hallway stand. The food has been ordered, and the wine. Probably she will forget something crucial, nevertheless. She laughs.

There has been a telegram from Dave: *Love to Emily and Adam. Waiting with fingers crossed. Dave.*

She decides to walk down to the post office in case something new has come in, but mainly because she wants to be part of summer. To stretch with all growing things towards the sun, to ease her restlessness. The house is infected with hope.

When she comes back, even Edward has caught it like a virus. He is unusually animated. She bends over him with pleasure and kisses him and he does not object. She has the neighbor's son carry him downstairs and she plays for him in the living room.

He drowses and smiles.

XVIII In Central Park

In Central Park the summer smell of Saturday morning is sharp with cut grass and the virtuous tang of sweat: joggers in an urban minuet, lawyers nodding at salesgirls from Bloomingdale's, couples furthering plans and quarrels between gasps. Ruth and Emily, with nothing at stake, jogged companionably, an easy rhythmic pleasure.

"Are you sure it's all right?" Emily had asked, leaving her son with Tory by the pond.

"Were you mugged when you lived here?" Jason demanded dryly.

"But it's supposed to be so much worse now."

"It's not as bad as they'd have you believe in London. Safer than Hyde Park probably."

Jason ran with discipline, a purgatorial exercise: in this extending of limits may I prove myself stronger than the collective anomie of my patients.

Once you got used to her, Adam decided, his Aunt Tory was not so alarming. Yesterday she had been afraid to go up inside the Statue of Liberty with him, but had hummed songs to herself all day. Besides it was perfectly acceptable to have a crazy aunt. Snelby had one who rode to hounds in her fifties and smoked a pipe and kept an assortment of bone corsets – not to wear, but as collectors' items.

My Aunt Victoria, Adam would say casually, sails toy boats in a park in New York City. She sits with her dress pulled up over her knees and her feet in the water and when one of the boats comes near she pulls it in with her toes.

Hey! children would call out. That's mine!

And Aunt Tory would look upset and put the boat back.

"Nobody shares," she whispered mournfully to Adam.

Smiling a little, though mindful of her sadness, Adam put his hand suddenly in hers. He felt rich with family.

"Jason," she said, hugging him. "It's so nice you've come back."

She often called him Jason, though at other times she seemed to know exactly who he was.

"When your mother was little, I used to give her rides in a wheelbarrow. But the young men were not allowed to touch me. Your mother went away so that the young men could touch her. You have his eyes, Adam. The young man in Montreal, you have his eyes."

Staring into the water, Adam saw the shadowy underside of his aunt's bare thighs, large whitish floats with a dark slash between, and he thought that she was full of secrets he did not want to know.

She leaned forward to see what he was looking at and they stared at each other's reflections. A tiny schooner cut cleanly across Adam's cheeks and sailed into the lapping cave of his aunt's mouth. She gasped and lunged at it with her toes and it scudded away, flakes of their disintegrating faces chasing it like spume.

"It's because I looked," she said. "I have to be careful not to look at people. Terrible things happen."

In spite of himself he was curious. "What terrible things?"

"I can't tell you. I came down the stairs.... And then the war happened. Father went to the war and he never came back. Someone else came back inside him. And then I lost Jason, he went away to school. And then I lost my young man."

Her sadness dragged at Adam's heart.

"Don't cry, Aunt Tory." He put his arms around her neck and kissed her. "Everyone comes back, I know they do. I thought I lost grandma and Uncle Jason but I was wrong. I lost Dave but he'll come back."

The large soft breasts against which she pressed him were warm as Australian sand dunes.

"Jason," she sighed. "You've come back."

(My crazy Aunt Tory, he would say to Snelby, thinks I'm her little brother.)

And then quite lucidly she said: "Please don't get lost, Adam."

Perhaps he would not after all discuss her with Snelby. In

his pocket he felt the unfamiliar American coins his Uncle Jason had given him.

"Come on, Aunt Tory" – pulling her by the hand – "I'll buy you an ice cream."

◆◆◆

From under his drenched headband, jogging by on his second circuit, Jason saw them standing hand in hand at the ice cream cart and thought: Tory loves the sound of "aunt." It does more for her than neuroleptics and tranquilizers. And when the child puts his hand in mine and says "Uncle Jason".... New life on our dead branches.

As the muscles in his calves and thighs rebelled, he ran faster. He was running from last night's dream. In the dream he had been trapped in the crawl space under an old house, hemmed in by boxes and a furnace that shuddered like a heart. It was impossible to move. From the sub-flooring above, postcards fell like goose-down from a slit pillow; stamped and addressed and unanswered postcards. And then, inexplicably, he and Stephen were sorting through a pile of mutilated bodies, their dead eyes open and staring: Sister Concepción's, Tory's, Nina's, Ruth's, Jessica's.

You have to close the eyes, Stephen said. That's required. You have to stop people from seeing their memories.

In Central Park Jason ran from the memory of those eyes. The pain in his legs and chest was acute, he ran into its embrace. I am in training, he thought, to withstand everyone else's despair. A stitch daggered his side and he gritted his teeth and drove himself on. But without his volition a cry for comfort shaped itself in his mind: Jessica. He could smell her in the sweet grass he smashed with his feet.

Pain seemed to inhabit his body like a tumor.

I could not, he gasped inwardly, countenance even the suggestion of torture. I could not live with what Stephen has seen.

Jessica, he called silently. Jessica, hold me!

He kept running until he had outdistanced the stitch. He had a disquieting feeling that he had behaved shoddily the day before yesterday, but Jessica would understand. He could not quite remember...; there had been pressures, time constraints. It was possible he had been something of a bastard, but considering Stephen, considering Ruth, considering Tory....

And Jessica would understand.

◆◆◆

"I heard you play the Sibelius... three years ago," Ruth said. "I feel... a kind of awe... jogging along like this... beside you. One realizes... the years of discipline."

"Why didn't you come backstage... with Jason?"

Their syncopated voices slid between the percussion of their feet.

"I wanted to.... You're off limits to me.... The family... is his private possession."

"He first told me . . . about you . . . years ago. In Montreal, eight... more than eight years. And none of us... ever met you."

"Not true.... We took your parents... to dinner once.... Not a comfortable occasion. Though your mother... is hard to forget."

Thud, thud, the punctuation of Adidas.

"I'd practically decided... he invented you. You understand... I adore Jason... my big brother, idealized.... But still... I'm amazed... you put up with him."

His other women, unmentioned, jostled them in ghostly clamor. Ruth and Emily jogged silently on. Their footfalls shussed over grass; cars passed distantly like meteors across the background of their silence; an occasional horse and carriage bearing tourists, a child with a kite, careened into view.

"I've been married," Ruth said. "And I've lived alone.... This is better.... We suit each other."

"You should be coming... to Ashville with us... this afternoon."

"It would be an intrusion.... It's all right, you know.... We both have 'no entry' signs strewn all over our lives."

Two boys on bicycles, riding full tilt at the women, parted at the last minute and made an ellipse around them.

"My first husband – " Ruth corrected herself – "My husband... he was an actor... which can be euphoric or harrowing.... That's why I'm in awe of you... the perseverance. One day I came home from work... and the bathroom door was locked.... I knew right away. One doesn't... encourage connections... after something like that."

"Oh Ruth!" Instinctively Emily touched her but Ruth flinched and veered aside to scoop up a dandelion flower. She slackened to a walk.

"We're bred for outer space, I suppose, our generation." She shredded the dandelion stem with her thumb nail. "Isolated atoms. But we want to stave off desolation. We want someone in the room when we wake at night. And you see, it works. Here we are. A social network."

Emily had a bleak vision of wraiths moving through twilight in patterns, of solitary figures hunched in a circle of chill caves, assuring themselves of community.

"Do you feel so desolate?" she cried involuntarily. "Does Jason?"

Ruth's eyebrows registered surprise.

"Doesn't everyone? Don't you? You live alone."

Ruth might as well have said: "You're grossly overweight," so astonishing was the perspective. Emily had thought of herself as backing away from the overheated blaze of family and lovers, but never as alone.

"I have Adam." A shorthand form of contradiction.

"An additional cause for terror, I should have thought."

"Oh no!"

"I am always amazed when anyone has the courage."

"You and Jason don't intend...?"

"Never. In any case, how can a child fill the void? What can you say to your son? You're still alone."

"No. There's the family...."

"Which you're very anxious to avoid."

"But that's the point. I can't. It's impossible. They're always with me, woven into me. And audiences. I have my audiences. And other musicians."

"And I my career. Power. Influence. People and finances at my beck and call." Indicating that these things did not count. "It doesn't hold back the night, does it?"

"It's because of the suicide you feel this way. We are quite different. I feel...connected to the sun."

"And yet you impress me as solitary. Always keeping a distance, a sort of nun. Why did you leave Montreal so suddenly? And Australia?"

"There they are!" As though fleeing from contamination, Emily ran down the slope toward the ice cream cart where Adam and Tory stood hand in hand with the sun between them.

◆◆◆

"He has the young man's eyes," Tory said. "The young man from Montreal."

And Sasha, slighted, stared at Emily from Adam's huge brown and wary irises.

"She's mistaken," Emily said softly. "She has never met your father."

"He has the young man's eyes," Tory persisted.

Emily did not wish to say: It is your half-brother, Sasha, she has met.

"Dave was there when I was born," Adam said staunchly, urging a different paternity.

"Yes, he was. That's true."

"He held me when I was just a few hours old. He told me so."

"Yes."

He wanted to ask: Why isn't he with us now? It seemed to him a criminal breach, at a season of family. His Sasha-eyes pleaded mutely and he saw the nerve in her cheek begin to flutter.

"Will you run with me, Adam?" she asked.

"Who will stay with Aunt Tory?" he countered.

"We won't be long. Aunt Tory won't mind, will you, Tory?"

"Emily always runs away from me. Whenever I look at her."

"She's not running away, Aunt Tory, she's just jogging. She goes around in a circle. But I'll stay with you. Do you mind, mummy?"

"Of course not." She kissed the top of his head. "He loves you, Tory." And she was genuinely, profoundly glad to care so lavishly by proxy.

Adam, it seemed to her, was extraordinarily more than the reciprocal preoccupation of Sergei and herself; he was definitely Dave's child also, a child of earth and sea and sky, of natural immutable loves.

"See you shortly," she called, jogging south, careening into the sun which even in summer was not at all like the sun in Australia.

Australia.

When she stood on the deserted strip of beach below Dave's house and looked out across the Pacific, or when she stared west toward Bathurst and beyond, across the never-never of cracked brown earth and ghost gums, she thought: This is freedom. Now I could write to father: sprightly letters full of historical and botanical and geological fascination that he will love to read. I could write to mother and Jason and Tory (as I promised) and sound tranquil.

Perhaps, at this distance, even friendship with the stern old man would be possible. There would be no point in disturbing him with unnecessary news, with any hint of a grandchild he had no reason to expect.

Just as there had been no point in telling anyone in Montreal, before her hasty departure. She wanted no sympathy. She could certainly live without Sergei. That was all behind her now.

Nevertheless when the telephone rang, she would catch her breath. It would be Denny or Ian or Dave. Not that it mattered. She would tense herself against the spasm of want. She would agree to go to another party.

On the beach below Dave's house, on the Harbour ferry, she was self-sufficient. Warmed. Unscathed. But at night she would calculate the time difference from Montreal and lie awake thinking: If Sergei calls, I will be nonchalant. I will tell him nothing. Perhaps he would say: "I want to know about my child." Because surely he must have some inkling. Surely he must wonder. Not that she wanted him to know, ever. Sometimes the strain of not minding that he did not know would keep her awake all night.

Ridiculous, she could say as soon as dawn spilled in from the east. An emotional tic, merely. Like feeling the rocking of a boat when the voyage is over and done with.

Tory's first letter arrived late in August when Emily was four months pregnant but not, she was confident, visibly so to anyone.

Dear Emily:

There are lawns and trees but there is also chain-link and I am not allowed outside. Australia is much larger but if they put a high fence around it you would want to escape. Something there is that doesn't love a wall.

A fence is a fence is a
fence.
When I feel the screams coming
like hurricane warnings
I go swimming.

Honeysuckle is everywhere
like seaweed.
Swim to me
so that I can open my jaws
like a shark.

But I love you
and would not bite.

Please write, Emily, please write so I won't drown. I cannot tell you about the screams that come like shock-waves through the water, and the loneliness. It is a cave very deep down without light.

Emily, Emily, Emily,
How does your baby grow?
With silver bells, and cocks and shells,

And men waiting all in a row.
The young man in Montreal does not sleep well,
dreaming of you. Please write. Love, Tory.

Somewhere between the Blue Mountains and Bathurst, the little plane came down bumpily on a dust strip hummocky with spinifex. Instinctively, Emily had turned to Dave. It seemed natural. He had offered friendship and rural retreats.

"I just need a few days," she said. "I'm extremely grateful to you."

"It's not quite like a country weekend in Massachusetts or Quebec, you know. You may go off riding only on condition that one of my stockmen goes with you."

She gave a mock salute. "Yes, sir."

"I'm not kidding. The bush is littered with unfound skeletons – last year's campers as well as escaped convicts dead nearly two hundred years. Why do you want to do this?"

"I love the emptiness. It's just...I came straight from the Montreal season, and before that New York, and now even the ferries seem crowded and the harbor small as a teacup." She laughed awkwardly. "I'm not making sense. Perhaps it's delayed culture shock. I just want not to have to see anyone for a few days, not to get phone calls or mail...."

"You'd have to drive to Bathurst for mail. I'll show you how to operate the radio in case you need help. You can reach Bathurst. Or me in Sydney."

An advancing cloud of red dust turned into a jeep and Dave's chief stockman held open a door.

"So the little Yank wants to rough it?" he asked cheerily. "Welcome to the outback, love."

"Oh, look!" Emily stared at the triangular-winged butterfly quivering on the jeep's windshield. "What an incredible color!"

"Blue Wanderer," the stockman said.

Dave held out one upturned hand – a trusting child waiting for a present – and stillness settled on the three people like a spell. Never quite motionless, the brilliant turquoise wings with their velvet tracery of black trembled like a pulse of the sun. The butterfly moved, paused above one headlight, alighted for three seconds on the branch of an iron-bark. Then it was gone.

Released from a spell, Dave dropped his hand. Grinned at Emily in a lopsided sheepish way.

"One of my idiosyncrasies. When I was a kid, a Blue Wanderer landed on the palm of my hand and stayed there for about five seconds. I'm always waiting for it to happen again."

Back in Sydney there was a letter waiting from Tory. Emily could not bring herself to read it and she could not destroy it. She put it in a box and offered certain obsequies: a fragrant bunch of dried gum leaves, a green ribbon tied around the box. She bought a postcard of the harbor and scrawled across the back: *Dearest Tory: I do miss you. When I come back I will take you to some place where there are no fences. Love, Emily.*

She bought another, the bridge and the Opera House against blueness, and wrote on the back: *Dear Sergei: Having a wonderful time.* She did not mail it.

September.

Dawn.

Air full of the soft sounds of sleeping.

Emily stepped gingerly around a maze of camp cots – evidence of a weekend-long party at Dave's Sydney house – walked out into sunrise and down the wooden steps to the beach.

Shading her eyes against the sun – a great burnished ingot emerging from the ocean like salvaged treasure – she could see in the extraordinary distance the curve of earth's spine, the Pacific crawling up and down hill, clinging crab-like to the ocean floor.

I am hanging by my feet on the underside of the globe, my head dangling into the cosmos. Behind me, two million city people are dreaming or reaching for alarm clocks or making coffee. In front, there is not a soul between me and fishermen hauling nets on the shores of Chile. What time is it there?....

Still last night? They are sleeping in huts scattered like driftwood around Valparaiso.

She took off her sandals and the white sand was cool with early morning. She thought of taking off her light cotton dress, but perhaps others would come down to the beach early too. At the water's edge she walked along the foam line, breakers expending their last energy around her ankles. Every fifth or sixth breaker was especially virile and would thrash against her thighs and foam up inside her skirt. Then the undertow would go careening off towards South America so that she would have to brace her heels against it, her drenched skirt plastered to her body.

"You should come in."

She gasped. Ahead of her was an area of white blindness, a glittering pathway to the sun that burned on the water. She shaded her eyes and squinted and saw Dave, naked as Neptune, diamonds of water glinting off his brown-gold hair at head, chest, genitals and thighs. He stood smiling at her, his hands on his hips, with no trace either of embarrassment or of sexual suggestion.

"Come on in," he repeated, extending his hand.

"All right."

She tossed her sandals far up the beach and took his hand and followed him back into the waves. As the water lapped higher, her dress billowed out like heavy sails, an impediment.

"Are you sure you want to keep it on?" Dave asked.

"It is a nuisance. I'll go back and take it off."

"Just let it go. The tide will take it in."

And she let the cotton garment and her underwear relay themselves toward the line of rocks, little flagships of recklessness.

Surf was new to her. When the first big breaker came, she was hurled in unceremonious cartwheels into the shallows, strafed with shell grit, lungs full of brine. She coughed and spat, humiliated.

"Not that way." He administered a salutary backslap or two and lifted her seaweed hair from her eyes. "Are you a decent swimmer?"

"Average, I guess."

"We'll go beyond the breakers then. It's another world."

He took her hand and showed her how to ride the waves, how to glide up the glass-green cave wall to the crest, to toss oneself over it buoyantly as a cork, to coast down the far slope. Beyond the breakers, they were atoms suspended in the earth's womb-fluids, insignificant life-matter under the vast sky.

Emily trod water, enjoying, Narcissus-like, the ghostly pearled glow of her own breasts, the swell of the growing child mooning up through the green lens of ocean. Rock-a-bye baby, in the sea's heart. In all her orifices, the water was cool and astringent.

She floated on her back, thinking of the Aztecs and Akhenaton, history's sun worshippers, and wondering how Australians had managed to cling to European traditions and churches when their dreams must have been flooded with pagan urges to deify the sun.

I am hanging on to a skein of water with my back, strapped to the downside of the wheeling world, my breasts and belly gilded with light, an offering to the burning eye of the void that drops away beneath me.

"I should drag you," Dave said, surfacing fish-silkily beside her, "to my cave on the ocean floor while I have the chance."

She smiled lazily, liking his nearness, but lost in her sun trance.

"You are extraordinarily beautiful," he said. He rested his large brown hand gently on her belly. As if in benediction. "And also pregnant."

"Nearly five months. I thought no one realized yet."

"I didn't till now. Though it explains things."

"What things?"

"Your...abstraction. Your self-sufficiency. A baby and a man back there to absorb you."

"No. No man."

"Ah." His pleasure did not escape her, but he added dryly: "An immaculate conception."

"Practically. For all intents and purposes."

Without being particularly conscious of it, she put one of her hands over his, but only momentarily. Her balance in the water was threatened and she spread her arms again, lazy fins.

Since she made no resistance he moved his fingers lightly over her body, caressing softly as seawater: her breasts, her throat, her face, her breasts again, her belly, the wet tuft of hair, the soft space between her legs. She had thought she would never feel sexual desire again. She would have panicked if it were not for the narcotic of ocean and sun.

He kissed the curve of flesh that covered the child and asked: "When is it due?"

"First week in February."

"Aquarius. The water sign."

He swam in slow circles around her, surfaced just behind her head, his hands on her shoulders, his body floating up towards hers like a life raft on which she could lean. "May I make love to you?"

"Dave." She trod water, facing him. "Don't. I don't want to be disturbed. I feel complete now. The baby is all I need."

"I'll wait."

"I mean, now and always."

"You're forswearing man?"

"I think so. Not your company of course. Not your friendship. I love being with you. You don't...*crowd* me."

"Massive self-restraint on my part. I've been lost since the first day I met you at Ian's."

"I didn't know."

"I didn't want to scare you off. It's my Blue Wanderer technique. I thought if I kept perfectly still for long enough, you might settle into the palm of my hand. Like this."

She felt the smooth current of his fingers brushing her inner thighs and was suddenly buoyant, pivoting on his wrist, her crotch in the hollow of his hand. Swayed there, her eyes closed, caught in a primitive tide of desire.

She kissed him. "My body seems to have a mind of its own."

Afterwards she lay on her back and he pulled her shorewards, his body curving below hers like a safety net.

"My sea mammal," he teased. "My beautiful whale. I consider myself to have contributed something of prenatal significance. I claim half the pregnancy."

"Dave," she warned, reaching below her, caressing his body

to soften the words. "Don't expect anything."

"That's all right. I was married once, a good way back. It took me a long time too."

"It's not a matter of getting over someone. It's a matter of escaping unscathed and wanting to stay that way."

"I'll let you. But this is Sydney and I'm offering you respectability plus private freedom."

"I'm indifferent to respectability."

"Just the same, I'm staking a birthright claim."

"How can it matter to you? Someone else's child?"

"I'm very persistent when I know what I want. You'll see."

About them the line of breakers heaved and frothed.

"Ride them in!" he called. "Like this."

And they flew like porpoises in to the sand.

By December the green-ribboned box was filled with Tory's unopened letters. Because it was Christmas, because Sydney was fragrant with frangipani and the slick of suntan oil and beer and watermelon, because it was a time of sun-courage and good will and impending birth, Emily opened the letter that came in mid-December.

She skimmed it, her eyes darting to the poetry.

> *I saw three ships sail away from me*
> *On Christmas Day, on Christmas Day.*
> *The young man, the baby, and Emily*
> *On Christmas Day in the morning.*
>
> *Jason will take me there for Christmas Dinner and father will try so hard to be kind he will lose his temper.*

She did not want to read any more, she folded the letter quickly and put it in the box. There was always such terrible penance to pay for happiness.

"What is it?" Dave asked, finding her staring out the window at the ocean. He kissed the nape of her neck, linking his arms around her large belly.

"My family." She showed him the letter.

And heard the little catches of breath as he read it.

"When you said her letters were frightening.... We could fly over and spend Christmas with them."

"No! That's the last thing I want. I haven't been home for Christmas since I left Ashville for New York. I couldn't bear it. I don't know how Jason does."

"Have you told them about me?"

"No. I don't intend to. Well, I'll probably tell Jason eventually. And mother, I suppose."

When it's all over, she did not add.

"Emily." His eyes reproached her.

"At least I write to them now. I'm far enough away that I can do that."

"How will you explain the baby?"

"I won't."

"But Tory already knows."

"No," Emily said. "Sometimes she's right by accident. She's been like this almost as far back as I can remember. It's probably inherited. One of mother's uncles killed himself when he was thirty. He was said to be schizophrenic."

"Couldn't we make her happier? If she lived with family?"

"No. Yes. One day, I always promise myself. Oh her life is awful, but you don't know.... We tried for years. She lived at home but once she feels all right she won't take the medication and the paranoia starts and the accusations and the fears...you don't know...all my adolescence I was hostage to her. The trouble is it's not possible to love her *enough*, nothing makes her feel safe. I had to get away to survive. How do I know it won't surface in *me*? If I stay around father and Tory, I feel I'm doing nothing but incubating madness."

Dave held her and stroked her hair. "Poor Emily. Poor Tory."

His eyes, as he looked into hers, were somber. She was to see the same look six weeks later when, unable to speak, he held newborn Adam in his large hands, and she forbade him to phone her parents.

"It's not their affair," she said. "It has nothing to do with them." His eyes clouded with the same stunned distress.

When he could trust himself to talk, he murmured: "Their

first grandchild. They have a right. You can't extinguish people like that."

"I can when I have to."

◆◆◆

"It's not that I want to exclude you," Jason told Ruth.

They leaned against an oak, their eyes on treetops and the Fifth Avenue skyline, their bodies splayed on the grass like two hands of a clock. "It's just that our family dynamics are sufficiently complicated as is. Father would consider you fair game, which would make me brutal with him and there'd be mayhem all round."

"It's perfectly all right. I'm glad to have met Emily and Tory though. After all these years. I partly envy all of you for that bonding, but I can feel the suck of it like a maelstrom. I'd be afraid of being smashed."

"Much the way we feel. Ruth...?" He took her hand. "I watched you with Tory Thursday evening when you brought her back from your downtown spree. For a moment I saw her as I like to remember her – young and glowing. I wanted to say thank you."

"It was lunch in the restaurant that seemed to do it. First I planned to take her to the Met but she panicked and wouldn't go in...."

"We were lost there once as children. Mother forgot about us and went off to the Cloisters. Tory was terrified."

"She calmed down when we left. And then in the restaurant...it was quite moving...she became very dignified, almost regal...as though she'd just rediscovered herself in a role that she once knew well. I felt glad that even moments of healing are possible. And I thought of you with your patients and felt so...*grateful* that you do what you do."

He reached out and touched her cheek with his fingers.

"You are...quite..." – he could not seem to find a word – "exceptional, Ruth."

She leaned toward him and put her head on his shoulder so that he would not see her cry.

This is sufficient, she thought. Just this.

As he stroked her hair he saw Stephen's face, and Jessica's. It is not impossible, he decided, for seriously flawed people to do good. But praise made him uneasy.

"I'm such a bastard, Ruth. You deserve better." Then, kissing her lightly on the forehead: "Well, have to get in shape for the upcoming bout with father. Better run another circuit or two."

◆◆◆

"The sun is different there, Aunt Tory. When I grow up I'm going to go back and I'll take you with me if you like. You could live at Kurrajong. That's Dave's sheep station."

"You want to go away already. Everyone goes away."

"But if I did, I'd come back. If you let people go, they'll come back eventually, that's what Dave says. You could trap them and keep them, but if you keep a butterfly in a glass case, it's no good to you. You don't see the light on its wings."

"They keep me in a glass case."

"When I grow up I'll take you to Kurrajong and you'll be free."

"You're going away."

"I would always come back because you're my aunt and I love you."

◆◆◆

Under crab apple boughs Jason overtook Emily. Companionably they slowed to a walk.

"How does this feel," he asked, "after ten years out of the country?"

"Three years. You're forgetting my New York concert."

"Willful thinking. Father's heart attack! What a chaotic night!"

"Doesn't augur well for family reunions. I keep saying to myself: I must have been mad to come for this."

"He's had time to adjust by now. You *were* rather tactless.... I mean, five years old! You could have given him years to become accustomed at a distance. To tell you the truth" – he turned and put his hands on her shoulders – "I was incredibly hurt myself that you'd never told me. As a matter of fact, in London last year I paced my hotel room for a day before I called you. Partly because I was still so wounded. And partly because I was afraid you'd shatter my necessary image of you. I'd rather not have seen you and preserved it whole. I steer by perfect moments: I remember Tory when she was sixteen. I remember you at a Juilliard recital when you were twenty, a pre-Raphaelite virgin with a violin."

"Oh Jason, you construct your own myths."

"I do," he conceded, releasing her shoulders and walking on. "But they're rooted in reality. As it happened, I needn't have worried. You're as virginal as ever. And Adam... Adam is like the world's beginning."

"Virginal! Honestly, Jason."

"But I still don't understand. I'm still hurt that you never told me. Why didn't you?"

"I don't know. I always meant to, sometime. Too much to explain that I couldn't bear to talk about, I suppose."

"But I wouldn't have demanded explanations. Surely you knew that?"

"Anyway, what have you ever told me about what went wrong with Nina? I saw the statue last night, it was the first thing I noticed...."

"It's another of my compass points. I remember Nina giving me the carving."

"And what have you ever told me about Ruth? She may be right. We're just random atoms bouncing against each other. We orbit around the family nucleus because there's no choice."

"That's rubbish. I feel – I have always felt – literally *attached* to you and Tory."

"Exactly. There's no escape. But otherwise...?"

"I meant, when you bleed, I bleed. It's not a question of lack of choice, it's a matter of...." But he did not want to say the word *love*. Instead he asked: "Remember how we did everything together when I came back from school?"

"I remember your outrageous dares. Climb on to the gazebo roof! Jump! Crawl in the broom closet with the spiders! You always liked to control. Though you also protected me at school. I admit I did adore you for fighting Ernie Cromwell."

"Who?"

"Surely you remember Ernie? He dragged off my shoes and stuffed them with snow. You fought him and got awfully battered."

"If I fought someone on your behalf, I would undoubtedly have beaten him."

"Don't you remember it?"

"No. But I do remember you jumped off the gazebo because I said to, and sprained your ankle. I rushed in to tell father it was all my fault. I couldn't wait to be whipped because I couldn't stand not to be hurting more than you were. Father obliged, of course."

"We're very big on atonement, aren't we?"

"Do you remember I showed you the red whipping marks? My proof of concern."

"Vaguely. I certainly remember spraining my ankle. I'll take your word that you atoned."

"Are you atoning for something now?"

"What's that supposed to mean?"

"Why did you leave Australia so suddenly? And so obviously to Adam's distress?"

"Any move is upsetting to children. I was offered London and Europe and I would have been crazy to turn it down. Every Australian musician and artist would say the same thing."

"And Dave wouldn't go with you?"

"I didn't ask him."

"Why not?"

"I'm not on your couch, Jason."

"Adam talks about him constantly. He was obviously important. To you too?"

"Yes."

"Do you miss him?"

"Why don't you sleep with Ruth?"

"I do. We just can't spend the whole night in the same bed. Restless sleepers. My nightmares frighten her and her fears trigger my nightmares. It's a domino virus, neurotic panics zipping back and forth like ping-pong balls. You're avoiding my question."

"You don't seem very good for each other. Do you still have other women?"

"From time to time."

"It doesn't make much sense. Why do you stay together?"

"Look, let's not pretend that any one in our family is normal – though that's a most imprecise word, professionally speaking, there being as many norms as there are contexts. I'm absolutely rotten for Ruth, or for anyone, but she stays by choice. Our relationship is adequately functional. She is gentler and more patient with Tory than either of us."

"It wasn't Ruth I was criticizing."

Jason reached out and broke off a sprig of mock orange blossoms, creamy and heavily fragrant. He handed it to her.

"I've come to believe in the supreme importance of redemptive actions. Ruth makes them often. Believe it or not, I am occasionally capable of them toward her. And I also believe in redemptive people. This isn't without scholarly and philosophical support, and it's certainly based on years of clinical observation. Adam, for instance; you just have to watch him with Tory. He's what I would call a redemptive person. As you are for me. I'm not one – though I'm capable of the occasional halting redemptive act. And I thought that perhaps, from the way Adam dreams aloud, Dave might be one for you."

"Jason, don't.... I can't...."

"He still matters."

"Yes."

"I knew it. So it's some form of self-punishment."

"No. Far cruder and more selfish. Ever since I finally got away from home, I've put survival first. And I felt as though Dave was busy reshackling me to the family. It had to do with Tory's letters. They came once, sometimes twice a week, for five years."

"I know." He sighed wearily. "That started when I was in boarding school."

"I couldn't read them, I couldn't destroy them. I kept them

in boxes. After a while I couldn't stand to see the mail at all so Dave always handled it. He read them actually. He would've written to her if I'd let him. He kept suggesting we bring her out to Australia and I began to fear I'd come home one day and find her in the living room."

She hunched her shoulders and spread her hands in a gesture of despair.

"I did write to her, Jason, a postcard or a note every month, but she never acknowledged it."

"I know. She still doesn't believe I wrote from school."

"Anyway, the sense of claustrophobia got worse. And then a visiting conductor wrote back and invited me to London and it seemed an irresistible escape. Not to mention the career advantages. Dave suggested half-year rotation, which I could probably have worked out."

"But here comes the twist," Jason interjected sardonically. "You had to punish yourself for fleeing from Tory's letters."

"You're dead wrong. The trouble is, Dave was part of the claustrophobia. And then something happened, a silly thing in a way, but spooky. There was a party at Kurrajong (that's Dave's sheep station) and I was standing looking out the window across the veranda into the desert. Someone had a Polaroid and took a picture and gave it to me."

She shivered.

"The most disturbing sense of *déjà vu*. I thought it was mother. I looked exactly like mother as I remember her one night staring out of the French windows at the gazebo. She'd been playing Beethoven and stopped suddenly in the middle of it. I must have been sixteen or seventeen and I remember watching her from the garden and promising myself: I will never be caged like that."

"You're so wrong about mother..."

"I stared at that photograph and felt swamped with panic. I cabled London the next day and said I was coming permanently."

"And Dave made no attempt to follow?"

"I was afraid he would and I'd never forgive myself. To give up his life when I knew I could never be reliable.... I left earlier than planned, without warning, and then wrote and told him I was having an affair with the conductor."

"Don't tell me this. I shoulder the brutality for all of us. You mustn't do it. I can't tolerate it."

She shredded the mock orange blossoms with her fingers. "There's nothing redemptive about me, Jason. But" – on a note of harsh irony – "I've stayed free and sane and I make beautiful music. I punish myself by staying absolutely celibate and by a grueling practice and performance schedule. A savage beast in sheep's clothing."

"*I am myself indifferent honest*," Jason said sadly, "*but yet I could accuse me of such things....*" He grimaced. "Always hated father's pompous way of dragging Shakespeare into everything. The point is, Emily, considering our family... you do give the world exquisite music, you've given us Adam, you've done all the atoning required of you. You mustn't punish Adam and Dave."

"I can't help it, Jason. The sense of being closed in becomes physical, it affects my breathing. It's happening to me now, the closer I get to father. I must have been crazy to agree to this."

"I was determined you'd come. Mother and I planned to give you no time to back out."

"Thanks."

"It was after I met Adam in London. And mother felt the same when she went, that we had to bring Adam and father together. Maybe it's just intense wishing, but I have the most extraordinary sense that something remarkable will happen."

Emily stared at him. His eyes had the hungry fervor of a pilgrim's.

"Before father dies," he said, "I would like to be able to love him."

The constriction in Emily's chest felt much worse.

XIX Adam

We've been driving north on Route 7 all the way from New York and now we're in the mountains. The Berkshires, Uncle Jason says, and almost at grandpa's and grandma's. It's quite different from home but very beautiful. It really is. You would think so too, Dave, except you'd be watching mummy all the time. She looks the way she does when she's playing in a concert or when she's riding with us at Kurrajong. You used to say: "She's got bushfires in her eyes."

I wish I was riding with you now. Sometimes at night I pretend I'm up on Clancy's back and I can feel the saddle between my legs and your arms around me and Clancy's mane blowing in my face.

Mummy keeps saying: "Oh Jason, I'd forgotten how lovely...."

It is lovely. It smells different from the bush at home but it is a good smell. Most of the trees I know from England: oaks and chestnuts; the elms are lacy like gum trees but they have a disease and there are hardly any left. There are other parts which are just pine forest and that is nicest. I would love to walk there because it makes me think of rain forest in the Blue Mountains. I don't really know why – it's quite different – but it has a magic smell like that and the same green shadowy look like a cave.

I'm going to have to keep talking to you, Dave, because I'm scared. Remember when you took me camping back at Kurrajong on my fifth birthday? We were lying in our sleeping bags and the sun was coming up between two ghost gums and a snake came slithering between us, a deadly one. You whispered: "Don't move, mate!" and we didn't breathe for the longest time. Over and over in my mind I practised the snake bite things you taught me: the tourniquet, the two cuts with the razorblade, the sucking and spitting. It seemed like hours and hours before the snake disappeared. That was the most frightened I've ever been, and the second-most was when we got on the plane to go to England and you weren't there, and this is the third-most.

Aunt Tory is in the back seat with me and she is holding my hand. You would think she was watching a snake licking its tongue in and out. Mummy and Uncle Jason are sitting in front and sometimes they talk very fast and remember stuff and giggle a lot the way Snelby and I do at school. Other times you can tell they are waiting for a snake to slither away.

I know this can't be because of grandma. I told you she came to London for my birthday and she smells of English lavender and other soft things and when she plays the piano I want to cry because I remember mummy playing her violin and you and me sitting on the veranda and listening and watching the bush or the ocean. Grandma is also a Blue Wanderer. She is very beautiful and she flies away from behind her eyes like mummy does.

So it's grandpa everyone is afraid of, and so am I.

I have got a room that was mummy's when she was little. It has pine floors and a bed with posts and casement windows. You would love this house, Dave, you really would. It has a circular driveway and verandas and French windows just like our house at Kurrajong and there's a little building like a birdcage in the garden and I can see the moon on it now. It is covered in honeysuckle which I have never seen before, but which smells nearly as good as frangipani.

When we arrived grandma came out to the car and hugged us all, me first, and I could smell the lavender and also her snake-fear. They didn't exactly push me but they sort of made me go in first, like Snelby and Dickinson did one time outside the headmaster's office. I didn't want to let go of Aunt Tory's hand but she was shaking so much that it made me feel worse. I knew I was going to get caned.

That time at school I just said your name to myself and I thought: Well, it will be *interesting* to be caned. All the most interesting boys in storybooks get caned. Snelby's father got caned lots, and he's in Parliament now. It will only hurt for a few minutes and afterwards Snelby and Dickinson will like me better and maybe they won't tease me about my accent. And I held my head high and walked in. It hurt much worse than I thought and for longer, but they did stop teasing me afterwards.

And that's what I did this time. I whispered to myself: Dave, stay with me; and I pulled back my shoulders the way headmasters like and I walked through the door.

But he wasn't like a headmaster at all. He was just a little old man in an armchair and not the least bit frightening. So I went up to him and put my arms around his neck and kissed him and said: "Hello grandpa, I'm Adam."

I don't know why I felt like crying but I did, and so did he. I sat on his knee and hugged him and we both cried. He kept saying my name softly as though it was one he'd never heard before.

And then he said: "So you've come home to America."

And I told him that I was a citizen of the world really, that America wasn't exactly home because I was conceived in Montreal and born in Australia and was being educated in England.

I said: "I do love the Berkshires though, and I love your house, especially that birdcage thing in the garden."

Then his laughing and crying got all mixed up and so did mine.

XX Prelude

When the old man woke on Sunday morning, he felt first that there had been some fundamental change in the quality of the air. He was alone in the bed, something he usually enjoyed, but it was not that. And not the sun or the trees at the window, though these seemed to him strangely beautiful. He felt pervaded, that was it, by well-being. As though he had ingested a massive dose of beatitude.

The memory of Adam came to him as bits of dream come back after waking – first, only the most fleeting fragments, easily lost again; elusive hints, a tantalizing glimpse of the whole; and gradually a coalescence of recalled parts.

Then, in a slow dawning of wonder, his mind turned over the knowledge that the child was still in the house. He sat up in bed and reached for his canes. Small marathon: lurching to his chair (damned legs!). And en route fresh astonishments assailed him: last night he had laughed with the boy. *Laughed*! He looked at the image of himself laughing as at an artefact of the Bronze Age. That such a possibility should have existed. That the vocal cords and facial muscles had remembered how to perform. How long, he wondered, since he had laughed? He did not think he had laughed in the lifetime of his daughter Emily. Perhaps briefly, at her birth, in a fond moment of hope.

He sank into his armchair, and breathed deeply, grumpus-like, waiting for his muscles to have the decency to stop twitching like a beached flounder.

Last night. A dangling in the void, that was how it had been. He would add it to his scrapbook of pivotal moments: Marta's arms extended in the gazebo; Emily's raised wine glass in New York; the slamming of car doors in his driveway last night.

"Here they are," Bessie had said, and the pacemaker itself seemed to stop; everything, blood and breathing, pausing, waiting to see if it was worth continuing. He had been aware of a shadow, he knew someone was approaching him, he had been afraid to look up. And then the child was in his arms.

The smell, the touch of a grandchild, was like an armful of hyacinths.

He leaned forward, his forehead against the screen, and saw Bessie and Adam, hand in hand, by the gazebo. The *nunc dimittis* came to him: *Now lettest thou thy servant depart in peace*. Some shuddering of emotions long dormant began to buffet his body. He folded his arms on the windowsill and rested his head on them and began to weep. Not in decorous quietness, but with a guttural animal sound like demons escaping. Helpless, he grasped a cushion from the chair and held it over his mouth and sobbed into it. He could not stop. It had nothing to do with sorrow, it was quite beyond his control. He began to fear that he would use up more strength than he had, that the pacemaker would not support him. But there was nothing he could do.

Eventually – he had no idea how long it took – the hurricane passed. He felt ravaged and empty. He felt as people do who return to homes flattened by flood, fire, storm: one would simply begin again.

Pieces of memory came drifting by like confetti fluttering from an old wedding album: the bleating blue vein in Bessie's neck; Tory on the stairs in her nightgown; Tory clinging to him on the Ferris wheel; Jason waving from a dormitory window at school; Emily in a white dress for her first public performance.

But something brackish, like a soiled rain perhaps, began to percolate through this drift of blessings; something dark; a cloud no bigger than a man's hand.

Oh god, he moaned, remembering.

A telegram had been sent. It could not be unsent.

Suppose, though, that nothing came of it? It was entirely possible that nothing would come of it. In fact, to look squarely at the matter of probability, it was completely implausible that Marta would step out from the potent aureole of myth and incarnate herself on his front lawn.

He had thought the same, he realized now, about Adam.

There was this about fantasies: they did not always stay tidily inside their proper fences. They roamed like gorgons.

What had he done, what had he risked? Even if Marta did not come, even if she only sent a telegram, Bessie would surely realize. Perhaps she would not forgive. Perhaps they would deprive him of the child. Could he not, after all this time, have sustained the illusion for his wife a little longer? Bessie was so fragile, she had so few resources. He would have spared her this, if they had only told him Adam was coming. It was because he had not known, because he had been so afraid, that he had had to take protective action.

But of course Marta would very likely ignore the telegram entirely.

This was surely what he hoped?

He thought of her, the sheer impossibility of her, standing before him, flesh and blood. The world well lost. He thought of old Mrs. Weston, immortal monster with her icebox of infant limbs. He thought of indelibility. He thought of Faust. It seemed to him that in the last twelve hours his heart had grown larger, hungrier.

He knew that he would not altogether object to a final act that was violent and bloody, his nerve ends crackling in a last orgasm of life, himself center stage.

◆◆◆

Jason sat on the front porch drinking coffee. He breathed deeply, consciously taking into his lungs great reserves of country-morning air. As though it could be stored, could leak forward into time, purifying and protecting him. He tried to remember other occasions when he had felt: I am content. He was not sure there had been any.

Certainly he savored memories of certain moments with Nina, especially in the beginning. And with Natalie, Jessica, Ruth. But it was in retrospect that these events had become tinged with a haunting quality. He did not think that at the time he had ever said to himself: Now I am happy.

Had he thought it as he walked beside the Thames with Emily? Almost. He remembered thinking: It's good to be with her again. A great rush of gratitude that there was someone who didn't require explanations for idiosyncratic behavior, someone who took *all that* (father, Tory) as a given.

But he could not go so far as to say he had been happy then, not with that sense of his own and Emily's emptiness. (What are we to *do* with life?) He would have liked to say, as they sat looking at Westminster Bridge and seeing instead the impossible tangle of family: Look, let me sponge up your share – the *angst*, the futility, all painful adjustments past and future. It will hardly make any difference to me. Enter into a contract of sane familial commonweal with this man in Australia, the one Adam's gilding with myth, the one you will scarcely speak about because he seems to mean so much. Be happy!

That, he realized, was what it took to redeem himself in his own eyes. One act of unambiguous benediction to set in the balance against the frightful weight of his destructiveness. That was why, this morning, he could think: I feel contented – for his connivance, for his part in ensuring that Emily and Adam came to the reunion.

To have seen the old man laugh and cry!

Somehow, out of all their flawed histories, had come Adam.

He watched his mother and the boy wandering around the garden together. "This is a dogwood," he heard her say; "you don't have those in England." Jason knew this could not last. He knew the most one was given in life were brief reprieves, intimations of paradise lost or only dreamed of. The art of happiness, perhaps, was simply to be conscious of such moments while they were happening.

He foresaw dangerous pressures on Adam – against losing that choirboy quality of translucence, that trusting innocence; so many people demanding of him the quintessence of purity, not wanting him embroiled in girls, cars, dubious opinions, possibly faulty career decisions, all the imperfections and wrong turnings of growing up.

He hoped they, collectively, would not stifle the boy. He hoped Adam would not come to resent them. But perhaps this was unavoidable between one generation and the next, perhaps even a biological necessity, as unremarkable as dead leaves in the fall and new buds in spring. Perhaps the point where you could forgive your father was only reached when you suddenly saw him frail and broken, his perverse pride in tatters: a lonely old man who could laugh and cry like a child, shamelessly, in public.

Was it simply this: the banal, almost ugly, realization of powers reversed?

Jason sighed. No motives were pure, he consoled himself. Ever.

He thought that he would like to have his father sitting with him on the porch. They could smoke their pipes together. He could tell his father about the current exhibition at the Whitney Museum. No. Wrong topic. That would reek of cultural smugness. He cast about: the Royal Shakespeare Company on tour; he and Ruth had seen *Twelfth Night*. His father would reminisce about high school productions. This was the sort of thing fathers and sons were supposed to do. *Normal*. An intoxicating word.

But there was a dilemma. How should his father be brought downstairs? Last night it had not been an issue, the whole thing prearranged, a neighbor's son arriving promptly at ten to carry the old man up to bed. Significance noted.

He felt now a physical craving, akin to lust, to cradle that gaunt figure in his arms. To say with his body: I am sorry for all the unanswered postcards, but who can fathom the animosities of childhood?

Yet was it improper, this desire? A crass flexing of Oedipal muscles? Did it matter? Should he – knowingly a compound of imperfections (the gloating son, ascendant), yet truly desiring communion and his father's blessing – simply appear at the old man's door? Father, bless me for I have sinned. I am Jason, your devious second-born. Or perhaps he could radiate a heartiness that would obliterate innuendo. Should he hoist his father over his shoulder with rough affection, like a knapsack, chattering busily to spare both of them embarrassment? *Remember when you took me hiking in the Berkshires?*

No.

An unethical victory.

Lack of choice would push his father past endurance.

He went inside to look for Emily and found her in the kitchen.

"Just taking a breakfast tray up to father," she said.

"Do something for me. Tell him I said I'd be very happy... I'd like him to have breakfast on the front porch. With me. Ask him... if he'd like us to send for the boy next door."

Emily raised an eyebrow. She knew perfectly well what he wanted. "He won't change miraculously. You always want fairy-tale endings."

Jason shrugged. "I'll sit with him either way."

When she came back downstairs she stood with her hands behind her back. A childhood game: which fist is it in?

"Guess what he said."

Jason waited.

"He said, and I quote: 'What's the matter with Jason? Doesn't his woman feed him properly?'"

Jason grinned.

Ascending the stairs, he thought: Now I am happy.

He was in the room with his father. No acknowledgment, the face still pressed to the screen. Jason coughed. Edward did not move. Goddamn him, Jason thought, he's still at it. The school principal, the boy on the mat.

Then he remembered the deafness.

He crossed the room, touched the old man on the shoulder. "Dad?"

"Took a hell of a long time," his father said gruffly.

My whole life, Jason thought.

Though his father was light as a child, Jason's arms trembled. He might have been the curator of an art museum, the bearer of priceless treasures – porcelain perhaps, irreplaceable, uninsurable, impossibly frangible.

For the first time in his life, Jason craved for descendants of his own.

"Stop sniveling," his father said testily. "Never could stand a boy who snivels."

"Dad," Jason said, a seismic tongue of laughter beginning to lick through his body like subversion, "I have to say that you are the most cantankerous, narrow-minded, rude, bullying, and pig-headed old man I have ever known."

◆◆◆

Tory did not want to go out in the garden. Yes, she would like to walk with Emily to the Davison's farm where you could still buy fresh-churned butter and new-laid eggs, but she did not want to cross the front porch where Jason and her father sat talking.

"Come on, then, the back door," Emily said.

"But he'll see us when we cross the driveway."

No point, Emily knew, in telling Tory that this didn't matter. She switched tactics, dropped her voice to a conspiratorial whisper: "We'll climb the side fence. We'll creep along behind the bushes and no one will see us."

Tory's face became animated with nervous complicity. Lumbering over the fence, shambling along on hands and knees in the grass, she chuckled and babbled to herself: "He'll never find out. We don't have to tell him everything. Emily won't tell, she promised."

It occurred to Emily, crawling behind the great bulk of her sister, that if she were seen from the neighbor's windows she would not care. The realization came with the force of absolution. Growing older, the mere fact of it, did carry at least a faint promise of wisdom gained. One wasn't condemned to repeat every single mistake *ad infinitum.* For instance: she remembered doing this at the age of ten, when Tory was twenty-two. Enter mortification, of an absolute variety. The laughter of boys from her class at school, the mimicking, the long crocodile of bodies all crawling through the grass. *We're off to see the principal,* they chanted. *Follow the elephant, follow the elephant, follow the elephant's ass.* Tory thinking it was a nice game, laughing along with them shaking her fleshy behind. And Emily, wretched coward, joining in the song (her lungs bursting, her eyes stinging) until the moment when no one was looking. Then she stood up and fled, abandoning Tory to the pack. At home she had crept under the bushes that throttled the gazebo and sobbed and twisted the flesh of her arms into savage peaks. Penance.

That was when she had made up her mind to leave home and never come back. Just as soon as she was old enough.

Yet here she was.

In the Davisons' cow pasture she lay in the long grass while Tory collected dandelions, slit their stems with her thumbnail, and made a chain. Singing to herself. *How should I my true love know...?* Twisting the garland around her head, preening for the cows, an aging slightly grotesque Queen of the May.

If a circle of townspeople were to rise out of the soil, Emily thought, all much too polite to chant cruelties, but nevertheless whispering to one another, she would take her sister by the hand and walk past them with head held high. Or perhaps she would start for home on her hands and knees, calling Tory to follow.

Was self-congratulation in order?

This came to her: her largesse was a product of distance. Of indifference, cultivated like a rare hot-house bloom for so many years. Sham courage. If she had defied those tormentors when she was ten, that would have meant something. Now it was too easy to count, there was no cost, no one mattered, she did not care what anyone thought. Distance. It was what she loved about audiences – that space between the stage and the hall. If suddenly one day there should rain on her catcalls instead of applause, she would think merely: I've known all this before. It makes no difference. It doesn't affect me.

No connections.

Except for Adam.

About Adam there was nothing she could do, she was connected by every nerve end. No choice there. Whatever grief or joy should come from that...well, that was her fate, she was committed to it. But beyond Adam was a moat. Perhaps she could afford to let down a drawbridge to the family once in a while – at Thanksgiving and Christmas, say. She thought that would be possible. Though this reunion, the very warmth of it, had the smell of risk to her.

No medals for courage then, or compassion. Her epitaph

could read: She kept her distance. So be it. She was a survivor. Closing her eyes, she pictured herself on a crenellated turret overlooking a moat. Beyond the water a small army worked at her command, raising a system of earthworks and a great wall, stone by stone.

◆◆◆

Lunch in the kitchen, which was large and sunny and smelled of cinnamon sticks and scrubbed pine floor. The six of them around an oak table older than Victoria, Edward wadded with cushions into his chair at the head of the table. Adam on his right, Jason on his left. At the foot of the table, Elizabeth ladled out a cold summer soup that gave off a soft fug of cucumbers and cumin. Every few seconds, though so calmly as to be unobtrusive, she paused, rested the ladle in the tureen, and stroked Tory's arm – as though she were gentling the sweating flanks of a spooked colt. Twice Tory had risen and made to leave the table; Elizabeth had murmured to her, gentled her. Jason, sitting next to Tory, nodded imperceptibly to his mother, and held his sister's hand.

Emily, sitting opposite, found it almost unbearable. It was like being trapped in a steam bath: a convectional current of love, anguish, anger sucking around her. (How can he ever be forgiven this? And yet how could one hold to account an old man frailer than paper? How could one not?) She felt faint from the miasma of feeling, as though the room had no air. Tory's unease weakened her like an infection. It was one thing to defy hypothetical tormentors. Another thing entirely to enter Tory's pain. (What would she do, if the shell cracked, if the fortifications crumbled, with all the anger and all the love?) She was desperate for coolness and distance.

"Mummy," Adam whispered. "What's the matter?"

"Nothing, darling."

She focused on nowhere, played an entire Vivaldi movement in her head, gripped the table, felt its old scars and hollows. Was startled by a memory.

"Jason! Here's the gouge you made with the knife." She traced the jagged indentation with her index finger.

Jason laughed. "Poor Beethoven."

"Beethoven?" Everything excited Adam, the whole rich panoply of family and history. "Tell me, tell me."

"Uncle Jason was carving Beethoven out of a cake of soap," Emily said.

"Can you sculpt, Uncle Jason? Did you know that the world's oldest sculptures are made of bone? From the Old Stone Age. I learned that in school, I've seen them in the British Museum. Why were you making Beethoven?"

"I was making him for your mother's birthday. Let's see. Her tenth?"

"My eleventh."

"Right, her eleventh. Soap is about the only thing I can carve. I was taking a filler course in art in high school. Anyway, I was having terrible trouble with the curly hair when the knife slipped."

"Where is he, mummy? Did you keep him? You didn't use Beethoven in the bath, did you?"

"No," Emily said. "Poor Beethoven, he got..."

She stopped suddenly and caught Jason's eye across the table. Everywhere, impasses. To converse in this house, they acknowledged, is to cross a mine field.

Perhaps genuinely dangerous.

Emily thought of New York again.

Nothing, none of the debris of old battles, was safely defused. Anything could sputter into violence again.

Adam's curiosity was piqued. "What happened to him? What happened to Beethoven?"

"Adam, darling," Elizabeth said. "Would you like some ham and salad?"

"Yes, thank you, grandma. Mummy, what happened to Beethoven?"

"He just got... Uncle Jason never finished him, that's all."

But the scent of family mystery was in the air. It was as familiar to Adam as the cabalistic secrets of schoolboys in England. He knew the smell.

Carefully polite, he asked: "Why didn't you, Uncle Jason?"

Emily and Jason looked at their father. Did these memories shame him? Or would he still justify himself? Would he rage again for the desecration of the table, the scar on its antique surface? Would he grab the nearest equivalent of the waxy Beethoven and hurl it through the window, a shower of glass on the kitchen floor again?

No sign. No indication that Edward was disturbed by anything beyond a recalcitrant slice of ham which was not submitting docilely to the knife in his arthritic hand. He glowered at it, muttered under his breath.

"Grandpa," Adam asked sweetly. "Do you know what happened to Beethoven?"

"Hmm?" Edward was vaguely startled. Harumphed. Patted Adam on the hand. "What was that? Beethoven? Died in the early 1800s, I think."

"No, no, grandpa. Uncle Jason's Beethoven. The one he was making out of soap."

A knitting of the old man's brows. A sense of reaching for something. Of concentration, of confusion. Then nothing. A trail followed to somewhere else, a different memory. Adam was about to persist, but Emily signaled a warning, mouthed silently: I'll tell you about it later.

She saw a muscle tighten in Jason's cheek (How dare the old tyrant forget!) and then relax. Jason looked at her and shrugged. Conveying: the past is not absolute after all.

Edward followed his own memory to a bench in the gazebo, waiting for the moment when incandescence would implode. When he and she would stand there together and he would say her name. Nothing could stop it now, he could feel the momentum, the whole Faustian tragedy bearing down on its final act.

Adam knew his grandfather was waiting for something to happen. Tory knew it too, the air tight as a drumskin around her, sharp with splinters. She would have to retreat under water, she began to whimper, to pucker her mouth into gills, to paddle the air lightly with her hands.

"Look, Tory." Elizabeth's voice was soft. Not furtive, not a whisper, more the sound of lullaby. There was a bowl of fresh fruit in front of her. Apples, peaches, small melons. She lifted Tory's hand toward them, guided her fingers over pieces of fruit like a teacher with a blind child. Soothing. Sensuous.

She lifted a peach to Tory's cheek and rubbed its soft pelt against her daughter's skin. They both seemed oblivious to the room. It was as though the two of them had stepped through an invisible door. To Narnia, perhaps, or some other magical world that existed between one molecule of air and the next.

The victims, Emily thought bitterly, her throat constricted. You see, her eyes said fiercely to Jason. You see what I mean about mother.

He shook his head slightly: You are misinterpreting.

Edward's voice startled them, a peremptory fractious tone. "What are you doing, Bessie?"

A vibration began in Tory's fingers and spread through her body so that her chair rattled on the floorboards. Elizabeth paid no apparent attention but went on talking quietly, offering pieces of fruit one by one.

"Tory," her father spluttered, exasperated, "Tor – " He cut himself off, agitated, the habits of a lifetime dying hard. He reached for a slice of bread and tore it into little pieces which he scattered over his ham as though forgetting that the soup course was finished.

Adam, smiling at him, asked: "Grandpa, what are you doing?"

"Eh?" When the old man looked at Adam, he would seem to remember something. He would abandon the febrile and cantankerous trails in his mind. His facial muscles would pause shyly, as it were, like a bashful teenage suitor in a lover's presence.

Elizabeth said soothingly: "Edward, darling, perhaps you two would like to sit out in the garden? Adam, would you fetch grandpa's canes from the hallway?"

Jason thought of courtiers waiting uneasily for the exit of George III, mad monarch, from the stateroom, as old man and child made their slow way to the door. A suspension. When the voices – bass and soft treble – floated in from the lawn, the figures at the table relaxed.

"*Plus ça change.*" Jason, his peace made, seemed imperturbable; his smile affectionate and rueful.

Emily blurted out: "I don't know how you've stood it, or

why you've stood it, mother. Or why I've come back."

Elizabeth, still stroking Tory's hands, seemed to return from somewhere else. Her eyes, cloudy, withdrew their gaze from Narnia, or wherever, and focused clearly on Emily. "People do terrible things just by lifting a finger," she said. "We all do it, everyone of us. If we didn't understand that, and didn't forgive it, we'd be savages."

Think distance, Emily warned herself. Think infinite space. What was the point of getting impatient with her mother or angry with her father? Nevertheless she found she had to say: "Some things shouldn't be forgiven."

"Even though Dave was badly hurt, he writes me such warm letters." It came out calmly, idly, as though a comment were being made on the weather. For a stunned moment, the implications being so preposterous, Emily had a sense of time and space dislocation. Which country was she in, which year of her life? Vertigo. A reeling about among the discrete compartments of her history. When it caught up with her – the shock, the sense of violation, of betrayal – she gasped.

In Jason's eyes, first startled then amused, she read: You see. I told you so. You've always been wrong about mother.

Emily stared at Elizabeth. She could not have been more surprised if somebody – Van Gogh, say, with his crazy mutilated ear, his clotted oils – had painted in a snarl on the Mona Lisa. Her mother's eyes, always the essence of benign passivity, were bright with accusation.

"We are all capable of brutality, aren't we, Emily? I am. You are with Dave. We all do it as easily as breathing."

Emily thought she might faint, her breathing came in ragged little spurts.

"So you see," Elizabeth continued quietly, a math teacher summarizing proof of a simple theorem to a slow student, "there's no point in not forgiving the others. Tory, darling, would you like to help me make the punch, while Jason and Emily set up the tables under the trees? People will be arriving soon."

XXI The Tiger Pit

When clusters of guests began spilling out of cars, strolling under the trees, milling in the gazebo, Victoria shrank away into the house. She leaned on the windowsill of her old bedroom and watched the swirling about on the lawn below. Ants, they seemed to her, moving in intricate arabesques. How was it that so many people knew exactly what they were doing and where they were going?

Mother was like something delicious, a fresh peach perhaps, in her soft dress, the ants all converging on her, paying court. Victoria stroked her own cheek, felt the soft fur of peach skin, of other securities. Perhaps if she kidnapped her mother and they lived alone...? But even mother was unpredictable. There was nothing that could be counted on, there never had been. Suppose Jason knocked on her door and said she must come outside? She would not. There were safe and unsafe places, and only her bedroom was safe at the moment.

The people below sucked at her like a whirlpool.

Her knuckles gripping the windowsill were white with strain. If she did not hang on tightly, she might slip, fall, careen on to the guests, be battered on the rocks of their staring. She could feel it tugging at her, a vicious undertow, and felt ill and dizzy. It was pulling her toward the gazebo which she could not look at, which she had never been able to look at since that night, her eyes always bridling away from it – the way a person with a pathological fear of snakes or spiders will quickly close a book that is too vivid with photographs.

But the gazebo always lay in wait for her wherever she was. Even dreams would fall away into it, flattening themselves out and orbiting it at a crazy speed, dropping into its vortex.

Swirling, swirling, the current of people was trying to drag her back to that night. It was going to be necessary to flap her wings and rise above the flood. She wondered if it would be possible to fly backwards through her life, to get to the other side of the great wall which had flung itself up, a black barrier. On the far side of that barrier there had been hope. Not the absence of fear. No, there had never been a time when she was not afraid, but there had been a time when she had expected to be like other people. She had managed to keep certain scenes intact in the scrapbook inside her skull: the Boston grandparents and aunts taking her to a birthday dinner at the Ritz, treating her like a little princess. Perhaps she had been four or five? Father had scowled throughout, making her fearful, but her fear had squatted, toad-like, on the far side of the crystal cruet set and the silverware, and her Grandfather Hampstead, mother's father, had protected her with his raised wine glass: To our little Victoria, the prettiest granddaughter in the world, who will grow up to be a great lady.

Yes, they had all believed that, and she herself had believed it before the fears began reaching out like bats scuffling from eaves. Gradually all the little fears had rolled themselves into something vast, an army of spiders that crawled out of the bedding every night, advancing on her, beginning at her feet and advancing, advancing. The night she came down the stairs and lost mother the spiders had reached her neck. If she had gone back to bed they would have invaded her mouth, her nostrils, her eyes.

She had roamed through the garden in terror.

And then father had rescued her. Not scolding, not frowning even, he had held her against his chest so that she had felt the spiky coiled hairs below his cotton shirt. How safe that had been. But father was unpredictable. She never could fathom his changing rules.

Below her, she could see him now with Adam on the porch swing – royalty receiving guests. He pretended to be impatient and embarrassed, but he loved it, she could tell; all those people bowing and scraping. She watched mother greeting people, smiling, shaking hands, embracing old friends.

From above, she was shocked to see how frail and bird-like her parents were, infinitely smaller than the hulk of her own body whose accretions mystified her – layers of blasted hopes settling on her year after year. Was it possible that she had begun as half a seed from each of those slight figures? Perhaps this was the worst thing, to be larger than both parents together. The violation of a natural law.

Her mother looked up at the window and then spoke to Jason. Betrayal again. They would drag her down, her flailing wings punctured and snagged. Like a bumblebee on its back on a windowsill, to be tormented by thoughtless boys. She would have to retreat into water and swim out of their reach.

When Jason came to find her she was huddled in an underwater cave in the corner of her room, hiding behind coral, disguising herself with a shroud of seaweed.

◆◆◆

"This little gala will not be without surprises," Miss Perkins of the School Records Office, sender of eleventh-hour invitations, murmured to Mrs. Fitzsimon, widow, member of the Board of Trustees. "I could intimate something if my lips were not sealed."

They both nodded to a cluster of local dignitaries.

"We all know Victoria will appear, my dear." Portentousness, Mrs. Fitzsimon indicated, was inappropriate. "Poor Victoria. I can remember her from school days, you know, before it became apparent. A tragedy. From Mrs. Carpenter's side of the family, I believe."

"Oh I wouldn't consider Victoria a surprise." There was a delicate disparagement, a tone of ever-so-faintly amused dismissiveness. "After all, it would be surprising if she were *not* here, wouldn't you say?"

"How do you do, Mr. Meecham? Yes, such a long time. Lovely day...yes, and Emily too, I believe."

The small talk and acknowledgments, the constant scanning of the passing parade, were automatic things that occupied only the fringes of their energies.

"Of course it is interesting to see Emily after so long."

"Oh Emily." So passé, the exploits of Emily, Miss Perkins implied. "I will admit, one occasionally asks oneself whether or not there is a husband."

"Shall we try the punch?" Mrs. Fitzsimon was determined not to give the satisfaction of curiosity.

Miss Perkins was not fooled by the indifference. "The pink lemonade? Or shall we be daring and sample the rum-spiked concoction?" One did not, she thought to herself, give up a rare trump card so easily. She would volunteer nothing until Mrs. Fitzsimon paid due court.

"I suppose," the latter prompted, "that invitations have gone out far and wide? The records office *combed* for past colleagues and acquaintances?"

"Not on a large scale. Not on a large scale at all, really. Though I must say, some of the most surprising contacts, from way back, from before the war...." She took an open-faced tuna and cucumber sandwich and asked casually: "Do you remember the Wilsons? Joseph Wilson, the deputy principal before the war?"

"Faintly. Wasn't he killed in action? I seem to remember there was something slightly scandalous about *Mrs.* Wilson. My mother used to mention her in a certain tone of voice."

"That's what I thought," Miss Perkins mused reflectively. "I was working in Boston, my first job after college. When I came home on weekends, people would point her out to me. She used to wheel her baby girl around town in a stroller looking demure as could be but you could see black lace on her petticoats. And then she left town. Of course the war dislocated everything, didn't it? We simply never found out what became of people. And after the war I became Edward's – Mr. Carpenter's – secretary."

"Oh Emily, my dear child, how lovely to see you again... quite put Ashville on the map, such a thrill for us...and your little boy up there with Mr. Carpenter, I believe? Such a shame your husband couldn't...."

◆◆◆

His grandfather, Adam thought, was like one of Dave's sheep when its feet were stuck fast in mud after the rains. Its brown eyes would say: Nothing is the matter; nothing at all is the matter (it thought the problem would go away if it pretended for long enough), but its flanks trembled so that tiny flying insects rose in gusts from the clashings and small earthquakes of wool curls.

His grandfather was expecting something to happen. He stroked Adam's hair absent-mindedly, watching for whatever it was. It had nothing to do with the women in soft dresses and floppy straw hats, nothing to do with the men in summer suits and cigars.

Adam did not think it had to do with his grandmother or his mother, though the old man looked at them often. His grandmother and his mother were very beautiful, especially his mother. Everyone looked at them. The men looked at his mother as though it were an accident – while they were rubbing a nose or lighting a cigar or just thinking about the chestnut tree. They pretended she had bumped into their eyes and taken them by surprise; they smiled at her and turned back guiltily to their wives.

Whenever his mother looked at him she smiled. He knew she was very happy that he was holding his grandpa's hand and that sometimes he put his arms around the old man's neck and kissed him. He knew it was because she wished she could do it herself. He could tell.

Perhaps she was waiting for him to ask Dave to come because she was afraid to do it herself. He couldn't tell.

⬥⬥⬥

Jason climbed into childhood, up the worn stairs with their soft oval hollows. There was the V, darkened in against the blonded oak, that he had made with his penknife before he went to boarding school. There was the sitting stair, third from the top, where he and Tory used to camp (back in the time of peace, before the war ended) while she read him stories: Snow White, Rumpelstiltskin, Rapunzel. She was always half mother to him, being seven years older.

And half child.

Tory, come out to play.

I can't, Jason, I can't.

Why can't you?

The darkness is in the garden again. I'm afraid.

I won't let it touch you.

Daddy will see me shaking. He'll be angry.

I'll protect you. I'll hold your hand.

He had always tried to find out: how could there be darkness when the sun was shining? But she could not explain. It was simply a darkness, full of fear, that settled over everything. She would tremble and her trembling would irritate father.

What on earth is the matter with you, Tory? Probably it alarmed him, probably his gruffness was love. If you're cold put a sweater on. If you're not cold, pull yourself together.

In the time of peace, before father came home from the war, they slept sometimes, he and Tory, in their mother's bed, their mother in the middle. (How did he know this? Tory must have told him; or perhaps mother had.) He did not think Tory had been afraid of the darkness then. It seemed to him now (and yet how could he possibly remember? He had been three when his father came home) that sometimes he had been the one in the middle because he could remember the different kinds of softness: how he curled himself like a ladle around Tory's back, his legs brushing against the lower curve of her buttocks; how his mother curled herself around *his* back so that he could feel her nightie bunched up between her legs and the soft cushions of her breasts against his shoulders, her breath on his neck. He could remember – so it seemed to him – the different smells: the complicated yeasty spiced fragrance of his mother, the spring-rain-and-clover freshness of Tory.

He leaned now against the wall in the hallway at the top of the stairs, overcome by the sensuous immediacy of the memory. He could have turned and touched the satin arc of his mother's breast; he could have embraced his gazelle-like sister while she was still flawless, he could have held her and preserved her there and kept her from the terrible changing.

A warm valley. Cradled between his earliest loves. If he could have stayed there, could have gone back!

He breathed slowly until the disturbing smells faded, then he knocked on Tory's door.

"Tory, it's me. Can I come in?"

No answer.

He looked inside. She was huddled in one corner on the

floor, moving her arms in a slow ballet as though she were under water. Not the sylph of childhood nights, stifling giggles, wriggling up against him in bed. A shape shifter. An imposter, rocking like a small boat on the pontoons of her thighs.

He thought of Circe. Of Morgan le Fay. Of evil enchantments. There must have been something he could have done or should have done. If he had studied the Tarot instead of psychology? He was always searching for the power to reverse spells.

(But Jessica said: You manipulate. You use people up.

And Stephen: Your task is to iron out the exceptional... to bring everything down to the level of the well-adjusted.)

"Tory," he said tenderly, taking her hand. His voice broke over the shoals of her retreat, gravelly, cracking itself open on rocks. "Let's sit on the sitting stair."

A pause in the swimming movements of her arms. A focusing. She let him take her hand. She went with him down the hallway and they sat together on the third top step. His arm around her, her head on his shoulder, he began a story. Once upon a time there was a beautiful young princess who came under a wicked spell....

◆◆◆

There had always been safe places and safe people. Her bedroom had been a secure island, even father would never come in without permission. There were those rare moments when father had held her and pledged protection. And mother – mother's love was like an umbrella, a safe cloak, it was always there – except that it was also likely to spring holes when rain began. When Emily was little...and when Jason held her hand she had always been safe...and when Adam did.

And there had been the other best time, the golden time, when her young man held her in his arms. She could not remember his name. She had to swim through many caves to find him because she kept that picture in the furthest one, in a locked chest smothered with crustacean growth. Sometimes, not very often, she swam there and unlocked the chest and took it out and looked at it, her icon.

In the picture he was visible only as a radiance that enveloped her, but she could feel again the silk of his skin. She called him Gabriel because of the brush of wings, light as eyelashes or angel's feathers, on her breasts and thighs. Gentleness came from him like an aura, and absolute peace and safety. But always, as soon as she felt him like a swollen arrow filling up her emptiness, the cave water would churn with predators: bloodied shark jaws and octopi squirting foulness over his beautiful golden body.

She was always afraid she would not get him back into the locked chest, that even this glimpse of him would be taken from her forever. She would vow never to disturb the memory again. Just to know it was there, not looked at, would be sufficient.

But today, as she sat with Jason on the third top step, Gabriel swam unbidden from his cave, he glided around her, he would not consent to being locked up again. His presence filled the house, she could hear the beat of his wings. Danger, she signaled. Danger! You must fold yourself up and become invisible.

He did not seem to care, his vulnerable golden skin exposed all over again to whatever might happen out there.

"Shall we go outside now, Tory?"

"I can't, Jason. I can't."

"Just for a few minutes. To say hello to everyone. I'll hold your hand. No one will hurt you, I promise."

◆◆◆

Emily ladled punch. She made small talk. Yes, she did remember the school play in 1957. And now Maureen was living in Houston, married to a NASA expert, and had three daughters! How time flies! Oh yes, she expected there would be more concerts in New York. And Boston too. No, for the time being England was the most suitable.... Yes, it was a shame his grandparents saw so little of him...the price of a concert career.... Actually no, she was living alone at present.... Oh of course, one always dreamed of Ashville, the old home, the old friends, but one can't, as they say, go home again.... Yes, Tory would be down presently; a strain for her, yes, of course...but as well as could be expected...yes, how kind of you....

She looked up at the house and saw her family entire, in one glance. The French windows reflecting the gazebo and herself; in front of them her son and her father on the porch swing. Her mother's face was pressed against the windows from the inside (as always remembered), a disembodied head superimposed on Emily's own shadowy image. They were all contained – her parents, her son, and herself – by the mirrored gazebo, raffish under its disheveled strands of honeysuckle, an oddly *décoiffé* Medusa-like frame for a family portrait. And above its reflected finial, at an upstairs window, like the eye of God in illuminated manuscripts: Tory. Behind her, Jason.

All present, real and surreal, merging and swaying apart. If Magritte were to depict The Family, its symbiotic layers and floating detachments and arbitrary disjunctions...? Or perhaps Escher...? The Family in ceaseless mutation?

She leaned over the punch bowl of cut crystal and saw the underside of the chestnut leaves and her own face rising and falling on a slow swell of rum-laced juice. Ice cubes floated across her cheeks.

Someone, that pompous Mrs. Fitzsimon, leaned over, importunate, crowding her reflective space. "Just a drop more, Emily dear." Like those irritating people who whisper during a concert. Emily stirred with the ladle, once, twice, a savage momentum, and Mrs. Fitzsimon's face disappeared with a gurgle down the vortex of mint leaves and rum-sodden strawberries.

"Oh, you've damaged it!" Mrs. Fitzsimon said, and Emily started as though caught in malice aforethought. But Mrs. Fitzsimon was referring to the pattern of leaves and fruit, in disarray.

"I'm sorry," Emily said stupidly. "I'm terribly sorry about everything. I just don't see what can be done."

Mrs. Fitzsimon looked at her sharply. You could see the

thought: They're all a bit strange, it runs in the family.

Emily leaned unsteadily against the trunk of the chestnut tree. In the same way that she sensed within seconds if an audience was with her, she felt now that she was in some kind of peril. She could scarcely breathe. She knew all the signs of another attack; had been through them before: the flight from Montreal, the flight from Sydney.

Perhaps it was the heat. She had a swooning sensation of surf and white sand, smelled eucalypts, was conscious of the presence of Dave as enveloping and ineluctable, like a weather system. She felt weak with desire, had to slide down the tree, lean on grass and trunk because of the heaviness between her legs – a throbbing inflammation surely audible as drumbeats and rampant now throughout her body so that even her arms, when she crossed them to protect herself, felt tender to her own touch, bruised with want.

There was no help for it, she saw. Years of fortifications slumping like ashes in a grate, the whole zoo of predators – risk, love, pain, vulnerability – barreling into the breach, the long battle lost.

Adam waved to her. Tory was coming through the door, clinging to Jason's hand, frightened as a child on the first day at a new school. And on the porch swing: her father, so pathetically pleased by all this brouhaha. His frailty was a taste in her throat, unbearable. He was the last translucent sliver of rind around the kernel of his death. Oh, she thought weakly, love is visceral and vicious. Love has steel jaws, the grip of a bear trap.

She began moving like a sleepwalker toward the porch, instructing herself, rehearsing: Sit on the step. Casually. Lean back as though stretching. Make contact, head against his knee.

The porch step.

She sits, casually.

No registering, in the old man's eyes, of her presence. Something else obsesses him. Emily thinks of young musicians waiting in the wings of performances that will make or break their careers. She clears her throat, leans back, a contact violent as a wound. The old man is shocked. His interior meditation has been violated. Without thought he prods at Emily with his cane as though rebuffing a scavenger dog.

This was the thing, she had known it all along. Once you stepped down off the stage and into the pit there were no guarantees. You became crazy as a gladiator, there was no limit to the number of times you could be gored. She wanted to beat on his chest with her hands and accuse: Bloody old tyrant! You demand our love but make the giving so impossible. Like Sisyphus rolling the rock uphill, an unachievable goal.

Perhaps she said it, perhaps she pummeled him. Emily, Emily, he was saying, just as distracted as when he jabbed at her with his cane. He was stroking her hair roughly, in agitated rhythm to his words: to be young, to be young, to be young. His hand was all knuckles and loose papery skin. She caught hold of it and pressed it against her cheek.

"The gazebo," he said, like a child begging for a treat. "Can you, Emily? I want to sit in the gazebo again."

Jason was nearby with Tory and she called to him. Adam helped. By concerted effort they hefted him along on his canes, careless of indignity. His throne room, verdant and rotting, received him, his guests paid court.

Elizabeth, concert master, watched from the porch. In her eyes, there glowed a secret and pleasurable knowledge: a composed ending, I have done it well. Only a few stray phrases to be drawn into the final chords: she was waiting for Edward to grow gentle with his eldest child, for Victoria to ripen into peace. Her eyes lingered on Tory, circling the gazebo in a twitch of nerves. Certainly there was still some anxiety, Elizabeth acknowledged, but also the calm expectation of promise. In exactly this way she had watched the first steps of all of them: heart in mouth, because of course they would fall, they would cry, they would suffer and lose hope; but then they would learn to walk. She waited, she believed. Life was mysterious and awful and senseless, a chaos of pain and celebration, so what could one do but have faith and make music of it all?

She congratulated herself. She was like a gardener who could coax trees into espaliered symmetry against a wall. She lured random notes into harmony. Prospero, she thought, was actually a woman, a white witch, benign.

A taxi pulled into the circular drive and a stranger got out, someone elderly who was small and vital as a hummingbird. A grandmother, one somehow suspected, to a number of small boisterous children. Elizabeth glanced at her fleetingly, then away, then back again, her line of vision jerked taut. Astonishment. And in the other woman's eyes: first caution, then a sort of proffered neutrality (I won't fire if you don't) and finally an ironically amused smile.

My god, Elizabeth thought. And it was like being young again, full of euphoric uncertainty, like the galvanic crackle of one's first concert, one's first love affair. Edward has done this. So *he's* Prospero after all. He has known all along. Is this an accusation? Or a seal of forgiveness with full knowledge? Is it peace or war?

God knew what the ending would be now.

She moved toward Marta, unprepared, defenseless, winded with agitation, exuberant. There was always this about life: some random note, winging away from the presumptive last phrase, would sing in one's head, would mock and entice, and one would chase it into another whole movement. She saw Marta's eyes rove, take in the house, the paper lanterns, the gathering. A dynasty. Elizabeth drew level, wondering: will she strike me, or take my hands?

They stood facing each other like warrior queens.

"So, Elizabeth." Marta's voice was still husky and low, only a little aged around the edges, her tone sardonic. "So you won. All the prizes."

Elizabeth said dryly: "There've been one or two losses over the years."

"Oh, losses." Who, Marta implied, should know more about losses than she herself did?

"You've won some glittering prizes yourself, Marta. Your career, your books, your son distinguishing himself in medicine, so I hear. And grandchildren?"

"Five of them."

"Well. You seem to have come out well ahead of me."

"If you only knew, Elizabeth. If you only knew." Her eyes

had the wildness of damaged birds. They fluttered about brokenly and then fastened on something. Someone. There was a quiver of fascination, a sorting out of information and memory. Elizabeth followed her gaze.

Marta whispered: "Is that...?"

"Yes." Elizabeth seemed both reluctant and amused, as though a concession were being made to a tax auditor deceived for so long that the statute of limitations had run out. "That's Jason."

"He's *Edward's*!"

"Unmistakably."

"And all my life I've believed...." Marta's hands bridled, they rubbed her eyebrows in bewildered pleasure, brushing away the folly of years. "When I got your telegram, I thought: that ruthless bitch. Before it's all over, she insists I see Joseph's other son. And then I decided, why not? I came to spit in your eye."

"He could have been Joseph's. He was born the day after I got word of his death."

"Joseph Junior was born a week later."

Marta was agitated, her hands twisting over old angers and griefs. Elizabeth looked at her own hands, makers of music and mayhem. She might have been Lady Macbeth, turning them vaguely over and back, over and back, bemused by the savagery of which she seemed capable.

"Do you hate me, Marta?"

"I survived on my hate. I fed on it. No husband, no money. Not even a funeral: no ritual for public grieving. And you" – Elizabeth winced from the energy of Marta's rage – "you filched even the possibility of private grieving. To have to assume he died thinking of you. I spent my nights crying and my days raging. That was my fuel – the determination to climb higher than you. I won't be modest, I earned my prizes, and I hope they made you envious."

"You're magnificent, Marta. You always were."

"For stooping to the indignity of scrabbling, you mean. Since not all of us were born to affluence."

Elizabeth thought: They never forgive you for that. Neither she nor Edward. "We were all mismatched," she sighed. "It should have been you and Edward, fighting together, tooth and nail, success before sex. Why do you think Joseph and I came together like...?"

Marta's face went white with betrayal, she swayed slightly.

Elizabeth thought she was going to fall and reached out. "That was unpardonable. I'm sorry."

"What a bloody-minded bitch you are, Elizabeth." Marta spoke quietly, almost with a kind of relief, as though she were absolved for the disgrace of losing; as though Elizabeth were the kind of opponent who, hitting below the belt, did not ultimately count. "Did you never feel a twinge of compunction? Why did you do it?"

Do it? Elizabeth looked into the past as through the wrong end of a telescope. Had there ever been that much control, a consciousness of *doing* something? She remembers it as being hurtled along in floodwaters. She remembers guilt and compunction as something that one drowning person feels for other victims of a cloudburst.

But Marta had not expected her to answer. As though still pondering Elizabeth's malice, still considering the crudely flippant suggestion of switched partners, she said: "There was a night, you know, the last night...when Edward and I might have turned to each other. We were both miserable. We both knew we were about to be deserted."

Elizabeth was startled. "Edward knew? No. You're mistaken. He's never known."

(But why else did he invite Marta today? He has known all along, he must have known.)

There was scorn in Marta's eyes. "You still amaze me, you know. Think white, and you're pure. Hide your head in the sand and no one will see you. Who *didn't* know, for god's sake?"

Elizabeth was shaken. "I've always been sure.... He's never given the slightest sign."

"Believe me. We discussed it. We pondered our fate. We might even have held each other for a moment, I forget. I think we did, for sheer comfort." Marta lapsed into silence, her eyes on distant and smudged events. "After they were both shipped off, I toyed with the idea of making something of it.

Baiting you. But I knew it would just make things easier for you. I couldn't bring myself to diminish whatever shred of guilt you were unlikely enough to feel."

"You really think there haven't been costs?"

Marta's shrug implied: the human condition, so what?

"You don't know about Tory."

"I know about Tory. I heard. I'm terribly sorry." She touched Elizabeth on the arm and Elizabeth flinched, but thought: She's generous, she always was. "She was such a beautiful child," Marta said.

"You're right about my bloody-mindedness. I think it was my fault, Tory's decline."

"Elizabeth." An indulgent, almost affectionate smile. "You're so extreme about everything."

"You don't know what happened – "

"Even as a child she was unnaturally intense. I remember."

"Yes. But there was something I did. And something Edward did. We pushed her over a brink."

"Anything might have done it. Much as the thought of your writhing with guilt appeals, Elizabeth. But everyone knows it's neurological. Inherited."

Elizabeth reached out uncertainly, like a duelist gauging a distance, and touched Marta's wrist. She was sifting the evidence for absolution, seemed to be weighing something. She said quickly: "I'll regret telling you this, I know." A long pause. "I was not confident...about Joe. We quarreled that last night. Your pregnancy changed things, I could feel a tide turning." She sighed. "After the war...probably...he would have gone to you and his children...." Though who can know? she thought.

Marta said only: "It was such a long time ago." But her eyes were bright with tears. And then an imp of a smile began playing about her lips. "Doesn't this strike you as bizarre? Two scrawny old ladies with gray hair and arthritis...discussing passion."

They smiled, they began to laugh. Gusts of mirth shook them as a cat shakes a bird. They gasped and held on to each other and laughed and the guests turned to watch in amazement.

Sobering up, Elizabeth said: "You have to say hello to Edward. He's in the gazebo." And thought: What will he do with this rabbit he has pulled from a hat? Will he brand me with a scarlet A?

Well, the music would play itself, no matter what she did.

◆◆◆

When his grandmother walked into the gazebo with the stranger, Adam knew. It was the moment his grandfather had been waiting for. Adam thought of the sheep. This was what he remembered:

When the shearing began, Dave used to say: It doesn't hurt them. They remember the smells – the men, the machinery, the tar, the lanolin slick of the clipped fleeces. That's why they tremble, not because it hurts. Adam hated to watch them standing so perfectly silent and still except for that shivering as the shears moved between flesh and wool.

His grandfather was trembling like a sheep standing next in line for the shearing pen and it was because of the woman, the stranger. She was small and old, though in a way she didn't look old. His grandmother was like that. He thought it was probably the way his mother would grow old. Their skin turned as leaves do, but only their skin. Not their eyes or the way they moved their hands. Those things stayed young.

He knew he had shaken like that, like the sheep, when the loudspeakers in Sydney boomed that it was time to get on the plane and he had asked his mother: "Isn't Dave coming to say goodbye?"

He whispered: "Who is she, grandpa?"

But his grandfather didn't hear him, he didn't notice anything at all, so Adam wandered off to look for Uncle Jason.

◆◆◆

Edward looked up and she was there. In the gazebo. He waited, unable to speak. Out of grief or discretion or ignorance – he didn't know which – Bessie left them alone. Other guests, stray talkers, drifted away.

"Dear Edward," she said, and took his hand. "After all these years."

Marta. He had never said her name aloud. He still could not do it.

"I have a grandson," he said. What he wanted to say was: I love you as I have always done and yet I choose my family again. "I have a grandson called Adam."

"And I have five grandchildren, Edward. Can you believe it? Three are Sonia's. She lives in Philadelphia. And two belong to Joseph Junior. He was born...during the war. He never saw his father. But you knew that, of course."

"I didn't know...you had a son."

She was amazed. "Elizabeth didn't...? No. I suppose she wouldn't speak of it."

"Bessie?" This confused him. "She wouldn't have known. She's never suspected...." Until today, he supposed, until today. What must she be thinking now? He would have to worry about that later.

But Marta was agitated and walked to the doorway and looked across the lawn at the house and then paced the little octagon of the gazebo, leaning at last against its honeysuckle-thick lattice. "The potency of *place*," she marveled. "Forty years and it seems like yesterday. Wasn't it hard to forgive? Or did it all seem irrelevant after the war?"

He was not sure what she meant, he waited for clues.

She brushed away time with her hands. "Oh well. I expect I would have done the same. If he'd come back." She sighed. "They were rough years, weren't they?" And when he didn't answer, she said brightly. "Well, we're both survivors. We should toast each other: To the wounded who never fell. And you, Edward. Fifty years, all this, it's astonishing. I'm so glad for you."

"What...did you...." His lips worked at shaping themselves, it seemed difficult for them to build words. "What did you...do...with your life?"

As soon as words flowed evenly again, he would say: It is still impossible and we will still survive. Your grandchildren. My grandson. I love you as I have always loved you, but it is still impossible.

Again she seemed surprised. "You don't know? I did a doctorate in history. I was teaching by the time Joe Junior was five. I'm still teaching part-time although I was supposed to retire a couple of years ago. You never read any of my books? The war in the Pacific, that was my area."

He was dumbfounded.

"I went to your daughter's concert in New York," she said. "When I saw the name first, I simply wondered idly...and then I read somewhere, Ashville, and I thought: it *must* be. So I went. Extraordinary."

She was there. He might have seen her. Even through such connections.... His Beatrice, always thinking of him. Now he would tell her. He would touch her. He would say: A million times I have come back here and walked into your outstretched arms.

She said: "I can stay for less than an hour, Edward. Terribly complicated arrangements, and such short notice, you know. When the telegram came, I thought I couldn't do it. The associations. Everything. But I'm glad I did. It was certainly high time to cauterize old wounds. Yes, it was good to come."

She put both her hands out to him and he took them.

Now he would tell her.

"Marta," he began.

⬥⬥⬥

The darkness had been thickening around Tory. After Jason let go her hand, the air turned brittle. Lacerations, with every breath she took. People came up to her and spoke and when she opened her mouth to say don't, please don't, please leave me alone, it would bleed.

People stood staring at the blood trickling out of her mouth. They took photos, they poked at her through the bars of her cage, they offered peanuts.

She closed her eyes until she knew the waves had come and hidden her completely. Lullaby. Lulled in the water. She swayed, steering herself with her fins.

She knew a place.

She swam to it, gliding from rock to rock unseen, sliding in under great trailing fronds of seaweed. Under there, in the dark against a cave, was something infinitely long and green, coiled like a sea serpent. It mesmerized her, and filled her with horror, both. She touched it – all scales and slime. She picked up its limp reptilian head.

And then the waters receded with dizzy suddenness, as though a plug had been pulled in the ocean floor. Clarity. She was under the honeysuckle, her face pressed up against the slats of the gazebo, the garden hose in her hand.

She could see her father and a woman holding hands. She could read the rhythms of air around his body. He smelled like an old stallion watching a mare in heat. Tory's mouth filled with salty juice, the taste of the taboo.

Something hummed piercingly inside her head, something primitive and coercive like a wolf howl or the scream of a ruptured blood vessel. She knew by instinct where the brass faucet was. She turned it as far as it would go, she dragged out the hose which cavorted like a sea serpent, she took aim, she watched the water hit her father and the woman like a flogging administered on a quarter-deck.

She screamed incoherently, on and on and on.

◆◆◆

Now Edward would tell her, her hands in his.

"Marta," he began to say as the water struck him. It pounded his face and chest, freakishly darting aside and then leaping back like a cat-o'-nine-tails. It was in his mouth, his nostrils, his lungs. He was gasping and coughing. Judgment. Now he would die. He tried to stand and there was a torrent around his feet and he fell.

For a moment, beneath the arc of water, he looked up and saw Victoria and then the whip of water was lashed across his face again and he cried out, he remembered, he tried to say: But you didn't understand. I was saving you. I wanted to keep you pure. You were perfect, Tory. I loved you.

Then there was blackness.

◆◆◆

And Jason remembered, as he scrabbled beneath the honeysuckle for the faucet while others clasped Tory with rude hands. He remembered what even his dreams had sheered away from. He stopped the deluge and ran to rescue her.

"Let go of her!" he was shouting. There was a man pinning back her arms and Jason lifted him up as though removing a burr from Tory's clothing.

"Get your hands off her. Tory, it's all right, it's all right. Don't cry."

Pandemonium all around them. Doctor, someone was calling, quickly, get a doctor! Ambulance. Guests milling around and shrinking back, already formulating gossip. Elizabeth, white-faced, leaned over the sodden bundle on the floorboards, chafing Edward's hands between her own and ordering urgently: "For god's sake, Marta, get into dry clothes. In my bedroom. Please!"

Marta was dazed. Her look perhaps meant: it's a violent place, this. Always has been. But she said as though talking in sleep: "Yes. Thank you. Then I'll call a cab." She wanted to get away, wanted simply to be elsewhere, but seemed for a moment incapable of the effort required to achieve this. She was somewhere in New Guinea, leaning over the fallen body that had never been found.

Perhaps Elizabeth knew what she was thinking. Elizabeth's eyes said many things: You are exceptional, Marta, I have always thought so. Would it mean anything, to ask for forgiveness?

But she only touched Marta's wrist and murmured again: "Go and change, for god's sake. You'll catch cold."

Marta said: "I'll call you tomorrow. I hope he'll be all right."

Through a parting of bodies, Jason saw his father on the floor of the gazebo and felt a chill as of icicles forming in his blood.

"Oh daddy," Tory whimpered in terror. "Oh daddy, I'm sorry I'm sorry daddy. I didn't mean it."

She lay down beside him, shuddering violently, and Elizabeth moved so that her daughter's head was in her lap. She stroked Tory's hair, stroked her arms, crooning: "Hush now, it's all right. Hush now, Tory."

Helplessly, Emily held Adam against herself. He was shivering with fright.

Jason whispered to her: "Do you remember?"

"Something. It's vague. Something horrible. *Déjà vu.*"

"You were only five."

But it hung there in the memories of all of them, like a lantern seen through mists, now fading, now candescent. Emerging from blur like a print being developed.

For Elizabeth it had always been overly vivid, too bright to look at.

Tory's seventeenth birthday party. Japanese lanterns in the garden. Dancing in the living room, the French windows open, young couples on the veranda sipping punch. All the right teenagers from all the right families present, Edward mellow and beaming.

"A toast!" he called, striding into the swirl of the dancers. "To my birthday girl."

But where was Tory?

Edward embarrassed, then joking. Retreating upstairs, to where Jason and Emily, too young for the revels, played card games and made spying forays: peering from the staircase, watching the lawn from an upstairs window.

"Is Tory up here?"

No, daddy, she's not here.

How long after that before the shouting began? Before they ran to the window? How long had Tory been in the gazebo with that boy?

First the veranda floodlights hitting the honeysuckle. Edward did that: the shadowy area out of bounds to the partygoers now glaringly center stage. And Edward, incoherent with rage, the garden hose in his hands, lashing about with his watery sword of justice. At the end of the long silver arc of anger were two strange little dancing figures, like puppets – paper white, naked – tied to the end of a crystal rope. They gasped and begged and danced and fell and tried to get up and tried to run and the beam of water followed them relentlessly.

Under the harsh flare of light, the watchers could see how

the water punched into Tory's jangling breasts and foamed at the V between her legs and how it hurled itself at the boy's jiggling penis and spumed around his testicles.

It seemed to go on forever, Edward's cries and Tory's sobbing and the dreadful lashing of water and the wide-eyed horror of the teenage guests (though already some of the boys were snickering), and Jason and Emily clung to each other at the upstairs window and shuddered, and afterwards Emily was sick.

Adam, white faced, still shivering. Still clinging to Emily. Arrival of the doctor. General confusion. Guests hovering and discreetly leaving. The massaging of the fallen body. The injections. Tory weeping quietly. Elizabeth leaning over Edward, stroking his hand.

"Heart's still functioning," the doctor said. "Bit of a miracle. It's weak and erratic. I don't recommend this sort of excitement for my heart patients. Let's get him inside till the ambulance comes."

XXII Coda

Vacuum. The ambulance gone with Edward and Elizabeth, the guests vanished, the silence overwhelming.

On the porch four figures, still as a painting, gazed across a lawn full of tables abandoned in mid-revel, a litter of half-empty glasses, dwindling ice cubes, stigmata of single bites on sandwiches and pieces of cake, ice cream slowly drowning in itself. It might have been a garden bewitched, mysteriously deserted without trace or sign of cause.

Only the slow creak of the porch swing on which Jason and Tory sat suggested life. And also, to a close observer, the eyes of the child – which missed nothing, monitoring and translating every nuance of facial expression.

He said to them earnestly: "Grandpa's not going to die, I know it."

"Of course he's not, darling," his mother said quickly.

And he understood that she was not at all sure. He realized they all thought he had been stating his fears. It would be a waste of time trying to explain that he *knew*, that he could somehow tell, from the touch and smell of his grandmother as she hugged him and then climbed into the back of the ambulance, that all would be well.

How would he say it? Simply: She can make things happen. Or maybe: When she holds something in her hands in a certain way, it cannot slip through her fingers and get lost.

He was confident she would not let grandpa's life slither away from him. When he thought of his grandmother, he thought of something strong and anchored, like a maypole. He thought of everyone else as ribbons braiding themselves around her.

Could this be put into words they would understand? Probably not. Grown-ups were exasperating, noticing so little.

For example: he suspected that his mother and Uncle Jason were not aware that Aunt Tory was... *different* somehow. She had terrified him with all that crying and shouting and the garden hose and the water, but now – yes, it was her eyes. They didn't drift as much, they focused. And also, even the way she was sitting was different: as though someone had tightened up all her loose strings.

The telephone rang, a spattering of sound, and everyone jumped. Jason went into the house to answer it and the others waited, suspended. Five mintues. Six. Tory's feet began to stutter against the porch floor like typewriter keys. Then Jason returned.

"Reprieve," he announced. "Doctor says he's out of the critical stage. He hasn't regained consciousness yet, but of course he's sedated. Mother's going to stay with him tonight."

The child wanted to remind them: I told you.

Tory hugged herself and smiled and said suddenly: "Now that he's all right." And then, as though there were a link: "Adam, when will we visit Australia?"

Even the boy, who followed his aunt's switchback logic more easily than anyone else, was caught off guard. Every nerve in his body hummed like a telegraph wire. So much in the balance. He was afraid to speak. He crossed his fingers behind his back and looked at his mother – a mute plea.

Emily felt herself to be ten years old again, poised terrified at the tip of the high diving board, a crowd of children watching from below, others waiting impatiently behind her on the ladder. She'd had no idea how far up this was, how much the board swayed, how hard and deadly the distant surface of water would look. There was no way back. She had to close her eyes and dive in full knowledge of risk.

She breathed slowly and said: "I'll call Dave tonight. We'll discuss it."

Adam did not move until he had counted to ten. Just in case he was dreaming. Then he was all over her like a jubilant terrier, hugging and kissing, his happiness a halo of incoherent sound. Tory began to produce something like a singing from deep within herself, and the garden filled up with their strange duet, non-verbal, high-pitched, and atonal – as though some avant-garde composer had written a new *Ode to Joy*.

Jason, not unaffected, touched his younger sister's shoulder. "I think," he said – though he had trouble speaking, and had to clear his throat – "that I'll go to the hospital for a while."

XXIII Elizabeth

The greatest mystery, Elizabeth thinks, is the wildness of the beast within us. At any moment we may move in some primal way, take a mere step in the direction of private desire, stretch an arm: and our claws have left blood in their wake.

Nevertheless she believes unswervingly in the efficacy of hope. Simply the growing, she thinks, the movement from day to day, ruptures old forms and is violent with beauty.

Is there a way to minimize the damage? To stretch into our jostled strip of time without harming another living thing? This is the quest. Each morning's waking thoughts scatter a million seeds of possibility.

She lifts Edward's hand to her cheek and holds it there, but his arm is heavy with sedation and sags back toward the bed. And yet it could flex itself into savagery. Who knows what might happen? It could snap its sinews in the cause of outrage, like Othello extinguishing Desdemona.

What is he dreaming?

What does she know of him? After fifty years: intimate aliens.

And yet how well some strangers know us.

She thinks of Marta who called her by her proper name. No diminutives. This pleases Elizabeth. They have never underestimated each other, she and Marta.

She supposes they have both spent a lifetime wondering what might have happened after the war. If Joseph had come back. Is it possible to resift all that? Is it necessary? Elizabeth would rather think of Adam whose voice rises into her mind like a benediction. She would rather stroke the dead weight of Edward's arm and coax it back to warmth. She would rather listen for the nurse's step in the hallway.

Is that Jason at the door? It seems so. He stands behind her chair and rests his hands on her shoulders. She turns to look at him and thinks of a tuning fork – something giving off a hum of excitement. Words float from him. "I really think, from now on, I'll be able to *do* something."

With his life, he means, with his patients.

She knows it is simply that he has discovered hope.

Sometimes she has tried to picture Jason functioning in his office in New York. His waiting room presents itself to her as teeming with unhappiness: subway crowds in hell, a cramming of people exhausted by the lives they drag around behind them like monstrous dragon-plated tails. Clank, clank: the sound of so many tormented pasts. All waiting for Jason to hand out the magic. And Jason waiting for the alchemist's stone. But *from now on*, he believes.

Elizabeth touches such moments as though fingering silk. She has always preferred today to yesterday.

Though sometimes yesterday intrudes, blundering back like a drunken guest after the party is over. Jason leaves, the past arrives. Elizabeth thinks of Marta. She remembers youth. The recklessness. The intensity. The awful heedlessness to consequences. The conviction (quaint now) that it will not be possible to go on living without the one most fervently desired body tangled into yours.

Elizabeth finds that some atom of memory stores everything. It lies around, this smoking chunk of history, in abandoned corridors of the brain, a hand grenade, waiting. A pin is pulled and it is all still there in undiluted vibrancy. The senses reel. Elizabeth sees, hears, tastes, smells, touches Joseph.

It is so disorienting, this visitation, so intense, that she covers her face with her hands. She shuts out the war, but cannot stop the ringing of the fateful phone call. She covers her ears. Futile. She knows all over again, as she knew it then, by the mere weight of the receiver, by the burden of dread in the air.

She watches herself: pregnant as a beached whale with Jason, her hand poised, afraid to lift up the news, afraid not to. Will it be about Edward or Joe? Which will be the more unbearable? And if it is Joe: will Marta, also eight and a half months' vast, be reaching for the phone in New York?

Elizabeth ponders this now. The labyrinth of simultaneous events, it has always fascinated her. What was Edward facing on the beaches when the jungle swallowed Joe? Had she and Marta received synchronized phone calls? Or sequential ones from the same disengaged official voice? (Joe must have listed them both: in the event of . . . please notify. . . .)

Elizabeth is agitated, her hands over her ears, her body buffeted by outer shock waves from the distant jangling of that telephone. She thinks: Perhaps we stiffened like that for every telegram, every phone call, in those days, and only afterwards told ourselves: I knew it. I knew it from the first ring.

She remembers lifting the receiver. Remembers the words, a telegram intoned. Joseph Wilson. Dead in action. Death confirmed by comrade who tried to recover the body under fire. Central highlands of New Guinea. She does not remember whether she replaced the receiver. She does recall the slumping, the touch of the carpet where she sat hunched and cowering. She might have been hiding from Japanese patrols. She remembers reaching out with her arms – to enfold Marta, perhaps, in New York. To howl with her. Though perhaps Marta would have clawed her like a cat.

Elizabeth mourned, prowling through New Guinea in her mind, imagining trees like twisted ropes and leaves vast as sails and vines like honeysuckle gone savage. She sat in the hallway all day, and all that night – except when like a sleepwalker she fed Tory and read to her and tucked her into bed. And Tory, with her white face and wide eyes, clung and whimpered, waiting for her fear to be put into words. But Elizabeth could not speak it.

She remembers the tug of the little girl's arms. The frightened whisper at last: "Mommy, is it daddy?"

"Not daddy, darling. Sonia's daddy."

Then Tory's quiet crying, the trailing off into sleep. Elizabeth returned to her vigil. She sat in the hallway all night. She felt safe with her back against the wall, beside the phone, close to the last filament of contact. On the following evening, she went into labor. It was Joe she wanted, a new edition, rising like a phoenix from between her legs.

But when Jason was born, when he came forth with Edward's eyes and nose, with Edward's fair hair burnished with copper, she was overcome. The rush of life took her by surprise, its variousness, its richness, its inexhaustible offerings of irony. She cradled the tiny body between her breasts. Mere hours from a death, minutes from its own before-life, its bawling grip on the day exhilarated her. She crooned to it....

Elizabeth realizes that she is fondling Edward's sluggish arm between her breasts, that Jason, hesitant, is watching her from the doorway. She lowers the arm gently onto the bedding and rests her face on it. Jason is transfixed, as though stumbling on the primal love scene. An echo of the afternoon eddies into Elizabeth's brain, Marta's voice, full of bewildered pleasure: *He's Edward's*!

Elizabeth sighs. Why had she never let Marta know? Another facet of the mystery, she thinks. Where do we store all this cruelty? She strokes her arms and is surprised to feel flesh. She realizes she was expecting something coarser, the pelt of a tiger perhaps.

Why is Jason filling the room like a vapor? How long has he been here? She considers telling him to leave the air alone, to stop pacing. She is afraid of dislodging another slag heap of memory. This is the problem: nothing is settled in the past, it is a shifting region of fault lines and instability. Consider what a random conjunction of *now* and *then* can do, consider Tory rampant as a thunderstorm....

Tory, Elizabeth thinks, is *essence*: pure childhood, pure terror, pure anger, pure pleasure. Elizabeth has always – in spite of the sin of favoritism – loved Tory uncritically and best, before all the others. Though it must be admitted she thinks this of whichever child she is holding in her mind's eye at a given moment.

"And as for Adam," Jason says.

Oh especially Adam. "Adam can pull love from the air," she agrees. It clings to him like pollen.

Jason is smiling. "If only the non-sequiturs of my patients were half as dazzling." He is tossing words into the room like catherine wheels, they buzz and glitter around Elizabeth's ears.

She makes an effort, knitting her brows. "And Adam?"

"He's beside himself with excitement."

She smiles absently and Jason shakes his head. "Oh mother, mother. Did you hear me? I said Emily is calling Australia."

Something sings inside Elizabeth, she moves her hands, if she were at home she would go to the piano. Excellent, she thinks. I have composed it well. Though one's control is never total.

Jason has gone, the air settles, Edward stirs.

She waits like a bird coasting on nothing. She reads his dream in the spasm of a muscle along his jaw. She waits for him to sit up and declaim from *Othello*: *O curse of marriage! That we can call these delicate creatures ours, and not their appetites!*

And how will she explain? How account for a whirlwind, a flash flood? Why does he want to know *now*? Forty years and he pulls the past out of a hat like a rabbit.

Behold, he says, swirling his magician's cape: Marta!

Explain, he demands.

Or had planned to demand. And was forestalled by Tory's spraying the air with indictments.

J'accuse, j'accuse, it has grown to an epidemic.

Look at him now, Elizabeth thinks. Even sedated, his face contorts itself into a frown. Preparing the case for the prosecution. It is irresistible, his rawness. She raises his still-clenched hand to her cheek, bends to kiss him. A witch's kiss: since the war she has schemed to bring him peace, has worked on a spell of contentment, has conspired to have happiness stalk him and startle his features with laughter.

It has been like a game of chess with Adam as queen's bishop. Last night he laughed! And she had thought: *Checkmate!* With a head full of dreams she had climbed to his bed.

His bed. Oh Edward, my puritan, she sighs. How comic that when she first saw him so obviously ill at ease in her father's drawing room, he looked like salvation. His hair rumpled, his tie altogether too carefully tied, his eyes hungry. Elizabeth remembers her answering hunger: I must have him. I must have those knotted muscles, that tamped-down rage.

She thought it would slither like lightning through decorum, she imagined it exploding between her thighs.

Fantasies, fantasies. While she dreamed of fire, he dreamed of ice.

Of course she learned to lie still like a virgin on an altar.

It was Tory who was punished.

He would have preferred three immaculate conceptions, Elizabeth thinks. Not that he was inclined to celibacy. Oh no, his hungers consumed him. It was only her participation that affronted him.

When Joe came like a new season at the end of winter, when he spoke to her eager flesh with his body, she had no more sense of a decision to be made than parched earth thinks of refusing rain.

After the war, she thinks, if I had taken my babies and left Edward, the scandal (back then) would have been indelible. It would have clung to her like an odor of garbage. Not that she would have cared.

It was not why she stayed.

These days, she thinks, in certain circles, it is a scandal that I did *not* leave him. In magazines she follows with amazement the reasons for which marriages are abandoned. Insane. It is true that her body has mourned for Joe, it is true that cravings have come and she has had to bury her head in the honeysuckle or play the piano for hours. But, she asks herself, for the price of solitary climaxes, for fifty years of licking my finger and sliding it between my legs, would I have forfeited this family and this marriage?

But where is the significance? clamor the writers of articles, crowding her. What of the stoppered passions, the lost concert audiences, the music composed for unlistening air, the waste?

But then who, she wonders, escapes waste? And who has time for all the opportunities that *are*? Why all this *angst*? People paying small fortunes for a listener, asking: What is the meaning of my life? It astonishes her. Elizabeth thinks there is more meaning between one blink of her eye and the next than anyone has time to write a gloss on. She stuffs her senses with the smell of sheets, the sound of an old man snuffling through a filter of drugs, the creak of her chair. She rests her head on Edward's chest and hears the erratic, the miraculous, the plaintively vulnerable tick-tock of the heart.

The present is overwhelming, thick with import. How should the past dare to seep under it? Why should loss and waste, reeking of regret, sneak into....

Elizabeth is agitated again. She goes to the window, inhales the moment, mad with summer. Only today matters, she insists, only today.

Too late.

Here comes Joe, huge as a colossus, striding into her senses as he first loomed into this toy-town where only genealogies and recipes and last year's snowfall were suitable topics of discussion. He comes trailing clouds of childhood and college, shared memories. Reminiscence slides over their tongues with the sherry, the old cerebral addictions: talk of music and politics and college mixers and who is where now and is Chamberlain taking the right course and is the Lend-Lease Act morally sufficient and is it inevitable that we will enter the war before the end?

A voice in the wilderness. A quickening. That was all. Just small daily pleasures, Joe dropping by on his walk home from the school, the two of them sipping beer on the porch and talking endlessly. Who could account for why it changed?

Elizabeth wonders: When did I realize what was happening?

The first day Joe did not come, by the extent of my dismay. Here are the details that will begin to matter, she thought the next day, hearing his scrunch on the gravel (a cavalier, almost swaggering step): the particular way his hair fell across his forehead, the careless disposing of his body on a porch chair, the way he placed one foot across the other thigh in negligent ease. The body's codes: how unpredictably translated in her emotions – Edward's unease and Joe's nonchalance both meaning love. This is clearly an aberration, they told each other, she and Joe. We will come to our senses presently. And soon: How can we possibly inflict all this chaos? How can we not? And then the war, great decider, and the final party.

Elizabeth is stuck in the past now, it crashes around her like a landslide.

While the house hums with conviviality they quarrel in the kitchen in whispered snatches.

"The army, Joe! I can't bear it. You can't leave me, I've been waiting to tell you, I'm pregnant."

"Oh god Liz." Elation and dismay in equal parts. A momentary embrace. A hasty parting as someone comes into the room. Small talk and jokes. The guest leaves, they resume.

"Oh god," Joe says, "I keep trying to repress it, I didn't want to tell you. But so is Marta."

"So is Marta what?"

"Pregnant. Everything is madness. Madness."

Biting her tongue on jealous rage till three more guests fix drinks, joke, wander off. Accusing: "You've made love to her!"

"She's my wife!"

"You wanted her. You're still in love with her."

"Hush. It's you I can't live without. A baby!"

"It might be Edward's."

Stunned rage. "But I thought...you said you hardly ever, that he didn't...."

"I never said that. He just doesn't like me to respond. It wasn't me who made overtures. I simply submitted."

"You *let* him when I...."

"And you *wanted* Marta...."

Under the ebb and flow of party farewells, wartime frenzied hilarity, toasts to Joseph, a dark primitive undertow of jealousy and impending loss. And finally they are alone in the house, guests gone, Edward outside somewhere immersed in farewells (they assume), Marta gone to send the babysitter home.

"Joe, Joe, I can't bear it. I don't want you to go. I'm afraid."

"This isn't a time to decide anything, Liz. All this chaos. Do you think I'm not distraught? Leaving you. Leaving Marta with one child and a baby coming..."

"You're thinking about *her*."

"Two lives beginning and I've no idea how I'll learn to face death...."

There is a wildness of kissing.

"Liz, Liz," he moans. "Oh Liz, oh my god."

They are on the sofa, her dress torn at the shoulder, the skirt bunched up around her waist. A ravenous moment, two people conscious of time run out, of mortality, of apocalypse. Her legs are locked around him, she wants to suck him deeper and deeper inside, to keep him there. To offer in time of war the great velvet refuge of her vagina.

She hears a sound on the stairs, half sees a flutter of movement. It is peripheral, to be ignored. But she turns and there is Victoria, a nightgowned wraith, watching from the doorway.

"Tory!" she whispers, frozen with shock and shame.

The child stares back with eyes like moons lost in orbit. Then she turns and runs out into the darkness.

"Tory!" Elizabeth is crying, wrenching free.

No doubt she is brutally abrupt. And distraught. Some animal sound, some groaning sob, part rage, escapes from Joe.

"It's impossible, Liz, it's impossible. It will always be impossible."

Madness, madness, madness.

Elizabeth is floundering about in the garden, in the past, looking for Tory. She throws out an arm, hangs on to the chair and the bed, catching at the present. Collides with Edward all over again.

For every moment of passionate elation there is an equal and opposite cost. This, Elizabeth believes, is an axiom. And these were the sentences handed down: the death of Joe, the damaging of Tory. She does not imply a simple-minded vengeful God. She is merely aware of the intricate ecology of human actions, the consequences of recklessness.

And yet, and yet....

Elizabeth cannot free herself of the expectation of that which is good, she is a glutton for each new morning, she takes the marrow from it. She holds today in her cupped hands: it is rare and beautiful, like an orchid or a butterfly.

It is to be savored.

It will never be seen again.

Edward is stirring now, she is at his side, he is conscious at last of her hand in his.

He is trying to say something, she bends over him, straining to catch his words.

"Still here, Bessie?" A tissue of sound.

Will it be bloodiness he wants? An act of contrition?

"About Marta," he whispers. "Forgive me."

Elizabeth smiles. She kisses him on the lips. "It cleared the air," she says. "It was a good thing to do."

He marshals his strength to say something further. "I swear," he whispers – though the words are thinner than air, they brush Elizabeth's ears like the shadow of an echo – "I swear it never came to anything."

She smiles her incomprehension and he touches her hair. She thinks: it is all behind us then. She leans toward him, rests her cheek beside his, and murmurs: "I love you, Edward."

Soon, she knows, he will begin to complain testily of the bedding and the nurses. By tomorrow the hearing aid and the pacemaker will assault his sensibilities unendurably. But for this moment he smiles and touches her face.

Elizabeth is moved to tears. It has sung itself well, she thinks. She likes this ending.